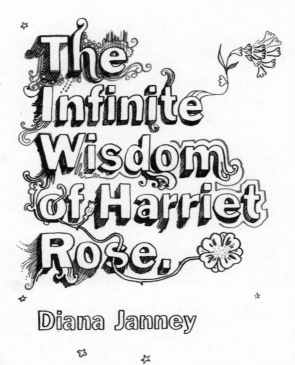

The Infinite Wisdom of Harriet Rose.

Diana Janney

headline
review

First published in 2007 by
HEADLINE REVIEW
An imprint of HEADLINE PUBLISHING GROUP

1

Cataloguing in Publication Data is available from the British Library

Hardback ISBN 978 0 7553 3769 9
Trade paperback ISBN 978 0 7553 3770 5

Typeset in Perpetua by Palimpsest Book Production Ltd, Grangemouth, Stirlingshire
Chapter heading illustrations by Nina Chakrabarti
Printed and bound in Great Britain by Clays Ltd, St Ives plc

HEADLINE PUBLISHING GROUP
A division of Hachette Livre UK Ltd
338 Euston Road
London NW1 3BH

www.headline.co.uk
www.hodderheadline.com

For my mother

I am grateful to all those at Headline involved in the publishing of *The Infinite Wisdom of Harriet Rose*, but my very special thanks go to Charlotte Mendelson and Leah Woodburn.

'I don't want any birthday presents this year – donate the money to a worthwhile cause instead,' was all I had said. How could I have guessed that such a simple suggestion would create uproar in our household?

I had not given the request much thought when I made it. In fact, the idea had only just occurred to me. Philosophers are like that sometimes – unfettered in their ideas, lateral in their thinking. That was why Plato was such a success. He would never have come up with his theory of Ideal Forms otherwise.

But my mother and Nana did not seem to understand such matters. And as a result, my simple, altruistic request appeared to have caused them a fair degree of unnecessary concern. I could hear them from my bedroom, where I had gone to escape their anxious glares and frosty silence.

'Did you hear what she said?' Nana was whispering, in the tone she reserved for her most important reflections. 'She wants us to donate her birthday money to a worthwhile cause! It's all your fault, Mia.'

'How on earth is it *my* fault?' my mother replied, forgetting her previous attempts to calm Nana down now that she herself was being blamed.

'You should never have let her answer the door the other day to those women handing out religious leaflets.'

'Harriet's an intelligent girl,' my mother responded, her powers of observation at their keenest. 'She enjoys lively debate.'

'It must have been some debate to go on right the way through *The Archers*,' Nana exclaimed.

'I thought it would be good for her,' my mother went on. 'How was I to know she would come away thinking she was Maria in *The Sound of Music*?'

In fact, my mother and Nana were mistaken. The exchange of views that had taken place on our doorstep between the two women and me had ended somewhat abruptly when I'd asked their views on Descartes' ontological argument for God's existence and the women had answered that they hadn't had a chance to discuss it with him yet.

No, if anyone had been responsible for my unusual birthday request it was not them. In truth, the idea had been entirely my own. Yet, like many ideas, as I had suggested in number 49 of my collection of Meditations, it had been brought to consciousness by the influence of my surroundings: Holy Innocents Church, to be more precise.

I had decided on impulse to go back to the church after an absence of a year and three months, a period that might seem disrespectful to those of a prejudicial nature, but in reality that was far from the case. My visit had had a purpose, although I did not quite understand it at the time. Indeed, it was not until I noticed the confessional box that my purpose began to take shape. Not being a Catholic, confessional boxes had always been a mystery to me. I think that was what drew me to it in the first place. Mystery appeals to writers, even if their work consists only of reflective meditations jotted down in a notepad they keep in their handbag at all times in case a thought slips away before it can be captured.

I walked determinedly towards the box – I didn't want the other worshippers to think I was a novice – and knocked on the wooden door.

'Enter!' a voice said, like Father Christmas in his grotto. A lesser person would have turned and run away, but not Harriet Rose, creator of *The Meditations of Harriet Rose* and the recipient of two school prizes, one for English, the other for philosophy.

It was dark inside. Once my eyes had adjusted and I could see him – Father – staring at me through the grille, awaiting my confession, I leaned forward and whispered, 'I think I should admit straight away that I'm not a proper Catholic – in fact, I'm not a Catholic at all.' It was only fair that he knew. I didn't want there to be any misunderstanding between us.

'Our door is open to everyone,' he said.

'That's my fault, Father,' I replied, closing it. 'I thought it might seem a little dark in here otherwise.'

Then it dawned on me: I had nothing to confess. Does that sound conceited in a thirteen year old? Perhaps so, but it was the truth, and I wasn't stupid enough to lie in a confessional box. But that was where I was. I had come here for a reason: there had to be something I wanted to say.

'I did want to have a brief word with you about something,' I said finally, cupping my left hand round my mouth in case we were overheard from outside.

'What is it, my child?' the voice asked into the darkness. 'I'm here to listen.'

'It's about my father,' I whispered. 'I wondered if you could pass on a message to him from me.' Suddenly it felt warm in the box, comfortingly so, like being asleep in a big soft bed and dreaming of a faraway place where the sun always shines.

'Do I know your father?' he asked.

'He's a handsome man,' I found myself explaining, 'with fair hair and pale blue eyes that twinkle when he laughs, and a dimple in his chin.'

'And does he come to Holy Innocents?'

'He used to. I can't say if he still does. I have no way of talking to him now, the way you do. But he always spoke highly of it. He loved its majesty, he used to say, its splendour, its mix of grandeur and humility. I remember one Christmas, his last as it turned out, standing not far from where we're sitting now. The pews were full to bursting so we had to stand, my father and mother and me. That Christmas was hard for us all. We knew how ill he was – he couldn't hide it from us any more. But he wanted to come here and sing his favourite carols. And how he sang! You can't have missed his singing voice, even in the midst of the crowd, which was spilling out into the street.' I had to stop for breath. It was airless in there. That was all it was.

'I understand,' he said quietly, and for a moment he sounded just like my father. 'And you have a message for him, you say?'

'Yes,' I said hesitantly – I hadn't quite worked out what the message was, 'if you happen to be speaking to him. I've tried to myself, but I just can't hear him any more. My mother says I will in time, but that doesn't make sense to me at all. I thought there was no time where he was, so what's keeping him? It's more than a year now, Father.'

'Tell me your message,' he said, in his low, thoughtful voice, which raised my hopes no end. 'What is it you want to say to your father?'

'Only that I miss him.' I choked — I wouldn't have if only I'd prepared something, but I hadn't. 'And I love him. And I can't believe how brave he was. And I wish we'd never argued, but sometimes it really was his fault, but I didn't mean the things I said when I was angry. And that Liverpool are doing well in the FA Cup. And my mother still can't stop thinking about him and wishing he was here with us. And much as I love having Nana live with us, it's not the same as it was before. But we're trying to be brave like he was. And trying to do things that would make him proud. Or make him laugh. It's his laugh I like to remember most.'

The silence that followed made me fear that Father had left the confessional box without me hearing, or had fallen asleep. Either would have been understandable, frankly. I'd gone on far too long. There must be time limits attached to these boxes. There was probably a queue a mile long outside.

'Be assured, my child, that Father has heard your message.'

It was exactly the sort of ambiguity I loathed. 'Do you mean *my* father, or you, Father?' I enquired — precision was such an important quality of the reflective mind.

'I meant both,' he replied.

'And what should I do now?' I continued, sensing that our meeting was being drawn to a close.

5

'You should pray, and I shall pray for you too. Concentrate your mind on all your talents and the positive aspects of your life – I feel there are many. Carry your love for your father with you into the world and make a difference to it, my child. Then you will begin to see that he is still with you.'

'I meant, Father,' I explained, 'what should I do now in the confessional box? How do I get out?'

'Push the door hard,' he said, a little louder than before, 'and it should open.'

His words had lingered with me after I left him. What did he have in mind for me? Which door was I to push hard? And if I did, would it really open?

As I left the church and headed for Harvey Nichols, it occurred to me that the Father and I might have been brought together for a purpose. I had needed help and it had been sent – and not just any old help but the most worthy, spiritual type you could ever wish to find. Didn't that prove something about this life and its meaning? Didn't that demonstrate something about me? What stronger proof could anyone hope to find that they were important to the world in a spiritual way? It was my duty to live up to the purpose for which I had undoubtedly been chosen, and I made a pact with myself, there and then in that incongruously noisy London street, that I would not let myself down by allowing the petty, materialistic elements of life to distract me any more.

And what better time to begin than on my birthday? It wouldn't just be a celebration of fourteen years on earth, it would be a landmark, a catalyst in my life. Given time, my mother and Nana would understand. They were intelligent, sensitive women themselves, how could they fail to? I would concentrate my mind on my many talents, as the Father had told me I should, and I would make a difference to the world. Maybe he was right and by so doing I would see that my father was still with me. And that would be the greatest present of all.

'I can work out sums in my head faster than Carol Vorderman because once I was criticised for my poor mental arithmetic skills.

'In church I always mime hymns so that no one can hear my singing voice.

'I play to win at chess, but I don't mind losing if it has been an interesting game.

'I believe in saying only what I mean.

'I always keep a notebook with me in case I need to jot down a Meditation to add to my collection.

'I used to think I would be famous when I grew up. Now I just want to be left alone.

'I always prefer a book with a happy ending, such as Kant's *Critique of Pure Reason* or, even better, his *Groundwork of the Metaphysic of Morals* – I love that one.

'I don't believe in God the way I used to because He didn't save my father's life.

'I prefer giving presents to people I like rather than receiving them.

'I get embarrassed easily, especially in a crowd.'

I couldn't think of anything else to say about myself so I sat down and studied the relative lengths of my fingers. It seemed an important thing to do just then, especially as everyone else in the class was silent. I wasn't used to speaking in public. It was harder than I'd thought it would be.

I guessed it was Jason's turn to talk about himself next. He would know what to say – he always did. Why couldn't he have gone first?

I could hear him shouting out about himself, his family, their home, his hobbies, his goals for the future. Why hadn't I thought of mentioning those things? Suddenly it seemed obvious that that was the whole point of the exercise. He was talking about the antics of his younger brother now, and everyone was laughing, even Miss Marlowe. If only I could find stories like that amusing. But I didn't. His younger brother sounded like an idiot to me. Did no one else in the class think he sounded like an idiot? And who cared that his favourite car was a Ferrari and his favourite colour yellow, or that he supported Chelsea and never missed a match?

He was going on too long and his voice was getting louder. Miss Marlowe was looking at her watch. It was time for Jason to sit down. I didn't want to hear the others talk about themselves so I stopped listening. At least that was one advantage of going first. I wished I hadn't mentioned thinking I'd be famous. They would all hate me for that, even though I bet they had all thought the same. So bloody what?

Suddenly I became aware that the others were staring at me, and even Charlotte had stopped mid-autobiography and was looking at me too.

'What did you just say, Harriet?'

It was Miss Marlowe's voice now, not Charlotte's.

I hadn't meant to say, 'So bloody what?' aloud. I'd thought I was just thinking it. It must have slipped out of my mouth.

'Did I hear you say, "So bloody what"?'

'Yes, Miss Marlowe.'

I couldn't lie. I must have said it – and so bloody what if I had?

'Well, Harriet, I think you owe Charlotte an apology, don't you?'

Charlotte? What had Charlotte to do with it?

'Why, Miss Marlowe?' I asked timidly, blushing at all the attention my inner reflection on my short-lived desire for fame had inadvertently caused.

'You may not hold her father's important position in the legal profession in very high esteem, but there are others in this class, Harriet, who do.'

Her father's important position in the legal profession? What had that to do with me? Was that what Charlotte had been whining on about?

I was about to explain that I hadn't the least interest in Charlotte's father when Charlotte began to cry – long, heartfelt sobs, interspersed with choking noises. She had returned to her desk and the rest of them appeared to be trying unsuccessfully to comfort her. I had once read about such attention-seeking tactics in *Cosmopolitan*, an article entitled 'Big Boys Don't Cry But Clever Girls Do'. But I hadn't thought anyone would actually take it seriously. What self-respecting female would resort to emotional manipulation at the expense of looking like a pathetic, weak-willed prat? I had asked myself at the time.

'Charlotte!' I announced, answering my own question.

Charlotte stopped sobbing as suddenly as she had begun. 'Yes, Harriet?' she replied quietly.

'Your mascara's running.' It was all I could think to say. And, besides, it was, in long black streaks all the way down her chalk white face.

'Thanks for telling me, Harriet,' she answered, smiling sweetly when she was aware that all eyes were upon her. I wished I'd read to the end of the *Cosmopolitan* article.

It was hardly what anyone would describe as the perfect start to a birthday. Not that I had expected a round of 'Happy Birthday To You' followed by fourteen bumps. How could I, when I hadn't told any of them it was my birthday?

Perhaps I had been a little harsh on poor Charlotte. Just because she wore extra thick mascara and hair extensions, that didn't automatically make her an airhead, did it? Well, perhaps it did, but Harriet Rose wasn't the type to patronise. After all, wasn't that what my experience in Holy Innocents had been about? Wasn't it part of my plan to be more charitable?

'Charlotte,' I said quietly, once Miss Marlowe had left the room, 'it's my birthday today and I'm going for a swim at my mother's health club in Kensington this evening. I wondered if you'd like to come with me?'

'A health club? Brilliant!' exclaimed Charlotte. 'Is it mixed?'

'Mixed?' I repeated, searching my mind for the relevance of the question.

'You know – boys as well.' She giggled, and for a moment I regretted all I was trying to achieve.

'Shall we say six o'clock at Reception?' I asked her. Then I wrote down the address – in capitals, of course – on a piece of lined paper.

'And by the way,' I added, 'you don't need to buy me a present. I'm asking for donations to charity instead.'

'Cool,' Charlotte said, and then she was gone, without so much as a 'many happy returns'.

My mother had joined the health club near our house in Kensington shortly after my father had died. It had been my idea, and Nana had agreed. We thought she needed to build up her strength after months of looking after my father as his health had deteriorated. Forty was too young to be widowed. It wasn't fair. But, as I'd expressed in Meditation 56, 'Fairness is seldom distributed to those who deserve it most.' Otherwise I wouldn't have lost in the final of the chess-club championship to Miles Brown just because my mind had wandered momentarily to what my mother might be cooking for supper.

Of course, Nana hadn't always lived with us. She and Grandpa had lived near Edinburgh, but then Grandpa had died, my father too, and we agreed we would be happier, the three of us, if Nana came to London to be with my mother and me. We had a bedroom each – Nana moved into the spare room at the front of the house, which looked out over the street. We lived in a quiet cul-de-sac but there was a street-lamp right outside her bedroom window that had kept Nana awake half the night at first, she said. But once she had replaced my mother's silk curtains with her triple-lined drapes from her old house, she was happy.

I liked it when Nana was happy. Her face exuded the warmth that her mind contained. There was no question that Nana was beautiful, by the standards of any generation. And she wore her looks naturally, unselfconsciously, like a lioness unaware of its age.

It made me feel safe to know that Nana was across the corridor and my mother on the other side of my bedroom wall in what had always been my parents' room – it was the largest and had its own en suite. I say 'parents', but I had only one parent now. It was a habit of speech I still found hard to change. And it didn't seem right to say 'parent' when I meant my mother, even though that was what she still was. But I was used to 'parents' in the plural. Somehow it made more sense. So if I couldn't have my parents I would just have to give up using the word entirely.

My mother was twenty-seven when I was born, and although she was now forty-one she looked much younger. Nana said it was because she had good bone structure, a beautiful figure and big eyes, which shone with steely determination. Whenever I went out with my mother, shopping, for example, I saw men turning to admire her. But she didn't react at all. It was as if she didn't notice – and maybe she didn't. But I did. What I liked best about my mother was her enthusiasm, her energy. She had a knack of making ordinary things seem exciting, like deciding what to wear or what to do on a rainy day or even styling my hair (there was too much of it for me to style by myself). She always did that. When I stopped to think about it, she was lucky to have a daughter like me to keep her feet on the ground.

At times like this, observing the two of them, so obviously related not just to each other but to previous generations of Highland warriors, I wondered if I'd been adopted. Never mind the steely determination, I didn't even have the auburn hair and pale skin that freckled in the sunlight. When I was in the sun, my skin bronzed almost immediately and my blonde hair became even blonder. Once, when I raised my concerns with my mother, she told me to look in the mirror if I needed confirmation of my parentage. I did. For several hours. From every aspect. She was right: our physical similarity was undeniable – the large, sea-blue eyes, the oval face, the thickness of the hair. It would be only a matter of time before I mastered the look of steely deter-mination too, especially if I practised it in the mirror now and again.

'Are we meeting Charlotte at the club or is she coming here?' my mother asked, while she was ironing my bikini.

'We're meeting there,' I said.

'Then you'd better hurry up and change – Nana's ready.'

'Are you talking about me?' Nana asked, as she jogged into the sitting room in her navy blue tracksuit. My mother had chosen it to encourage her to come with us. There weren't many seventy-four year olds at the club, but that didn't bother Nana. She had always preferred the company of younger people. Not that she or my mother would be staying at the club that evening. They thought it best that Charlotte and I swam on our own. But that didn't prevent Nana changing into what had become her favourite outfit.

'I'm relying on you, Nana, to tell me what to make of Charlotte Goldman. I've told her to wait for me at Reception. You could just pop in for a second.'

'I can tell you that already,' Nana said. 'She sounds like an attention-seeking troublemaker to me. How does she do her hair?'

Nana set a lot of store by how people did their hair. Hers was always immaculate, dark auburn in keeping with her Celtic roots, strong and defined like her personality.

'She's got blonde hair,' I said, 'the sort you can see through. And she has extensions.'

'Extensions?' repeated Nana, with a frown. 'What are they?'

'Bits of false hair they tie to their own to make it seem longer and thicker,' my mother explained.

'I knew it!' Nana exclaimed. 'She's a phoney.'

'Let's have a look at her first,' my mother advised, 'before we go jumping to conclusions.'

We set off in my mother's car and arrived at the club to find Charlotte engaged in conversation with Ben, the receptionist and swimming coach. It appeared from the snippet of conversation we heard as we walked in – my mother first – that they were discussing the club rates and whether there were any celebrity members.

'What did I tell you?' Nana whispered loudly, arching her eyebrows.

'You must be Charlotte,' my mother said, with an outstretched hand. 'I recognised you from Harriet's description.'

Before Charlotte could answer, Ben turned to my mother and said, 'Hello, Mrs Rose, you're looking fab this evening.'

Although 'fab' might not have been the word I would have chosen, Ben was right. There was a glow to her complexion that I hadn't seen since my father's death. And her hair seemed even shinier and more auburn than usual, falling round her face like a finely carved picture frame.

'You won't be coming in tonight?' Ben asked, observing her black cashmere sweater dress and the pale blue pashmina draped round her shoulders.

'No,' she replied, somewhat shiftily I felt, 'I've got something else to do.'

Curiously, she did not stay to dwell on what that something was, but disappeared out of the door with Nana, saying over her shoulder as she went, 'Nana will pick you up at seven on the dot.' And then they were gone.

It was not until we were in the changing rooms that I discovered Charlotte wore a bra. We were putting on our swimsuits and Charlotte seemed to be taking an unusually long time to wrap a blue and white striped bath towel round herself, then manoeuvre her little body inside it as if she were a caterpillar about to metamorphose into a beautifully coloured butterfly. Sadly, the similarity ended with her emergence in a black polyester swimsuit with barely a hint of bust as she attempted to conceal a matching bra-and-pants set depicting Winnie-the-Pooh at each nipple area. Until that moment I had admired Winnie-the-Pooh: he had always struck me as a bear with an amount of sense beyond his status and rather silly name. But Charlotte's little bra changed that. Thenceforward, Winnie-the-Pooh became a bear whose fate it was to expand in line with a pair of adolescent bosoms while clutching his ever-expanding honey jar as if to let it slip would be to deprive poor Charlotte of her hard-earned modesty. How could I ever take a bear like that seriously again? I had grown up thinking of him as a unique, individual thinker, a being to aspire to, and all of a sudden he had been transformed into not one but two bears of very little substance.

I removed my white cotton vest with dignity, and folded it tidily beside Charlotte's towel. Then, in my nakedness, I took a step back to observe myself in the wall-length mirror. I was proud of my shape – I liked being tall and slim, and it was true to say that I had the beginning of a bust, especially if I stood side on and breathed in. But the idea of housing it in an unnatural contraption that restricted its movement seemed to me like locking up tiger cubs at the zoo, then moving them to a larger cage once they became too big for the one they were in.

I looked hard at Charlotte as we advanced towards the pool, and I was sure that, deep down, she felt as I did. It was probably her mother's idea. What sensible fourteen-year-old would choose to curtail her liberty at such an early stage of her development? There was more to pity about Charlotte Goldman than I had ever realised. Take her swimsuit, for instance. It hadn't occurred to me, when my mother and I had been planning what swimwear I should take with me, that Charlotte would choose a no-nonsense black polyester costume. To see her in it beside me almost made me wish I hadn't worn my red bikini with the gold chain straps. It was just that everyone had always said that in it I looked like a young Bardot, and as Charlotte was half French, I'd thought she might find that comforting.

I used to be good at French before Charlotte arrived at our school. In fact, I was the best in the class. Our French teacher, Madame du Bois, used to praise me for my grasp of the language. *'Merveilleux!'* she said once, in front of the whole class. But Charlotte's French was better than marvellous. It was perfect. Within a week of her arrival at the school, I had dropped from top of the class to some-where in the middle. Second place held no appeal for me. So I aspired to be bottom from then on. But bottom took some working at. It didn't come as naturally to me in French as it did in science: I even came bottom in science when I cheated and looked up the answers in my file during the exam. When the results were read out and I heard my name first I'd had no idea Mr Shaw was starting at the bottom, until he added, 'Thirty-three per cent.' When he continued, 'You're not going to win the Nobel Prize for Science, Harriet, are you?' my worst fears were confirmed. I must have looked up the wrong pages.

I blamed my mother. She thought science was messy and dangerous for girls. I was too pretty to be good at science. I was created for language, communication, culture, the arts, drama, not playing around with substances in jam-jars. She had a point. Not even Charlotte seemed to take to science, and she had Louis Pasteur in her heritage.

I had piled all my hair on top of my head, as my mother had shown me, and held it there with a big gold clip to match my straps. Charlotte had pushed hers, extensions and all, into a white rubber cap she had brought with her. As I looked away, I couldn't help reflecting for a moment upon the aesthetic importance of visual contrast.

Charlotte and I walked in silence, both of us absorbed in our very different types of self-awareness. I sought out the springboard from which to demonstrate my aquatic skills. It was not that I was an extrovert by nature – far from it – but my reflections on Charlotte had left me feeling a little deflated. I needed to prove myself to her and the two other swimmers who had noticed our approach. At first, it was hard to tell whether they were male or female, so quickly were they travelling through the water, like dolphins, and the last thing I wanted was for them to think they had impressed me.

I veered towards the springboard with the confidence of a marathon winner, unperturbed by the shouting and gesticulating around me. On reaching it, I walked the plank with the grace of a ballerina and the poise of a catwalk model. That would do the trick. Here, at last, was my stage, and if the other swimmers and Charlotte sought to distract me with their screaming and waving, well, frankly, that was their problem.

I raised my hands high above my head and clasped them together in a position of prayer, poised to catapult myself high into the air, then twist and hurl my body head first towards the water.

The next thing I remembered was being lifted by two strangers to a lounger by the side of the pool. There was nothing heroic about my response to the blood gushing from my mouth as my upper front tooth was released from my lower lip. Neither could my reaction to the wobbliness of the tooth be described as brave. Yet I like to think that, on the whole, my stoic determination not to cry impressed the crowd that had formed around me. After all, it was not my fault that I had failed to understand the cries as they had sought to draw my attention to an inadequately displayed out-of-order sign above the springboard. I could hardly have been expected to know that it would collapse under the force of my magnificent manoeuvre and hit me in the mouth as I fell against it.

In seconds, the pool had been evacuated and a lifeguard was at my side. It struck me that the role of a lifeguard should be to prevent accidents rather than to attend to them from afar once they had happened. But I was in no position to be confrontational. So I accepted the attention and the hot water and towels, and wondered whether this was what it was like to give birth. From the other end, of course. The beauty of being a philosopher was that you didn't have to be specific. Precision was aimed at theories rather than practicalities.

Fortunately for me, one of the swimmers who had looked like a dolphin in the water seemed to have experience in first aid: he knew how to hold my tooth in the gum until it had steadied. His name was Jean Claude and he spoke English with a French accent, so I guessed he was French. He must have been sixteen or seventeen, with strong black hair and dark brown eyes. Of course I didn't tell him that I'd thought he looked like a dolphin – there are some thoughts a woman just has to keep to herself.

Unfortunately Charlotte had a very different philosophy. The moment she spotted Jean Claude at my side, his black swimming shorts just above the knee as he stooped to offer me a steadying hand, she was moved to exclaim: 'Harriet! I was *so* worried about you! Your poor mouth! It looks *horrible* – are you all right? Oh, hello, I'm Charlotte!'

But Jean Claude was too busy with his first aid to respond.

Once I was able to speak again, I thanked him in French for his help and he replied, in French, that it was his pleasure. For that, I respected Jean Claude, and it was clear that he respected me too. Here at last was someone who could see through the kind of tactics employed by the Charlottes of this world. Here was someone who was impressed by the absence of tears and an abundance of courage. Who needed womanly wiles?

Jean Claude got to his feet and began to walk away. His hair was still dripping water. It was running down his long, bronzed back and disappearing into his baggy black shorts. In seconds, he would be gone. I think it must have been a combination of shock and chlorine but out of the blue, I suffered a relapse.

The five minutes it took Jean Claude to fetch me a Coca-Cola was all the time I needed to come to my senses. I was not there to be picked up by some charming, good-looking Frenchman. There was more to this life than the pursuit of hedonistic happiness. No, Harriet Rose had a mind to develop – and yet, at the first opportunity, she had turned into a stereotypical waif, looking to be saved and protected from the traumas of life by a dashing hero. Not so fast, Harriet! Use your head! Think of poor Charlotte and how much she needs the right role model.

I was feeling better now. The Coca-Cola had helped to steady my stomach and my lip had stopped bleeding. I stood up to go. Jean Claude walked on one side of me while Charlotte manipulated her way to the other. A curious trio of decreasing height and silent embarrassment, broken finally by Charlotte saying, in French, 'You've been very kind to Harriet.' She smiled at her compatriot. '*Merci.*'

'You are French too?' He had no choice but to ask.

'*Ma mère est française*,' she explained, as if he would be remotely interested.

We had reached the changing rooms. Charlotte opened her mouth to continue her futile conversation, but was prevented by my saying: 'After you!' as I held open the door for her to enter the changing room first. Once she was safely inside, I bade Jean Claude a hasty '*au revoir*' and followed her in.

It took Charlotte even longer to change back into her white stretch jeans and orange Lycra T-shirt than it had taken her to get out of them. I sat on a bench in the corner to make sure I was fully recovered. The time it was taking her to style her hair was getting on my nerves. And she smiled at herself in the mirror as she was doing it. I had to get away, however charitable I wanted to be. It was too much for a thinker like me to bear.

'I've just realised,' I said, 'that I left my towel by the swimming-pool.'

'You can borrow mine, if you like,' she replied. 'I've finished with it.' She pointed to a crumpled wet blue and white striped heap on the floor beside her.

'It's all right,' I said, 'I'll go and find my own.'

Jean Claude was getting out as I returned to the pool. When he saw me he smiled and pointed to a lounger, where we sat side by side.

'Thanks for your help earlier,' I said lamely – it wasn't what I'd practised on the way there.

'I was happy to be of assistance,' came his gallant response. Then we sat. Silently. For several minutes. Staring at an empty swimming-pool as if there was something fascinating about pale blue chlorinated water. Surely as the author of *The Meditations of Harriet Rose, A*

Thinking Adolescent, I could come up with something more interesting to say. If I was going to get to know Jean Claude I had to find out more about him. I tried again: 'Do you mind if I ask you a question?'

'Of course not,' he replied casually, running his hand through his hair.

'Those shorts you're wearing, did you choose them yourself?' It was a question I'd wanted to ask him ever since I'd noticed they had the kind of legs you could see up.

I hadn't expected him to laugh – it was probably nerves.

'But did you?' I pressed, and he could see he would have to give me an answer.

He stopped laughing and said, 'As it happens, they were chosen for me. They were a present from a girlfriend.'

Suddenly I wished I hadn't asked. After all, what had his tasteless baggy shorts and unstylish girlfriend to do with me? 'Oh I see,' I muttered, turning away.

'I'm sorry,' he said, placing his right hand on my knee, as if it was quite natural to do so.

'You don't need to apologise,' I said, staring at his hand and wondering whether Nana would think I should remove it. Not literally, of course. Just from my knee. Not even Nana was that protective.

'But you look like I've upset you,' he went on, 'and that's the last thing I wanted to do, especially after such an accident.'

'Upset?' I laughed nonchalantly. 'Why ever would I be upset by a pair of *passé* Bermuda shorts? I was simply making conversation, that was all.'

I was happy to have used a French word he would understand to get across a point that was beginning to cause me a degree of

Diana Janney

irritation – until he withdrew his hand from my knee and I wondered if, perhaps, I should have stuck to English.

'You're right. They are a little *passé*, aren't they?' And he looked at me out of the corner of his eye before he added, 'Just like the girlfriend who bought them for me.'

'I'm in no position to judge her fashion taste without having seen her,' I remarked, as philosophically as possible.

'I wasn't talking about her fashion taste,' he explained. 'I meant that for me she is *passé* – how you say? Finished.'

'It's probably for the best,' I suggested – tactfully, I felt.

Jean Claude must have thought so too: his hand went back to my knee as he asked, 'I wonder if you would have dinner with me tomorrow? Maybe a bistro. I don't know London very well, but I expect you do.'

Was he hoping for a date or a tour guide?

'I could tell you where to go.' It was my casual way of accepting his invitation but for some reason Jean Claude looked uncertain, so I added, 'There's a little French bistro off Kensington High Street – perhaps we could meet there?'

Before he had time to construct an interesting way of saying, '*Oui*,' I was stunned into silence by the sound of Charlotte's voice behind us saying: 'Brilliant! I like it there too. When are we going?'

I learnt a valuable lesson that day: never pity small, stupid people with extensions, because what they lack in height and intelligence they make up for in brazen pushiness. I could hear Nana's voice in my head, sounding the warning over and over again. But, like an over-confident puppy, I had not heeded her words and had fallen headfirst into a trap for which I had only myself to blame. Surely not even the Father could have expected my benevolence to stretch this far.

24

But what to do? Explain to Charlotte that the invitation was meant only for me? Perhaps Jean Claude would fall into the same trap, take pity on the self-deceiving Charlotte and pretend that the invitation had been meant for her too. I couldn't take that risk. Then what? Miss out on an opportunity for a dinner date with Jean Claude because of the scheming guile of a *petit oiseau* with the brain of a fox? Certainly not. *Quelle tristesse!* Was my life destined to be one long tragedy? Had my mother been reading *Anna Karenina* while she was carrying me?

There was only one solution, and before I could reflect on its virtue, I found myself saying, 'Eight o'clock tomorrow? We'll look forward to it.'

4

As the moment for my birthday presents approached, I began to think my selfless, spiritual request might have been a little rash, especially when Nana said I couldn't change it, then gave my mother a furtive nod when she thought I wasn't looking. I had aimed for too much too soon. I should have begun by suggesting smaller presents for my fourteenth birthday, then worked up gradually to charitable donations by my twenty-first. But it was too late now: I had made the request and I couldn't go back on it without losing face entirely.

So, when my mother and Nana walked into the sitting room, my mother empty-handed and Nana clutching a solitary package, I braced myself and hoped that my mother hadn't taken me too literally.

'We've got you a joint gift this year, Harriet,' my mother announced proudly, as if, I feared, less meant more. 'I hope you like it as much as we do.' Nana patted my knee as she passed the present to me.

It was small, about the size of a DVD, beautifully wrapped in gold paper with a big red bow on top. As I opened it I tried to convince myself that a documentary on some third-world country or a talk on animal rights was exactly what I'd been hoping for. Yet when I saw it was a hardback book with a bright red cover and delicate gold lettering, my spirits rose. I scanned the front for its title and author. I was not disappointed. It was a title I appreciated by an author I was only just beginning to understand. It was described as *A Collection of Meditations* and the title was *The Infinite Wisdom of Harriet Rose*.

'Do you like the title?' My mother sounded nervous. I don't know why – it was exactly the sort of title I would have chosen myself. It went to the root of what Harriet Rose was about – the infinite nature of her ageless profundity, a wisdom that knew no bounds.

'Nana and I thought about it for a long time before we came up with *The Infinite Wisdom*,' my mother explained, fingering the embossed gold letters with pride.

'I like it,' I said, when finally I could get the words out. 'It distinguishes it from Descartes' *Meditations*, or the *Meditations of Marcus Aurelius*. It would have been confusing otherwise.'

'And in a way,' my mother went on, 'you chose the title yourself.'

'I did? How?' I asked eagerly.

'Don't you remember your Meditation Thirty-three at the start of Section Two?'

The words had seemed familiar, but I hadn't realised they were my own. I turned to Meditation 33 and read:

> In His infinite wisdom He took you away.
> I never shall forget that day.
> No fond farewell, no plain goodbye.
> Too ill to live, too soon to die.

I want you back,
I won't let go,
I need you here,
I miss you so.
In His infinite wisdom He took you away
While I still had so much to say.
Wise words now fill an empty space
Where once I saw your gentle face.
I want my words to make you proud.
I'm hoping you can see
The many thoughts you helped me form
By giving life to me.
I write them down.
They fill each page.
A thoughtful child, a youthful sage.
In His infinite wisdom He took you away.
But I, in mine, shall make you stay.
I'll bring you back with the stroke of my pen.
In my infinite wisdom I'll see you again.

My mother had tears in her eyes as she said, 'It's the present your father would have chosen for you too.'

There was even a price on it – £13.99. My own book for sale at £13.99! Anyone who wanted to read my Meditations would have to pay. And yet, moments before, they had been a private collection for my eyes only. But, then, that was before I had become an author, a published author, no longer plain Harriet Rose but *the* Harriet Rose, author of *The Infinite Wisdom of Harriet Rose* and not to be under-estimated.

I turned to the inside back flap because Nana told me to – she wanted me to see the photograph she and my mother had chosen of me. It was a happy photograph, a colour head shot, but at first I couldn't place it. Although I was smiling, there was something tragic about my expression, as if I'd just been shot but I didn't want anyone to know. And then it came to me – Sports Day 2003. I had won the sack race by such a distance that they had missed me, the judges, Miss Gold, Miss Silver and Miss Bronze. They had run up to my three runners-up, clutching brightly coloured ribbons, red, blue and green, but the fools had overlooked me entirely. I stood there for several seconds in my sack, wondering if perhaps they would realise their mistake and strip Molly of her red ribbon before she'd had time to grow attached to it. But, no, the ribbons remained proudly in place, and not one of my contemporaries had the guts or the decency to own up. Where is the honour in receiving an honour undeserved? I asked myself that night, and the next.

In retrospect, I should not have prevented my father registering a formal complaint, but at the time I thought his loud booing and remonstrating as he stood on his chair were more than enough. But justice was done, and I didn't have to wait long for it. The following weekend, there I was, front page of the local newspaper, snapped by an eagle-eyed member of the *paparazzi* with a sense of fair play – Harriet Rose winning the sack race at least three lengths ahead of everyone else. To my father and me it was not merely a result, it was a victory. An injustice had been corrected, and to us that mattered far more than winning a stupid race. And now the very same photo-graph took pride of place in my own hardback book.

My collection of Meditations had started out as a sort of dedica-tion to all the people who had influenced my life. It was clear who those people were. I began with my mother because she was the most important person in my life. I filled a whole page with descriptions of her good and bad points, her strengths and weaknesses, her triumphs and disasters. Then I wrote '2' at the side of the page and followed the same pattern in describing my father. It was easy. I knew them both so well. They were with me back then every day of my life. My life was them. I couldn't envisage a life without either.

I remember I began Meditation 2: 'My father taught me how to be myself.' Then I stopped, as writers do, to reflect on my chosen words. Was it clear enough what I wanted to say? Not that it mattered whether it would be clear to other people, for I hadn't imagined then that my work would ever be read by anyone but me. Rather, was it clear enough to me? What do twelve-year-old girls know about themselves? Who else could I be but me?

It felt strange, this reflection, like learning a new language, then saying something in it without knowing exactly what you've said. And although I was only twelve at the time, I had known there was something more to the reflection than I had captured. So I tried again. This time I wrote: 'My father showed me how to be true to myself.'

That sounded better, more sophisticated, and I was pleased with it until I asked myself how I would know if I was false to myself. I might think I was being true when in fact I was not. So I crossed that out too.

My third attempt was in fact my last because this time I was happy with it. It said: 'My father taught me how to play chess.' It was just the beginning I wanted. It went on:

He told me which were the most important pieces, and never to underestimate or undervalue the pawns. He said that some-times you need to sacrifice a piece as a means to a greater end. He taught me never to be beaten by 'fool's mate', and that if you are winning, not to take your eye off the goal. He advised me not to be too defensive as it suited my game to advance early on, and to watch out for other players' tactics of trying to make me lose concentration or to break my confidence. He said that if I managed to keep the goal in view, and did not give up under pressure, or because I was pieces down, then I would be a great player and, more importantly, I would enjoy each game.

I wished I had shown him that Meditation. I wished I had not hidden it away all those months when he was ill. I wished I had told him I could not let him win our final game of chess together just because he was ill, as he had taught me that in doing so I would not have been true to myself.

Nana was Meditation 3 – third time lucky, she would say, and Grandpa was 4. Granny Rose was 5 and Great Aunt Margo 6. Those six made up my entire family, coincidentally the number of different pieces there are in a game of chess – king, queen, castle, bishop, knight and pawn. That was what had given me the idea. Why not describe all the characters in this section to correspond with the pieces in a game of chess? Of course, it would be obvious which side I was on. Six were already on paper. But that didn't mean the other side was not equally important in the creation and mastery of the game. Which was why the first section of my Meditations contained thirty-two characters, one for each piece on a chessboard and two very opposing sets of influences on my life. One side was made up of the members of my family, alive and dead; the opposing side, Meditations 17 to 32, were an eclectic mix of characters I didn't particularly like. But that was what intrigued me. They made the game more interesting: they brought out the best in the other side, highlighting its strengths and weaknesses, and made victory taste even sweeter. Eight pawns, like Charlotte Goldman, chattered and schemed their way through Meditations 17 to 24, while at the helm stood Miss Mason, the opposing queen, who had criticised my mental arithmetic skills in front of the whole class on my first day at senior school, just because her poor articulation had led me to mishear the question. They were all there, the players on my stage, good, bad, and a very grey area somewhere in the middle of the board.

When I had finished the first section, I closed the book and put it in an Emma Hope shoebox, like a buried corpse that would never see the light of day again. But like a corpse – and by then I had already seen one – it nurtured the life it left behind.

And that was why Section Two of my collection began with the very special Meditation 33, from which the title of my book had been drawn. I had written it on the day of my father's funeral to let him know that his death had not deterred me from continuing with my writing. And although he never had the opportunity to see my work, I knew without doubt it would have made him proud – its versatility, the keenness of the observations, the integrity with which I had written.

He had known I wanted to be a writer. That was why he had bought me a pen for my birthday the year before he died. I kept it in the loop at the side of my notepad like an exclam-ation mark. I lost it once in a taxi, soon after his death – it must have dropped out of my handbag. I thought it was gone for ever. But I was wrong. It had been handed in to a lost-property office by the driver. I cried when we went to pick it up. That may sound silly to non-writers, but other writers will understand. And not because you cannot write without a pen. Writers remember incidents like that one because they form symbols in their minds that they can never wipe out, however hard they try. My missing pen was never just a missing pen: it was a missing father, and every time I look at my pen, that is what I see, will see, always. And when I take it out of its loop and see my thoughts forming words with it on a page, my pen is a means of communicating with my dead father. Not just that pen, all pens, because once he had bought me a pen to encourage me to write.

Underneath the photograph there was a brief description of me: I had created my Meditations in a classical style but with my own youthful yet poignant outlook; I was an exceptional student, recipient of two awards for English and philosophy; I possessed a literary flair that I intended to develop when I left school; my book was unique, refreshing, an enlightening insight into the teenage mind.

I read on with amazement. Would anyone believe this of me? And if they did, wouldn't they resent me for being such an exceptionally talented individual? In short, hadn't Nana and my mother exaggerated just a little too much for my own good? But so bloody what if they had? It was my birthday and I was going to enjoy it. Tomorrow, in the words of the great Scarlett O'Hara, is another day.

'You must have wondered why I was in such a rush when I dropped you off at the club this evening,' I heard my mother saying. 'I had to collect the first box of books from the printers. The rest will be delivered – we've ordered a thousand.'

That brought me back to myself. For a moment, I had forgotten all about my publishing team, my mother and Nana, Mia and Olivia, or rather Miandol Books as they called themselves, while they sat patiently awaiting the author's response. Nana passed me my rollerball pen and my mother opened the book at the page containing the title and my name, and said, 'May I have the first signed copy?'

From her expression it was obvious that she expected me to write something special for her. But what? The page suddenly seemed so white and big and empty. 'To Mummy, with all my love, Harriet,' seemed inadequate. I needed to think of something witty or meaningful. I needed to investigate how other authors signed their books. I needed time to practise my signature. 'Write something in it later,' she said, taking the pen from my hand. I knew she would understand.

It was the greatest present I had ever received, but I couldn't quite get the words out to express it, so instead I gave them both a hug and wiped my eyes, which always watered when I least expected them to. 'Thank you,' I whispered. But neither of them wanted to hear that.

'Let's have something to eat!' Nana said. 'And then you can blow out your candles.'

It was not until later that night, when I was browsing through my book on my bed, that I discovered they had even included a dedication. It read: 'To my late father'. They knew me so well.

There was no point in having a thousand copies of a published book if they weren't out there in leading bookshops, to be purchased by discerning readers, who had been directed to them by a powerful publicity campaign. The following day, once the shock was wearing off a little, it was decided that my mother would be in charge of marketing and publicity, and that Nana would be sales representative (on the understanding that no one was allowed to call her 'rep'). My role entailed remaining silently in the background, cloaked in practical introspective creativity and oblivious to the required efforts by those around me.

It sounded quite easy when the publishing team explained it to me. How could it fail? Nana, the formidable persuader, my mother, the ingenious organiser, and me, the enigmatic thinker. It was as if Fate had always had the project in mind, moulding our individual characters for this purpose, guiding our paths towards this very intersection. Really, we had no say in the matter from the moment I had picked up my prolific rollerball for the first time. There was only one pressing matter: that of the launch party on the publication day, which had been organised for the following Saturday. That gave me just three days to decide what to wear and to work on my speech to the guests — but guests — who were to be the guests? It was a question that only the publicity manager could answer.

'There's nothing for you to worry about,' my mother assured me. 'Just read one or two of your Meditations and thank them for coming.'

But who was I to thank? My friends would barely fill our sitting room, never mind a reception at the London Portrait Academy.

'You don't invite your friends to a book launch!' my mother exclaimed. 'You want people there who'll be encouraging and buy your book.'

I could see her point. But where would we find such people?

'There have been fifty-five responses so far,' she said, reading from the guest list. 'I'm waiting to hear from another forty-five.'

I had never heard of most of the guests. Total strangers would be attending my launch party, buying my book, discussing its merits, listening to my speech, sipping my champagne and orange juice, and gossiping about my outfit. Booksellers, local newspaper editors, critics — there would even be a representative from the *Evening Standard*'s London column. Overnight I had lost a mother and gained Max Clifford.

The invitations had described the evening as a reception to celebrate the launch of *The Infinite Wisdom of Harriet Rose*. I guessed that meant I had to be there. The invitees had also received a copy of the book's jacket, so at least they would be able to identify me when they got to the London Portrait Academy. I found myself wishing they hadn't cropped the sports-day photo to just a head shot — that way I could have hidden inside my sack.

'You can forget all about sacks.' My mother smiled as I was getting
ready for my date that evening with Jean Claude and Charlotte. 'We'll
all go shopping tomorrow and choose a beautiful new outfit each –
it's too important an event not to. All those people coming to the
London Portrait Academy just to see you – and there might be the
occasional glance at your publishing team!'

'Couldn't I wear these?' I asked, pulling on my favourite hipster
jeans with strategically removed back pockets – people didn't give
enough thought to what they looked like from behind. They should:
a parting impression was just as important as a good entrance, if not
more so. 'They're perfect for tonight, but you'll need something
smarter for the London Portrait Academy,' my mother explained
diplomatically. And I felt confident that she would make the ideal
publicist.

'I've arranged for the reception to be held in the Rembrandt Suite
on the first floor,' she went on.

'Not the room with the parquet floor and triple chandeliers,' I
gasped, 'and six sash windows along one wall?'

'That's the one.' I could see from her eyes that my mother was
impressed with herself. 'They let me hire it at a special rate because
I've had a portrait exhibited there.'

It would never have occurred to her to submit a painting to the
London Portrait Academy if my father and I hadn't talked her into
it. We knew she needed encouragement. She always did. She lacked
confidence where her own talents were concerned. She hadn't even
told her friends that she had been awarded a first in fine art in her
youth. I had been just eleven when my father had driven us to the
Academy. I waited with him in the car and we made my mother go
in alone with her portrait. It was quite large – four feet by three –
in an ornate gilt frame. She had locked herself away for days in the

attic room she now called her studio. No one was allowed to see it until it was finished and the varnish had dried. She was still finding fault with it as she unveiled it from the sheet that had covered it on the way down the stairs at home – 'If only I'd had longer, I could have added much more detail to the eyes. If you don't think it looks like you I'll take it away and start again. If the skylight window had been larger I could have spent hours more on your hair.' And so on. All the time she was making excuses she was scrutinising our faces for a reaction.

No one but my mother could have read our open-mouthed silence as disapproval. It was the most beautiful, moving portrait of a young girl either of us had ever seen. *Harriet's Smile*, was the description on the back of the canvas, just above 'Mia Rose pinxit'. She was the only one of the three of us to be surprised when the London Portrait Academy said they would like to exhibit it, just as she was the only one of us to be surprised when the commissions poured in.

And now my literary creation was going to join *Harriet's Smile* at the Academy. How proud my father would have been of us both. What better venue could there have been for our special event?

'Just because it's an elegant building doesn't mean I can't be comfortable. You never saw Van Gogh in black tie and he wouldn't have been turned away from the London Portrait Academy.'

'We'll think about it tomorrow,' my mother suggested, as she helped me on with my white Cannes T-shirt. I thought Jean Claude would appreciate a subtle reference to the Côte d'Azur, and it would give us something else to talk about if we needed it. I had gone to Cannes for my last holiday with my parents and I would never forget it.

'Just wait until he sees you in that,' my mother enthused. 'Charlotte Goldman might as well stay at home.'

*   *   *

Unfortunately she didn't. There she was in the bistro when I arrived. I could see her sitting alone at a circular table in the window. There was a large white dripping candle in front of her, which was just as well because if it hadn't been there passers-by would have been able to see down the front of her low-cut turquoise blouse. Not that there was much to see, of course, but with the help of a maximising bra, they weren't to know that. At least Winnie-the-Pooh had a night off, I thought, as I pushed open the bistro door and joined her at the table.

'Have you been here long?' I asked, eyeing her empty milkshake glass.

'Not really,' she lied, looking towards the door. 'He's late,' she added. 'I'm surprised – he looked the type to be punctual.'

'You obviously know more about men than I do,' I mistakenly confessed.

'It's quite easy,' she explained. 'There are only two types, really – the ones who want to please you, and the others who want you to please them. Jean Claude seemed like the first type to me.'

Stunned into silence by the exhaustive simplicity of the alternatives, I decided to study the menu, which had been placed on the red and white checked tablecloth in front of me. I hadn't actually eaten in the bistro before, only passed it on my way to school.

'The steak frites is usually good,' I said. It was an abstract theory – steak frites usually *is* good.

'I don't eat meat,' Charlotte replied, and for a moment I feared I'd underestimated her.

'I know how you feel,' I said, 'all those beautiful animals slaughtered just to be left half-eaten on a greasy plate.'

'It's not that,' Charlotte replied blankly. 'Meat gets stuck in my teeth.'

We were halted in our interesting moral debate by the arrival of Jean Claude. My first impression was that he looked better in jeans and a T-shirt than he had in his baggy Bermudas, and I was encouraged that he had chosen an outfit similar, in what Charlotte would describe as 'type', to mine, rather than the less casual outfit for which Charlotte had opted.

'Sorry I'm late,' he said, 'but I had a philosophy assignment to finish for tomorrow.'

Naturally this remark was of no little interest to me. 'You're studying philosophy?' I said. 'What a coincidence. So am I.'

'*Vraiment?*' he replied, as if Charlotte wasn't even there. 'I've just arrived in London at a sixth-form college in South Kensington to improve my English. Philosophy and English are part of my Baccalaureate.'

'That's uncanny,' I said. 'I received the school prizes for English and philosophy. I'm particularly interested in Descartes at the moment.'

'As am I,' he said enthusiastically, moving his chair a little closer to mine. 'There are not many philosophers who believe in the existence of the soul.'

I was just about to embark upon a subject I found particularly fascinating when Charlotte exclaimed: 'I like Descartes too! I know all about his "*incognito ergo sum*".'

'*Cogito.*' I had to correct her. '*Cogito*, not *incognito*.' I didn't want Jean Claude to think I was a total idiot too.

Charlotte broke off a piece of baguette with such vigour that the crumbs went all over what there was of her little black skirt. 'Descartes was French,' she said suddenly, as if she'd only just realised it, 'like us. My mother comes from Brittany,' she went on, which was news to me – I'd always understood she was from Boulogne. 'She came to London as a bilingual secretary and met my father, who is a lawyer.'

I couldn't quite see the relevance of the last part of her remark but it seemed important to Charlotte that Jean Claude was fully informed.

'A lawyer!' Jean Claude repeated, then turned to me and asked, 'What about your father, Harriet? What does he do?'

'He doesn't do anything any more,' I told him. 'He's dead.'

As I spoke I could see Charlotte fidgeting uncomfortably. I couldn't think why. Perhaps she had forgotten my father was dead.

'I'm so sorry,' Jean Claude said, placing his large bronzed hand on mine. '*Quel dommage!* He must have been quite young. *Ta pauvre maman.*'

'Forty,' I said, but I didn't want him feeling sorry for me so I went on, 'I live in Kensington with my mother and grandmother. We have a two-storey house with a roof terrace where we sit in the summer. You can see all the way to the Albert Hall on a clear day.' I sounded like an estate agent trying to sell a house that had been on the market for too long.

'I live with my parents in Islington,' Charlotte interjected, and I was sure she emphasised 'parents'.

'I don't know that area,' Jean Claude replied politely – I could tell he wasn't interested.

'I'll show it to you, if you like,' she had the audacity to suggest.

Just then the waiter arrived to take our order. Jean Claude and I chose the steak frites and Charlotte went for a French omelette.

It wasn't a long order, but it gave all the time I needed. 'If you like philosophy,' I said, addressing Jean Claude as if Charlotte had fallen asleep, 'you might be interested in my book, which has just been published.'

'You have a book?' he said excitedly. 'I didn't realise I was having dinner with a famous author.'

'It's a collection of Meditations I've been writing for the last two years. The launch party is at the London Portrait Academy this Saturday.'

My last words were almost inaudible above the clanging of Charlotte's knife against her glass, an activity she seemed to find particularly absorbing. But that didn't matter. I had a more important dilemma to resolve. If I asked Jean Claude to come to my party, I would have to invite Charlotte too – I'd been brought up to be polite. I weighed up the options swiftly and decided against it.

'There are going to be lots of important people there,' I said, hoping that even Charlotte would realise that excluded her. 'Intellectuals and philosophers – even a reporter from the *Evening Standard*.'

For once, Charlotte Goldman was lost for words.

The steak frites was as delicious as I'd hoped, and Jean Claude agreed. Charlotte complained that her omelette was a little under-done, which seemed like an excuse to cover it with tomato ketchup. 'At least it won't stick in your teeth,' I remarked, which was lost on Jean Claude.

Jean Claude and I ordered the *tarte au citron* to follow. Charlotte didn't want anything, or I'm sure she would have chosen the orange and lemon charlotte she'd spent so much time talking about.

'What about a cappuccino?' Jean Claude suggested.

'No, thanks,' she replied. 'No pudding for me.'

I could tell that the dinner was drawing to an awkward conclusion, but I couldn't think of anything else to say. I had reserved my Cannes T-shirt for a topic of conversation in a situation such as this, but somehow the Côte d'Azur did not follow on naturally from a foolish mistake about the meaning of 'cappuccino'. Fortunately, I didn't have to ponder for long – Jean Claude was obviously more capable in such situations than I was.

'So, tell me, Harriet,' he said, looking hard into my eyes, 'what do you want to be when you leave school?'

I had never really thought that far ahead before. Of course, I'd always wanted to be a writer, but did that answer Jean Claude's question? 'I want to be interesting,' I said finally.

Jean Claude smiled. 'But you already are.'

It was then that Charlotte began to attack the table noisily with her unused spoon.

Charlotte got to her feet, which took her a few inches higher than when she was sitting down, and said, 'I think we should be going.'

Jean Claude was far too polite to resist a command from the haughty Charlotte. He rose from the table and escorted us to Kensington High Street where we stood searching for taxis. As Jean Claude and I lived in the same direction, it was natural for him to suggest that we share a taxi together and find another to take Charlotte to Islington, which we did. At last we were alone, Jean Claude and I. It was the opportunity I had been waiting for all evening. Charlotte hadn't even left us to go to the ladies', which I had counted wrongly on her needing – all those mirrors for her to smile into, how could she resist? But she had. Yet now that we were alone we were silent until we were approaching my house and I said, 'This is where I live.'

'I am close to you,' he observed, which, I confess, I misunderstood for a moment. 'I live in South Kensington with my mother.'

'Walking distance,' I said.

'Perhaps we could meet again?' He raised his voice at the end of the question French-style.

I knew this was my moment. 'We could probably squeeze in one more guest at my launch party if you'd like to come. The numbers are tight, but I could ask my mother.'

43

'Really?' He seemed delighted. 'Are you sure?'

'It starts at six o'clock. There's a champagne and orange-juice reception at the London Portrait Academy. I'll be giving a short speech.'

'I would like very much to come,' he said, kissing my hand. 'But you give me your telephone number before you go?'

Neither of us had any paper, so he used my pen to write my number on the back of his hand. It was a long number, even for a hand the size of Jean Claude's, but he managed to fit it along the side of his thumb.

'It suits you!' I laughed as I climbed out of the taxi. It was my attempt to sound witty and light at the same time, a passing remark over my shoulder as I disappeared into the intriguing shadows of my home. 'Don't look back,' I told myself. 'Leave him wanting an encore.'

The day before my launch the telephone kept ringing but I was instructed not to answer it — the author should be mysterious and elusive — so it came as a surprise when Nana ran into my bedroom to tell me that Sacha Distel was on the telephone for me.

'Who?' I asked.

'Your Frenchman,' she replied.

It was a worry that Nana's hearing should begin to fail when I was about to give my first ever speech. 'You mean Jean Claude,' I said loudly.

'He wants "speak with you"!'

Nana's French accent was appalling — if the book went international, we would have to find someone else to deal with the overseas buyers.

I had already asked my mother whether Jean Claude could come to

the party. 'Why not?' she had replied. 'We want the book to go international.' Besides, it would have been rude of me not to invite Jean
Claude. London could be an unwelcoming city if you didn't know the
right people and the best places to go, as my mother pointed out.

'I've had a word with the publicist and she says you can come to
the party tomorrow,' I told him – I believed in getting straight to
the point.

'When you said you were a published writer, I did not know you
had your own publicity team,' he said.

'There are many things you do not know about me,' I replied
mysteriously, racking my brains to think of one.

'Then perhaps I will discover them while I am in London.'

I had been famous for just three days and already a Frenchman
was flirting with me. I had become a *femme fatale*, and I didn't even
wear lip gloss. I paused long enough to think of a witty response,
then said, 'How long will that be?' It wasn't what I had been hoping
for but I was Harriet Rose, not Dorothy Parker.

'At least a year,' he replied.

'It would take much longer than that!' I laughed. OK, so I wasn't
Dorothy Parker, but I was learning fast.

'Tomorrow at six, then?'

'I look forward to it.'

My mother was right – what to wear was an important decision with
an audience to impress and a literary reputation to promote. I could
see that she and I had to give a great deal of attention to creating
the right image – not just for me, but for the sake of the reading
public. I owed it to them.

Usually I asked my mother what she thought I should wear, but
this time I made the mistake of involving Nana too. Nana knew a

great deal about matters of style – otherwise she wouldn't have taken us to a McFly concert in a full-length fawn cape and big black sunglasses – but when it came to her only granddaughter, it was a different matter. 'You want to have your hair nice and curly and pulled back with a lovely bright Alice band so people can see your beautiful face,' she suggested, as the three of us set off down the King's Road. 'I'm sure I've still got a set of heated rollers in the house somewhere.'

'She doesn't want curls,' my mother explained. 'She needs to come across as intellectual and serious. I think she should tie it back with a black velvet clip.'

'Look,' I interrupted, as we entered our first dress shop, 'it's *my* hair and *my* face and *my* book launch and *I* really would like to choose what I look like for myself, thank you.' I was beginning to feel as if I was shopping with Trinny and Susannah.

'Can I help you?' a sales assistant asked me. 'Are you looking for anything in particular?'

But what was I looking for? We hadn't discussed it. We should have done. With all the talk about my hair it had gone out of my mind. So I let my mother answer for me. 'We're looking for a cocktail dress for my daughter,' she explained, pointing at me – I don't know why. The girl would hardly have thought Nana was her daughter.

'What about something black?' the assistant suggested.

'Black?' Nana exclaimed. 'It's not a funeral she's going to. She wants to wear pink, maybe with a few frills. That Jean Claude would like that. Men always like pink.'

'I'm not dressing for men, Nana,' I snapped. 'I'm dressing for myself.'

'But why would anyone want to wear black?' Nana persisted, as the assistant went to fetch a selection of little black dresses.

The trouble was that some of them made me look too young and others too old. And the assistant would have had me looking like a cross between Kylie and Bonnie Langford. It didn't matter, she thought, if the dress was short enough to see my bottom (or 'great arse', as she described it). With my beautiful long blonde hair I'd look 'wicked'.

Wicked. Why did everything have to be 'wicked'? I didn't want to look wicked. I had never aspired to *be* wicked. I wanted to look interesting, inspiring, enigmatic.

Nana didn't understand it either. 'Who do you think you're calling wicked?' she roared, getting to her feet in the changing room and heading towards the stunned girl, who took a step back and fell into a display of designer handbags. 'There's not a wicked bone in that girl's body! You'd better apologise or I'll show you what wicked really is.'

My mother and I tried to intervene, but there was no stopping Nana.

'It's just an expression, Nana,' I said, 'like sexy.'

'Sexy? A fourteen-year-old girl being described as "sexy"? Is she mad?'

The girl apologised and said she'd only meant I looked very pretty in the dress, and I did, but I didn't want to look pretty – I was an author not a weather girl.

Eventually we found the perfect outfit: black silk with a pattern of red roses to keep Nana happy.

My mother's outfit was much easier to choose as she knew exactly what she was looking for – a pair of flared white linen trousers and a blue silk blouse, worn loose but well cut to show off her figure. Not too much, though – the art of understated mystery was important to her. And, besides, Nana wouldn't have let her – not since she had a bairn to bring up. It only took her three-quarters of an hour to find the perfect outfit in Harvey Nichols, which she knew exactly how to accessorise with a long pearl necklace.

By lunchtime my mother and I had bought our outfits, which left the afternoon free to concentrate on Nana's, which we both knew would take the longest, even if Nana didn't.

'You don't need to bother about me,' she said, in a voice that didn't convince either of us even though Nana truly thought she meant it. 'I'm easy.'

If we hadn't stopped at a street café for organic fruit cocktails and Caesar salad, I don't know how we would have coped. Now, there was another emperor who had known what he was talking about: it took a stroke of genius to think of the anchovies.

We started the search for the perfect Nana outfit in Peter Jones, until Nana took offence at being shown a collection for 'the older woman'. So we headed up Sloane Street and eventually found a shop that appealed to Nana's dress sense.

'Have you seen the price of this one?' she protested, in one of her loudest whispers, which she thought no one would hear.

'Quiet, Nana, they'll hear you!' I urged, replacing the pale brown dress with the velvet trim.

'It's cashmere,' an elderly assistant explained haughtily. 'Cashmere's always more expensive.'

'You wouldn't be trying to tell someone from Scotland about cashmere, would you?' Nana replied, adopting the stern, fiery expression I knew so well; like a cross between Braveheart and Cleopatra.

'Perhaps this is more the sort of thing you had in mind,' the woman suggested, recklessly, I feared, holding up a brown polyester trouser suit with speckled feathers in the lapel. I could tell by the colour of Nana's cheeks that she hadn't taken kindly to the assistant's suggestion. What should I do? I couldn't just stand there and do nothing, and my mother had disappeared upstairs. So I did what I always did when Nana needed my help. I laughed. And it worked. Nana laughed too, until the tears were running down her cheeks. It didn't take long after that for Nana to see the situation from a new perspective. She took the trouser suit from the assistant and began to stroke the feathers on the lapel, saying to the assistant as she did so, 'It's beautiful – I expect you plucked the chicken yourself?'

Just then my mother came back, holding a smart navy silk dress with white cuffs she had found upstairs. Before Nana could say another word my mother had ushered us all into a communal changing room at the far side of the shop. Nana wasn't used to communal changing rooms. She liked her privacy. But with my mother and me to shield her from curious eyes, she began to undress. I had never seen Nana in her underwear before and couldn't have failed to notice her pants.

'Are you admiring my French knickers?' Nana asked me, hitching them up. I'd heard of French knickers, but I hadn't known until then how they differed from English ones. I had imagined that French knickers would be seductive in some way, probably black silk with lots of lace and high legs. But these were off-white with a reinforced gusset and an elasticated waistband. These French knickers were not just ordinary knickers, I decided. Nana's French knickers were surely a symbol of liberty and abandonment, worn only by women who didn't care for conventional frills or superficial nametags. These French knickers were flags blowing in the wind like a statement of victory. Suddenly I felt ashamed of my Marks & Spencer beige satin thong. I longed to be the owner of a pair of cotton French knickers like Nana's.

Once my mother had arranged the dress on Nana correctly, even Nana seemed pleased, finally, after three hours of searching. She glided out of the changing room to look at herself in daylight as though she was Greta Garbo, poised, majestic and ready for anything.

'You look beautiful, Nana!' I cried, squeezing my mother's arm approvingly.

'She certainly does!' my mother agreed.

Only the assistant was silent – until Nana turned to her and said, 'How do I look?' with a knowing smile.

'We've got it in larger sizes,' she muttered, and we knew Nana must be looking good.

The day of the launch began for me at four a.m. I saw no point in staying in bed when I couldn't sleep. Far better, I thought, to get up and practise my speech. The others wouldn't hear me if I mimed the words into my bedroom mirror. I'd spent the previous evening watching my mother's video recording of the BAFTA awards to get me into the right mood, so I knew what I had to do: thank as many people as I could think of, which for me meant my mother and Nana, so that wouldn't take long, and keep mentioning whatever I was there to plug, in my case *Infinite Wisdom*. It seemed that if that didn't hold their attention, the last resort was to cry and make my voice quiver while I told them how far I'd come in such a short time. But I was Harriet Rose, philosopher, thinker, so that wasn't an option. As I'd stressed in my Meditation 55, 'Women who cry when they are not feeling sad are like men who speak through a smile about serious matters — untrustworthy.'

Watching the awards ceremony had taught me one important lesson, though: no matter how insignificant you feel you are, there is always somebody far less significant in the audience. And usually not just one person. Most of them, in fact. That is why they are listening to you rather than you listening to them, after all. I arranged my three teddy bears and Bugs Bunny in a line in front of my mirror to give the impression of an audience. Their eyes made them seem intent on what I was about to say. I hoped my real audience would be as animated. But what about Harriet Rose? How did she appear?

I moved a little closer to my mirror. Then I picked up my own copy of *Infinite Wisdom*, the one in which I kept a photograph of me with my parents, as a bookmark. I had already decided which Meditations I would recite — I had even made a note of one or two more in case I was asked for an encore. It wasn't a sign of over-confidence, quite the reverse: I didn't want to be caught out with nothing to say. I had the reputation of Miandol Books to consider: they had put their faith in me and my Meditations. I couldn't let them down.

I kept the book closed as I studied the gold lettering and red cover. How much effort, I wondered, had gone into its creation? How many hushed conversations had there been while I was asleep upstairs? How much attention had been paid to each tiny printed detail? How many memories were triggered by the words my publishing team had read? Which of them had thought up the name of the publisher? Had Nana said she wanted her name to come last? I knew without doubt that my mother would have chosen the colour scheme, but which had picked out the paper and the fonts? Had they taken it in turns to proofread? When had they found time to go to bed?

So many details had led to its creation, and I, in my infinite wisdom, had seen only a book. Like staring at my face now in the mirror, I should have looked beyond what I could see. I should have recognised their effort and attention. That was what their birthday gift should have meant to me.

I opened the book and, for the first time, looked beyond the words I found there. I felt the weight and texture of each page. I found the special reference number for which they must have applied. I saw the copyright, which they'd ensured was in my name. I removed the paper cover to reveal the hardback binding. Red like the cover, with gold writing down the spine. The title, my name and 'Miandol Books'. A culmination of our separate efforts, a unity of three in one.

I closed the book and placed it on my bedside table. The light there caught the letters of my name. *A Collection of Meditations* was how they had described it. An expression of love was what it meant to me.

As I ran my bath, with drops of my mother's Jo Malone bath essence, which she had left beside the taps the night before, I decided not to practise what I'd written. I didn't need a rehearsal. The book would speak for itself.

The London Portrait Academy was a truly imposing building, with massive gates leading to the pillared entrance. A guard was there to greet us and take us to the room they'd reserved for us on the first floor. We climbed the mighty staircase together, the three of us, each with different questions in our minds. I was wondering what I'd find when I got there, whether the room would be as I remembered it and where I would stand. My mother, no doubt, was asking herself why my father couldn't have been there, and Nana, where she'd find the loo.

We had plenty of time to prepare ourselves for the guests' arrival. We checked the list to remind ourselves of who they were. Eighty-six had said they would be coming. Ten hadn't bothered to reply.

'Several of the guests own independent bookshops,' my mother explained, as we studied the names. 'Others have written books of their own.'

'You didn't tell me that other writers were coming,' I said, the reality of the situation suddenly sinking in.

'Just minor ones who've produced academic works,' she replied – as if that would reassure me.

'Academics are going to be here too?'

'I don't know why that should worry you,' Nana said, sipping her first glass of champagne. 'You're an academic yourself.'

Of course she was right. I was an academic. I shouldn't have needed reminding.

'We need a good mix of people,' Publicity explained, 'from all walks of life. You can't just have guests like Jean Claude whom you feel comfortable with.'

I'd never said he made me feel comfortable – how did she know?

'That's why I've invited Melvyn Bragg,' she continued.

'Melvyn Bragg's coming to my book launch?'

Nana passed me her champagne – she could see I was in shock. 'Melvyn Bragg?' she asked. 'Who's he?'

'Only the country's most important person in the arts,' I explained.

'He can't be more important than Parky.' Nana's eyes gleamed with excitement. 'I hope you asked him.'

'I did, as it happens,' my mother said, as she examined one of the many oil paintings that covered the high walls of the Rembrandt

Suite, 'but he couldn't come. He wished you all the best, though. I told his PA that I would send him a copy of the book.'

'It's only a matter of time, then,' was Nana's philosophical response.

'So, is Melvyn coming?' She hadn't answered that, and I was beginning to feel faint. Maybe I should have practised my speech more after all.

'He may pop in if his meeting finishes in time,' my mother said, still studying a large dark portrait beside the last of the six windows. 'They're starting to arrive,' she said suddenly, and for once she seemed nervous too. 'I recognise that man down there in the grey suit from our local delicatessen.'

'What was the point in inviting him?' I asked. It was a come-down after Melvyn.

'He sells the most delicious salami,' she replied, as if that explained everything.

We had just enough time to organise the hundred and fifty copies of the book we had brought into piles beside my desk. I'd signed some copies in advance for Nana to sell. Forty or so – we couldn't be too hopeful. What mattered was that they talked about it after-wards, as Publicity explained. The sales rep, on the other hand, said they should all buy a copy. It was the least they could do when they'd drunk our champagne.

'It doesn't matter to me whether they buy my book or not,' I replied, from a corner I found particularly appealing at that moment. 'I just wish they'd all gone home.'

My mother thought it would be all right for me to have my own glass of champagne with orange juice, as long as it was only one. And after a while, I was feeling better, especially once Nana and I had joked about the clothes some of the guests were wearing.

We had decided that I should address them from beside my mother's portrait of me, to give an extra dimension to Harriet Rose. Not just the serious, studious intellectual they saw before them, but a younger, less developed *Harriet's Smile* too. A depiction of a happy girl placed incongruously beside portraits of older, more worldly faces.

As I rose from my desk to address my guests, I knew we had chosen my outfit well. Eighty-six pairs of fascinated eyes fell upon me. *The* Harriet Rose was about to give her speech. Cameras clicked, and somewhere in the background a female journalist from the *Evening Standard*'s London column was noting my every word.

'Thank you all for coming to my launch party this evening. When my mother told me the names of the guests she had invited, I have to confess that I had no idea who most of you were. Except important people like Melvyn Bragg, of course, who, I understand, might be coming tonight if his meeting finishes in time. Successful people like him are always so busy.' I could sense it was going well, even if their faces weren't as animated as those of my teddies and Bugs Bunny had been in rehearsal. I continued: 'That's not to say you have to be famous to be important. There are some non-celebrities here this evening who are nevertheless very important indeed – and talented, and interesting, and intelligent.'

I smiled at them as I spoke and my warmth was reciprocated by a gentle nodding of heads and a murmuring of agreement.

'I'm talking, of course, about my mother and Nana.' I looked in their direction. 'Two people who so obviously stand out from the crowd.' I started to applaud, as I had planned the night before, and after a moment, some of the guests joined in, although I have to say I had hoped for something a little louder and more persuasive. But I wasn't going to be deterred by such lethargy. My publishing team deserved better than this. So I decided upon a course of action I had not intended and called, 'Hip, hip!' then broke the silence that followed with my own 'Hurray!' That would show them.

'I know some of you have come a long way this evening, and I don't just mean intellectually.' I laughed to emphasise that this had been meant as a joke. But no one else did. I should have stuck to being philosophical. I wasn't a natural comic. My mother had warned me. I could see her standing proudly at the side of the room with Nana, both urging me on with their expressive eyes. Were my eyes as expressive as theirs? I wondered suddenly. If not, they should be; they were the windows to the soul. I opened mine wider and wider until the muscles ached and I had to blink a few times to stop them watering.

A woman at the front, in a low-cut black dress that revealed her cleavage – too much I felt – whispered something in her partner's ear and he laughed out loud. My mother gave him one of her looks and they were silent again.

I had never heard my voice in public before. I had not expected them to actually listen to me. I had thought they would carry on chatting while I talked over them, like a pianist in a hotel lounge. One or two even nodded when I said something they agreed with. That really put me off – I tried to make a mental note of what I'd just said, then forgot what came next. I had talked my way through the first page of my introduction when a thought occurred to me: What if there was a heckler? I stopped speaking and looked at the crowd gathered round me. None of them looked like hecklers to me, but did I really know what hecklers looked like? I would just have to risk it, and if anyone started to shout out, I'd put them firmly in their place with an intimidating glance or a *mot juste*. And if that didn't work, I'd get my mother to deal with them.

No one was going to interrupt me tonight, not even Charlotte Goldman. Charlotte? What was Charlotte doing here? I hadn't invited her, and my mother certainly wouldn't have. 'She seems like an airhead to me,' was the only comment my mother had made about Charlotte after our evening at the health club. I tried not to notice her but it was difficult as she was dressed in bright pink with frills.

'A common cause unites us here this evening,' I went on. 'My Meditations.' I hoped no one had noticed that my voice was shaking. I sought out my mother for approbation, but I couldn't see her – she was obscured by an oversized guest. She should have known I would need her in view – surely that was the whole point of motherhood?

'So I shall let my Meditations speak for themselves.' It was beginning to sound like a party political broadcast. I should have thought of something snappier to say at this point. I flicked through the pages of my book until I found the bookmark I had placed there the night before.

'Meditation Forty-one.' I paused to ensure that everyone was keeping up. That was when I first noticed Jean Claude – the only guest I had invited – walking towards the front of the madding crowd. He nodded to me, just once, before being obliterated by a mass of pink frills.

'Meditation Forty-one.' I looked down at the written page as if I needed to be reminded of the words I would find there, as if I had not taken the whole night to memorise every one, as if I didn't care that Charlotte Goldman was engaged in animated conversation with Jean Claude.

'If I were to choose a Meditation that best described myself to you this evening, it would be Meditation Forty-one:

'I am myself, nothing can change me,
I am myself . . .'

The bright pink frills were vibrating up Charlotte's arms as she spoke, layer after layer flapping in the air, like rows of flags heralding a coup.

'You can legislate, defy, manipulate,
But whatever lies airhead . . .'

Airhead! I stopped mid-Meditation and looked around me. Had I just said 'airhead' when I had meant to say 'ahead'? And if I had, had anyone noticed? The woman from the *Evening Standard* seemed to be sniggering into her shorthand. There was nothing for it. I had to carry on:

'But whatever lies ahead
You will not change me –
I am myself.'

I paused when I reached the end of Meditation 41. In rehearsals I had read on until Meditation 44, which was a reflection on women's right to equality and independence. But suddenly I was doubting my own words. Was this really independence – Harriet Rose, the thinker, pontificating in her subtle black dress about women's rights, while the local airhead exploited her femininity in lurid pink froth to the delight of a questionably intellectual male member of the audience? I doubted it. And if it was, it was not an equality I wished to be part of, whatever Nana might say about pink. I had my principles, and if pink was the new black, it was not a colour to which I would ever subscribe. I closed my *Infinite Wisdom* and left the room. It was not a statement, it was a state of mind. Someone, somewhere, some day would understand the difference.

'You shouldn't have left like that,' Publicity complained over breakfast the following morning. 'The woman from the *Evening Standard*
wanted to interview you.'

'I didn't exactly leave,' I reminded her. 'I was in the ladies' room.'

'But for an hour and a quarter! All the guests had gone by the
time you came out.'

'I'd had a lot of orange juice,' I replied unconvincingly. 'Anyway,
what did I miss?'

It was a question I'd been longing to ask ever since my mother
had driven us home from the London Portrait Academy and I'd
pretended to be asleep on the back seat. As soon as we'd got home,
I had disappeared upstairs to bed and they had known not to disturb
me even before I'd hung the '*ne pas déranger*' sign on the door
handle.

'There was a lot of talk about how beautiful you looked,' my mother said, as she poured herself a coffee from her cafetière, 'and how interesting your book seemed.'

'I bet none of them bought a copy all the same,' I suggested. 'They looked like a mean lot to me.'

In reality, it was hard for me to remember what any of them had looked like, other than Jean Claude and Charlotte, but my mother wasn't going to know that.

'What would you say if I told you we sold out?'

I knew she was telling the truth because she smiled as she said it and looked pleased with herself. 'All one hundred and fifty?'

'Every one. Some people bought two copies so they could give one to a friend. The sales more than paid for the evening.'

I shouldn't have described them as mean. I'd liked the look of them, really. They were the sort of people who exuded style and good taste – you could tell from the aroma of high-quality perfume and aftershave that had lingered in the empty room after they'd gone.

'Did all the guests buy a copy?' I asked, as I hammered at the top of my hard-boiled egg forcefully with my spoon.

'Nana was in charge of sales,' my mother replied. 'I was mingling with the guests.'

'I don't suppose anyone bothered to speak to Charlotte Goldman in that daft pink dress?' I had to know. Holding back only gives you indigestion. There was something about my mother's hesitation that I didn't like – even though she was finishing a mouthful of croissant.

'She disappeared soon after you did,' she replied. 'I thought she might have gone to look for you.'

'She wouldn't have found me if she had,' I said. 'I locked the cloak-room door.'

'I thought it went very well.'

Did she really think I'd be persuaded that easily? 'And what about Jean Claude?' I continued. 'I expect you chatted with him?'

Before she had a chance to answer, Nana burst into the kitchen in her red velvet dressing-gown saying: 'You wouldn't be talking about the dark-haired boy in the blazer, would you?'

'I thought he was rather good-looking,' my mother replied.

'Good-looking?' said Nana. 'So was Rhett Butler, but that didn't do poor Scarlett much good.'

'Surely the problem was of Scarlett's own making?' my mother suggested reflectively, but Nana didn't seem to hear her.

'You didn't answer my question.' They needed reminding.

'He left shortly after you did as well,' my mother replied, looking at Nana, who was frying some bacon for herself.

None of us spoke over Nana's sizzling bacon, which she liked well cooked on both sides with a piece of fried bread 'for company'. Once it was nicely settled on a plate, she joined us at the breakfast table and took a long, hard look at me. 'What's the matter with you?' she said finally. 'From your expression, no one would think you'd been a raging success last night at your sell-out book launch with everybody talking about how marvellous you are.'

Nana had a certain unguarded way of putting things.

'I think Harriet's unhappy about Jean Claude chatting to Charlotte Goldman during her speech, then leaving at the same time she did.'

Sometimes I wondered if my mother was a mind-reader. Her precision was uncanny.

'And you're fretting over a fool like him?' Nana asked, arching her eyebrows and staring into my eyes until I could barely believe my own stupidity. 'You're better off with a nice bacon sandwich.'

The sales rep set off with her big black briefcase at nine thirty on Monday morning. It wasn't a proper briefcase – in fact, it was a leather shopping-bag with the handles taken off. But tucked under Nana's arm it looked pretty convincing. Inside it there were five copies of my Meditations, an invoice book, and an apple turnover to keep Nana's sugar level up. Nana was a great believer in the importance of apple turnovers. They were her answer to every crisis. When she heard that someone was ill, she would personally deliver an apple turnover to them even if it meant travelling many miles to do so.

'She'll be all right once she's had an apple turnover,' she would say. And the funny thing was they usually were.

We knew not to wish her luck as she marched off down the road towards the heart of Kensington and Chelsea. Luck had nothing to do with anything involving Nana. She would make it happen, and if

Kensington and Chelsea weren't ready to succumb to her selling powers she would find somewhere else where they were. As she disappeared into the morning sunlight, in her dark brown overcoat, turban hat and black sunglasses, we knew it might be hours before we saw her again. I had tried to persuade her to leave the hat and sunglasses behind but she said they made her look like Katharine Hepburn, and in a way they did. I pointed out that I hadn't heard Katharine Hepburn was ever a book sales rep, but my mother said that wasn't the point.

It was a nerve-racking time for us all. My mother and I waited by the telephone in case Nana had news for us, but the only time it rang, it was a wrong number. A man at the other end of the telephone asked my mother if she was 'Gladys', and she replied that if she had been she would have changed her name by now.

'There's nothing wrong with "Gladys",' the man informed her with indignation and what my mother described as 'an attitude'. 'Gladys is my mother's name.'

'And if I were your mother,' she replied, 'I would have given you the wrong number too,' and hung up.

It may sound like panic but none of us was used to being high-powered businesswomen, so we called a meeting, my mother and I, and agreed that we should drive to a few bookshops in the area and see if we could spot Nana coming out.

My mother pulled up on a double yellow line outside the first we came to and I ran in. We had guessed correctly. Nana was engaged in conversation with a male buyer beside the counter. Her bag was open and the man was reading the back flap of my book. My spirits rose when I saw that the apple turnover was still in the inside pocket of the bag, as yet uncalled upon. I hid behind a pile of Harry Potter books in case the buyer recognised me from the photograph.

Eventually the man spoke. 'The author's only fourteen,' he said, then opened the book to sample a Meditation.

'Fourteen, but with the wisdom of a sage,' Nana replied, taking out her invoice book. 'How many shall I put you down for?'

It was her confidence I admired most from my hiding-place, her bravado. I wanted to applaud and shout, 'Well done, Nana, well done!' But all I could do was listen.

'I'm not sure it's right for us,' he was saying, as he handed *Infinite Wisdom* back to Nana. I removed a copy of Harry Potter from the top of the pile to get a better look at him. The man was twenty or thirty, with long brown hair and an earring. I could see him looking Nana up and down as if she had wandered into his shop through some sort of time warp, like Doctor Who without the telephone box.

'You won't be sure until you try it, will you?' She was removing her sunglasses to give him her full glare. I began to feel sorry for him. 'May I refer you to Meditation Fifty-three?'

The man flicked hurriedly through the pages, as he had been ordered to do by the formidable representative.

'Would you like to read it aloud?'

I could see his hesitation — it couldn't have been a situation he was used to.

'Meditation Fifty-three, you said?'

'That's the chap!' Nana replied.

'"Writing requires having something to say. Reading requires a capacity for understanding. Otherwise words are mere markings on a page. Every great writer understands the need for a great reader."'

'Are you a great reader, Mr . . . ?'

'Just call me Nick.' He smiled. 'I like to think I am, Mrs . . . ?'

'Just call me Olivia.' Nana smiled back, the sense that victory was within her reach shining out of her steely blue eyes.

'Olivia, put me down for four to start with, and we'll see how it goes.'

'Shall we make that a straight half a dozen?'

Nick laughed and shook his head in the direction of a female assistant, who had been listening silently in the background, clearly overwhelmed by Nana's command of the situation.

'Go on, then, Olivia. Half a dozen.'

I waited until Nana had left the shop before I dared to move. The two assistants were poring over my Meditations, smiling and reflecting happily with each other. It was just the reaction I had hoped for in my readers: excited incredulity. I looked back over my shoulder as I went through the door. They were transfixed – Nana had pointed them in the right direction and left them wanting more.

We drove her home, our heroine, and she revelled in unfolding her success to us in every detail. It transpired that Nick's order was the last of a long line – fifty books had been ordered and others were thinking about it. At that rate, there could be two or three hundred book orders by the end of the week. We began to wonder whether we had had enough copies printed.

We stopped at a red traffic-light and a man knocked on my mother's window to sell her a copy of the *Evening Standard*. Until then I had forgotten all about the female journalist. My mother passed the man a pound coin and told him to keep the change.

'You look!' she said, throwing the paper towards me in the back seat.

'No, let Nana,' I replied, throwing it back to the front.

'Give it to me!' Nana said, with a degree of irritation. 'I don't know what all the fuss is about.'

My mother and I waited impatiently while Nana flicked through the paper. 'There's a photograph of you!' she announced. 'Don't you look a picture! I've never seen anyone who can carry off black as well as you do.'

My mother stopped the car and we all stared at the page. That was when I saw it – the headline: 'THE MEDITATIONS OF A BUDDING ROSE'. It wasn't a bad start, if a little clumsily expressed – people might think she had been referring to my chest. And there was a picture of me below it, looking ponderously at my Meditation 41. I read on: 'Fourteen-year-old schoolgirl Harriet Rose celebrated the launch of her newly published collection of Meditations at a champagne and orange juice reception held at the London Portrait Academy.' Other than the reference – unnecessary, I thought – to the orange juice, there had been nothing too disastrous so far so I continued, reading aloud now: 'She doesn't just have good looks, she also has an enchantingly naïve way of making you think. It was an entertaining evening, especially when Harriet chose to read one of her unique Meditations to her transfixed guests:

> I am myself
> Nothing can change me
> I am myself.
> You can legislate, defy, manipulate,
> But whatever lies ahead,
> You will not change me.
> I am myself.'

So she hadn't heard me say 'airhead' – there was a God, after all. I read on: 'I defy anyone to pick up *The Infinite Wisdom of Harriet Rose* and not read it with a smile. The only downfall of the evening was that it ended too abruptly. Thank you, Harriet Rose, for brightening up my Saturday night. My only criticism – stay longer next time.'

I had hoped she would enjoy my work, but praise such as this was quite an achievement. On top of that, she had chosen a suitably serious picture of me. Some journalists would have supposed a smiling photograph of a fourteen year old was more appropriate.

'That journalist wasn't daft,' said Nana, and my mother and I agreed.

After the launch party I had no intention of seeing Jean Claude again. Anyone stupid enough to listen to what Charlotte Goldman had to say while I was reading my Meditations was not worth bothering with. I agreed with my mother about that.

My mother had a knack of understanding complex affairs of the heart and translating them into simple terms: 'When he rings,' she said, 'tell him to sod off.' So I did. Of course he rang back again and again after that – until Nana answered.

'I just want to speak to Harriet for a small conversation – five minoots,' he implored.

'You had your chance, Sacha, and you blew it. Now, why don't you go and practise your Prince Charming act on your bit of candyfloss?' Nana didn't believe in giving people the benefit of the doubt.

He didn't ring again after that. I have to say, I thought she'd been just a little too harsh with him – a simple 'She's not in' would have done. Besides, he would have had no idea what candyfloss was. He probably thought it was something to do with dental hygiene.

I decided that the best way to forget about Jean Claude was to write a Meditation about him. It would help to focus my mind on his insignificance. Jean Claude would be nothing more than a numbered Meditation in a book full of them.

I curled up on my bed, took my pen out of its loop in my notebook and wrote:

> I once believed in love,
> I thought it was all true,
> But I was so naïve,
> I once believed in you.

It said it all. Now there were more pressing matters to worry about. In two days' time I would be going back to school after half-term, which meant facing Charlotte. Nana thought I should take a copy of the *Evening Standard* with me. 'That'll shut her up,' she said, whereas my mother thought I should point out how common it is to gatecrash other people's parties, especially high-profile ones held at the London Portrait Academy.

I walked tentatively to my desk, armed with a copy of the *Evening Standard* and a head crammed with put-downs. It was a French lesson first. Charlotte would like that. At least she'd be able to keep up.

I could hear her heels clicking towards her desk and smelt her cologne as she walked past me. 'Hello, Harriet!' she shouted at me from her front line.

'Hello, Charlotte.' I was polite but aloof.

'I enjoyed your book.'

Did she think she could fool me so easily? But I was ready for her. 'Thank you,' I replied, and she knew.

'It was a fantastic photo of you in the paper.'

I stuffed the *Evening Standard* up the back of my sweater and prayed that no one had seen me do it. 'Which photo was that?' I asked nonchalantly.

'I think it was the *Evening Standard*.'

The rest of the class were listening now, open-mouthed.

'Harriet was in the *Evening Standard*?' Jason exclaimed. 'What for?'

'She's written a book – *The Infinite Wisdom of Harriet Rose*. It's very good.'

I have to be honest, it wasn't going according to plan. My best lines had already been rendered redundant and I had barely opened my mouth. Then, suddenly, I had a brainwave: 'Have you read it, then?' I looked hard into her eyes as she formulated her response so she would be in no doubt that I would know if she lied.

'No,' she said.

I smiled wryly at the rest of the class in turn.

'But Jean Claude read it to me.'

My mother had arranged for me to be interviewed on the local radio station that evening. It had not been difficult to persuade them – they had recognised my name from the *Evening Standard* article.

'We'd love to have a chat with Harriet,' Angela had said. 'Can you bring her in this evening – about five thirty?'

So I was duly brought in, whether I liked it or not. And I did not. I just wanted to be left alone. I had been humiliated, and nothing my mother could say on the way to the studios made the slightest difference – how could she know Charlotte would live to regret it, and so what if she did? That would only put her equal with me. I deserved to be ahead, didn't I?

'Remember Meditation Forty-one,' my mother urged, as we drew into the studio's car park. But that was the whole problem. As I had expressed in that Meditation, nothing *could* change me. Whatever lay ahead, I was always myself. My interests lay in expanding my mind, not my address book. No matter how much Charlotte manipulated, I would still be the same gullible, naïve, unworldly self.

'For God's sake, Harriet, think of your father. It's not sports day now. You can still win the red ribbon!'

It was the jolt I needed. Suddenly I was Scarlett O'Hara again.

'Take me to Angela! I'm ready for her.'

My mother squeezed my hand and I promised myself I wouldn't let her down.

Angela, my mother and I chatted over hot chocolate as a preamble to the recording. It was bitter, lukewarm in plastic cups, out of a machine. Angela swallowed hers in one gulp, as if it were medicine, and when she had finished I noticed that it had left a brown stain on her upper lip like a moustache. I wondered whether I should point it out to her, but decided against it – I had heard media people could be quite touchy. She might take it out on me later. Whatever I thought about Angela and her mobile mustachioed mouth, I needed her on side.

'So, Harriet, you've written a book. Fan*ta*stic!'

I doubted the sincerity of her enthusiasm even before she added, 'What's it about?'

My mother adopted her role of publicity manager and took out a copy of the Meditations from her handbag.

'Thanks! *The Infinite Wisdom of Harriet Rose, A Collection of Meditations.* Great title! So it's like, poems, Harriet?'

Surely the clue was in the title.

'More like philosophical reflections, really,' I explained diplomatically.

'Reflections – I love things to do with the mind and stuff like that, don't you, Mrs Rose?'

I knew what my mother was thinking because it was my thought too: thank God we didn't bring Nana!

'Just call me Mia,' my mother replied.

'As in Mia Farrow?'

Angela thought this was particularly amusing until I topped it with: 'No, as in "Mamma Mia".'

'"Mamma Mia"!' Angela shrieked with laughter. 'Good one, Harriet!'

Now that we were all getting on so well it seemed the right time to start recording, so we moved to another room filled with sound equipment and microphones and the interview began.

'Tonight we have with us fourteen-year-old Harriet Rose, author of *The Infinite Wisdom of Harriet Rose, A Collection of Meditations*, which is out now in hardback. Hi, Harriet!'

'Hello.'

'Tell us a bit about your Meditations – you describe them as psychological reflections.'

'Philosophical.' I couldn't let her make a basic categorical error without correcting it, however much she disliked me for it. I would just have to risk it.

'Quite the professor, aren't we?'

It was a tone I hadn't heard in Angela before. Suddenly I saw her in a different light – still with the same brown moustache but, instead of Laurel and Hardy, she had turned into Basil Fawlty. Remembering my promise to myself on our way into the studios, I replied, 'No. Professors charge for lectures.'

It was the beginning of a new Harriet Rose – feisty, assertive and ready for anyone. Scarlett, you would have been proud of me!

Not being in a position to debate the niceties of the philosophical/psychological distinction, Angela had no answer so, predictably, she changed the subject. 'The book is published by Miandol – I haven't heard of them before.' She took on a Charlottian expression and I guessed she had done her research.

'That's right. Mia, as you know, is my mother's name and Ol is short for Olivia – my grandmother. They published the book for my birthday. It was the best present I've ever had.'

It was obvious from Angela's demeanour that she thought she had found an Achilles heel. 'That's a lovely story, Harriet. You must have been so pleased when you saw it.'

The day before, when I was younger and more naïve, I would have taken her words at face value and thought I'd misjudged the woman. But today – today was the day after yesterday, and I was ready for her. 'I was very pleased,' I said, then waited.

'Especially as I expect it had been turned down by lots of main-stream publishers.'

So that was what she thought. 'Actually, no.'

I paused long enough for her to read hesitation in my silence. 'No? You mean no publishing house has seen your Meditations?'

'Not a single one. Until my Meditations were published, the only people who had seen or heard them were my mother and Nana, and now they're selling in bookshops up and down the country, with only my mother as publicity manager and Nana as sales representative. It says a lot about the book, doesn't it?'

Angela thought it was time to play Robbie Williams's latest single, saying, as she did: 'Here's someone with *real* talent.'

But that didn't bother me or my mother. No publicity magnate in the country could have got us better publicity.

'What a funny idea for a present.'

It was the response I had anticipated, but not from one of my teachers.

'How many copies are there?'

'A thousand,' I replied, as Miss Mason replaced the book on my desk without having read a single Meditation.

'A thousand? What are you going to do with them all?' she asked, her neck reddening right down to her chest.

'She's going to sell them,' laughed Jason, 'at book signings up and down the country!'

'Are they doing two for one at Waterstone's?' interjected Miles.

'No,' I replied casually. 'They're selling them at the full price – thirteen ninety-nine.' Then I added, 'But I might be able to get you one at a discount if you can't afford it.'

I could barely believe they were my words rolling out of my mouth like cannonballs, annihilating the opposition with ease.

'I haven't seen it on Amazon yet!' Miles retorted, with a sly grin at Jason.

'Then keep looking,' I said, wondering if I would ever be able to explain the workings of the Internet to Nana. 'It's just a matter of time.'

'There will be no sales in the classroom, Harriet!' Miss Mason announced, with irritation.

'Then I'll sell them outside in the lunchbreak,' I replied quietly.

I sold thirty copies in an hour, which made me realise the importance of the right publicity. By two o'clock I was used to signing books. The secret was to write the same in each one. Otherwise it took too long and you ran the risk of writing something in a hurry that you would live to regret. So I wrote: 'With all good wishes, Harriet', with a diagonal line under my name for definition.

If only I could have given a signed copy to my father. How proud he would have been. He admired my writing – he said it demonstrated my spiritual side. 'Have you met my daughter, the writer?' He would have practised saying it in front of my mother and me to make us laugh. And we would have laughed, the three of us, laughed and cried. Then he would have read the book, slowly, in detail, until he knew each word I had written by heart, pausing here and there to read a favourite Meditation aloud, until he reached the final page. Then he would have closed the book, wiped the tears from his eyes and said . . .

But what would he have said? I couldn't decide. I couldn't even remember what he had said when he was proud of something I'd done. And he *had* been proud of me. I knew he had. I racked my brains to think of all the times I'd made him proud. There was the time when I'd come first in my Latin exam, and when I'd been awarded the school prize for English after my first year at senior school, and when I'd stood up to Mark, the class bully, who had been picking on poor Alice because she had spots and wore a brace and was too fat to get over the horse in gymnastics. Then there was the time when my father had been ill and I'd carried on revising for my exams so that he wouldn't blame himself if I slipped back in class, and then, when he was almost gone, and he had turned to me and my mother, at his bedside, the morphine drip in his left arm, and he had taken our hands and said, 'I wonder at my good fortune.'

'I know not where you are, but I shall love you from afar,' I had written in Meditation 34 after he had died. I wanted to know where he was. At first I'd thought he would get a message to me, explaining what it was like, that place where he had gone that no one knows anything about. It seemed selfish not to let me know he'd arrived safely. What harm could there be in a simple 'I'm happy and well and wish you were here'? Obviously he couldn't have sent a post-card but his voice would have done, just one sentence. Perhaps not even those particular words – he might not wish I was there, it would be quieter without me, and he probably hoped I'd stay here a while longer. But words to that effect. Or, if not words, a sign – not a V sign, like he gave my mother when she drove by mistake through a red light in the Old Brompton Road just as he was about to cross it and he hadn't realised it was her, but a special sign that only I, and perhaps my mother, would recognise. But none came, or if it did I missed it. He had never been the greatest communicator – why should he be any different now? I suppose there was always the possibility that he wasn't anywhere any more. That would certainly explain his silence. Yet it didn't strike me as a satisfactory explanation, and that was what I wanted. I would just have to accept there were some things we couldn't explain, like why England couldn't even win the World Cup when they had beaten Germany 5–1. It may seem a trivial analogy, but that's what analogies are all about – to philosophers at least. Reduce the problem to its simplest terms, then look at what you're left with. Philosophers have done it with hares, tortoises, arrows, heaps of sand, brains in vats, even ravens. So what was wrong with using the England football team? Some people even seemed to think that David Beckham *was* God. And how many players are there in a football team? Twelve – there you are! Or is it eleven? Anyway, what really matters is the *principle*, not getting bogged down with too much detail.

'You think too much,' Nana would say to me, when she saw me in a reflective state. Then she would sing a song to make me laugh. Living with Nana was like being in one long musical – there was no situation too sombre for a song. Not even she understood the song's relevance sometimes: she would hear a word that reminded her of one, and off she would go.

Maybe she was right and I did think too much. But surely that was better than talking too much, like Jason. He never knew when to stop. Why is it, as I'd asked in Meditation 50, that those with the least to say always say the most? I had once read of a Greek philosopher, Cratylus, who had become so disillusioned with the futility of language as a medium to communicate thought that he had decided to remain silent and wiggle his little finger when anyone spoke to him. I wondered why he had chosen his little finger – probably as a symbol of the smallness of things. No one but a philosopher would understand that.

At the end of the afternoon I signed one last book, then headed towards the school gates. It was the time of day I liked best – just before teatime and *The Weakest Link*. I wandered towards freedom, feet firmly on the ground, my mind lost in contemplation. Was my father still with me? Could he hear my thoughts? Why did Jason speak so loudly?

It was the lights I noticed first – bright flickering lights accompanied by clicking noises on the other side of the gates. As I drew nearer, the sound increased, and not only with proximity. And the lights appeared to flash faster and faster. Was it a mirage? Hadn't I eaten enough chocolate that afternoon? Was it the sign I'd been hoping for?

'Harriet! Over here!'

My name! Had a voice called my name?

'Harriet Rose!'

I wasn't mistaken. There it was again. As I hurried towards the half-open gates I felt in my heart that something special was about to happen – a metaphysical event about to occur, a messenger about to arrive.

'Harriet! Can I have a word? Over here – the *Kensington and Chelsea Messenger*.'

I had heard of Gabriel, Michael and Raphael, but the Kensington and Chelsea messenger was a new one on me. Could it be that I was a little out of touch, celestially speaking?

'Harriet! Give us a smile!'

I did as I was ordered – how could I have done otherwise? – and it was as if the whole sky lit up, a majestic blaze overhanging our very own school gates, silhouetting Harriet Rose as she stood with angelic smile, radiant in wondrous anticipation.

'Who's there?' I asked, into the brightness.

'We're from the press, Harriet. Can we ask you a few questions?'

It might have been the shock, or perhaps the disappointment, but

I couldn't think of a single thing to say. Question after question they hurled at me, the press, as I stood there in silence, trying to think of something sharp or intelligent to say. But nothing came out of my mouth. Not a word. So I lifted my right hand in front of my mouth and wiggled my little finger.

It was the photograph that every one of them used, each with their own heading, Harriet Rose and her wiggling little finger. I liked the *Kensington and Chelsea Messenger* heading most:

HARRIET DOESN'T GIVE A DIGIT WHAT ANYONE THINKS

When fourteen-year-old schoolgirl Harriet Rose was asked about her sudden rise to fame since publication of her book *The Infinite Wisdom of Harriet Rose*, the enigmatic author had only one response – to wiggle her little finger. Anyone who wants to know more about her thoughts will have to pay £13.99 for them. Nick Brady, a buyer at Kensington Books, where *The Infinite Wisdom* has made the 100 Best-selling Hardbacks list in its first week, said, 'I think the book's success lies in its indi-viduality – it took a great mind to write it, but it needs an equally great mind to understand it, to paraphrase one of Harriet's Meditations. We're strongly recommending it.' Well done, Harriet. Perhaps you'll give us a wave next time.

The *Hammersmith Daily* was not nearly so flattering but, then, what do you expect from a neighbourhood whose main claim to fame is a flyover? It began 'A ROSE BY ANY OTHER NAME', then went on to suggest that the success of my Meditations was due to their having been written by a schoolgirl and published by her mother and grand-mother – the individuality of the concept, rather than its content, had made it popular, was what they were trying inarticulately to say, but what they actually wrote was: 'When you read the book you wonder whether it's all due to her mum and gran's efforts more than hers – any schoolgirl could have done it, and that's a fact, not a medi-tation. You can wiggle your little finger, Harriet, as much as you like but we give you the thumbs down.'

The article that concerned me most, though, was in the *Pimlico Press*. Again, the same photograph, this time with a more serious tone:

HARRIET LOST FOR WORDS

When Harriet Rose was invited to discuss her newly published tome, *The Infinite Wisdom of Harriet Rose*, she had nothing to say. All the fourteen-year-old schoolgirl was able to do was to wiggle her little finger at the cameras. Her petite schoolfriend, Charlotte Goldman, explained: 'Harriet is a very private person – quite shy, really. We were taught in philosophy about an ancient philosopher who went around wiggling his little finger at people, rather than speaking to them, and Harriet probably thought she'd do the same. She's quite impressionable like that, but underneath she's a really, really nice person.' Perhaps Harriet should take a leaf out of her friend's book instead of taking her own too seriously.

Impressionable? Charlotte Goldman had described me as impressionable? Charlotte Goldman, whose style fluctuated between Charlotte Church and Charlotte Brontë, depending on which magazine article she had just been reading? And what did she know about Cratylus? I'm surprised she didn't think it was a term used in human anatomy. She must have hung around the journalists when I'd gone, hoping to get her pasty face in the newspaper — she would have shown them her knickers for an opportunity like that.

'But where does it get her?' my mother said. 'They only spoke to her at all in order to find out about you.'

She was right, of course. I was the one they wanted to know about — I was the enigmatic Harriet Rose, while she was just a 'petite schoolfriend'. How patronising was that?

We decided to buy a red leather album for the press cuttings. On the front page we juxtaposed the two versions of the sports-day photo — the head shot from my book and the full-length one in my sack. It brought a lump to my throat, seeing them together like that. The two versions of Harriet Rose, author of *The Infinite Wisdom of Harriet Rose*.

My mother had taken several photographs at the launch party. She was a good photographer and had managed to capture most of the guests, chatting or listening to my short speech. I was surprised to find one of Charlotte Goldman, though. My mother tried to flick past it, but she couldn't hide it from me. Even with half her head cut off I could tell it was her.

'What does she think she looks like in that tacky pink dress?' Nana asked, tearing her out of the photograph to leave a crowd of guests with an empty space in the middle.

'I thought you liked pink, Nana,' I replied, picking up the remains of the photograph and stuffing it into my pocket.

'Not on someone with her colouring. She looks like the Pink Panther.'

When I studied the torn picture later, in the seclusion of my bedroom, I could make out Jean Claude quite clearly, especially when I held the magnifying-glass close to his face. I had to admit that he looked quite handsome in his navy blazer and pale blue shirt – I had only seen him in swimming shorts or jeans. It showed he'd made an effort for my special evening – unless he'd just thought lots of women would be there. That's the trouble with disappointment: it leaves you more cynical than you were before.

Surely he must have seen me in one of the local newspapers – he was living in South Kensington, the *Kensington and Chelsea Messenger* area. He could at least have written a note to congratulate me on my success. And as I had been left in no doubt that he had read the book, a simple '*bien fait*' would have done. How had he really behaved that night? I found myself asking. The truth was I didn't know. He had read my Meditations to Charlotte, if she was to be believed, but in what circumstances? She might have queued for a bus with him after the party – you can wait for hours for a number seventy. Or perhaps the lift had stuck at the London Portrait Academy on the way out. Again, entirely possible.

I was beginning to sound like a romantic victim from one of those articles in women's magazines: 'Are you sure it was really *his* fault? One hundred ways to test whether you made him dump you: score under 20, you have nothing to blame yourself for; 20 to 50, you probably could have been a bit more understanding; and over 50, the poor bloke had no choice – try complimenting him more next time (if there is a next time).' They should have had my mother write their articles – a simple 'Sod off' would save a lot of heartache in the long run. It was what English women had excelled at for generations – wasn't that what *Pride and Prejudice* was all about? Tell him what you think, then wait and see how he reacts. If he comes back, he might be worth a second chance. If not, well, so bloody what, frankly, Mr Darcy? All you read in magazines was how to get him, how to steal him, how to keep him, how to seduce him, how to manipulate him, how to win him back, how to marry him, how to divorce him, and how to make him pay for it. When did you ever read about how to love him? Did no one want to know how to act with pride and dignity any more? Why should anyone *want* to steal, manipulate, seduce or marry a man who was not entirely devoted to her for who she was, not what she had been told to be in order to get what she wanted? Not Harriet Rose.

If Jean Claude truly wanted to get to know me, as he had said, it was up to him to find out. He already knew something of me through my Meditations, which was a lot more than I knew about him. When I stopped to think about it, he had told me very little about himself. All he had said was that he was studying at a sixth-form college in London. I didn't even know his surname.

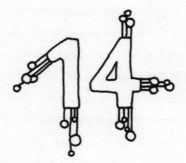

Once a term our class went on an outing to somewhere important in London. We were allowed to make suggestions of places we would like to visit, but they had to be 'culturally important' or of 'sociological interest'. I had suggested that Harrods would fulfil both criteria, but Miss Foster said I was being controversial.

It may sound silly, but I wasn't entirely sure what 'controversial' meant so I looked it up in my pocket dictionary, which I always kept in my handbag. It said 'fond of, or causing, disputation'. For precision, I looked up 'disputation'. It said: 'argumentative debate or disagreement'. Miss Foster believed me to be fond of argumentative debate because I had suggested that Harrods might be of sociological and cultural interest. I looked up 'sociological': 'studying human society, in particular, civilised society, or social problems'. I saw nothing controversial in the belief that Harrods was an ideal place to observe both civilised society (they sold Chanel, for goodness' sake) and social problems (wasn't that the reason they banned backpacks?). As for cultural – 'broadening or improving the intellect, tastes, etc.' – I had written some of my best Meditations over lunch in their tapas restaurant on the lower ground floor.

I came to the conclusion that either Miss Foster had used the wrong word – which was quite possible, given that she was a geography teacher – or that she herself was being controversial in accusing me of it. I replaced my dictionary in my handbag with the swiftness of a card-dealer and said, 'I can't honestly see why it's more controversial to suggest Harrods than the Princess Diana Memorial Fountain,' which had been Miss Foster's own idea.

To my surprise, I had the unanimous support of my classmates, none of whom were particularly keen to wander around a watery garden feature surrounded by tourists when they could be relaxing in air-conditioning with kiwi and passionfruit pick-me-ups in Harrods' Dress Circle Restaurant on the first floor. Miss Foster, who I suspected had a secret penchant for my idea deep down, conceded.

And so it was that Class 3B found themselves walking through the streets of South Kensington towards Knightsbridge in search of cultural or sociological interest. Miss Foster and Charlotte led the group. I could hear them babbling away about geographical regions of France and the vast number of French people who lived in South Kensington. Miss Foster joked that it had become known as 'Sud de Kensington', which Charlotte seemed to find side-splittingly amusing, for some reason best known to herself and Miss Foster.

I preferred being at the back of the group so that I could observe what everyone else was doing without them observing me. Not that there was a great deal for me to observe, other than Jason and Miles discussing how badly Chelsea had played at home that weekend and

Jason demonstrating how Lampard could have done better. We were a quiet group on the whole – even Charlotte seemed subdued that day. I put it down to a fear that she might not have put enough sunblock on her lily-white face. But I was wrong. There was something else on her mind. She slowed down long enough for me to catch her up, then, taking me aside, she whispered into my ear, 'Isn't that Jean Claude on the other side of the road?'

At first I thought she was teasing me, so I took no notice and increased my pace in the hope that she would fall off her high-heeled sandals. But somehow she managed to keep up with me, saying, 'I can't be sure, but it does look like him.'

She reminded me suddenly of a mosquito, buzzing in my ear, then biting me when I wasn't looking. Should I brush her off, like the blood-sucking insect she was, or was it time to be controversial?

'Look, Charlotte, why don't you just—'

'Hello, Harriet, how are you?'

His voice was deeper than I remembered, the French accent more pronounced. It had the effect on Charlotte of a bright light in a previously darkened room.

'*Bonjour, Jean Claude,*' she said, as if he had addressed her. '*Ça va?*'

Jean Claude did not respond, but continued to look at me as if he was willing me to speak.

'I am very well, thank you, Jean Claude,' I said finally in my best Elizabeth Bennet voice, hoping the intonation would be obvious even to a foreigner.

'I wanted to say thank you for your party – I enjoyed it.'

'Not at all,' I replied, adding, 'You remember Charlotte?'

'Yes, of course. Hello, Charlotte.'

I could have sworn he was irritated by her presence – even wanted to say, 'Go away and leave us alone!' But I might have been mistaken.

I was no expert where affairs of the heart were concerned. So I observed Charlotte's reaction, uncertain what I was looking for, until she said coyly, 'Thanks for the other evening. I really enjoyed it.'

I had all the confirmation I needed. I turned to Jean Claude and said, 'Well, goodbye, Jean Claude,' then walked abruptly away. It might not have been 'Sod off' but it was the best I could do. I wanted to look back to see if they were planning their next encounter, laughing at my naïveté, but I didn't. Instead I sat on a bench that was tucked back from the road and took out my notebook, intending to write a Meditation that would capture what I was feeling just then. But nothing came. I was suffering from what was described in literary circles as 'writer's block'. I couldn't just close the book on an empty page and replace my unused pen. I tried again, and before long I found myself writing: 'I have learned a lot about cultural importance and sociological interest today: if you put your trust in a smooth-talking Frenchman it is only a matter of time before you get bitten by a mosquito.' Now I was ready to return to my class-mates.

'You should have been here fifteen minutes ago!' Miss Foster exclaimed, as I approached them.

'Why? What happened?' I answered boldly. I had waited years to use those words, ever since my mother had told me that that was what she had said to her own teacher when she was late for school. The problem was that, unlike my mother, I was never late for anything, except assembly (and that was only because she didn't get me up in time), so this had been my first opportunity to use them. It should have come as no surprise to find they did not sound as witty when I said them. I should have practised their delivery over the years – I was not a natural extrovert like my mother.

'What happened?' I tried again, smiling this time as I spoke. But

Miss Foster and the others just stared at me, looking puzzled. I felt like a failed comedienne about to be heckled off stage. It was not the response I had anticipated — it had sounded so funny when my mother said it.

'Nothing happened, Harriet. We were waiting for you to arrive. Now that you have deigned to join us, we can go in.'

It was cooler inside than out, which only went to prove that Harrods had been the better option. Miss Foster told us to be back at the same entrance half an hour later. I suspected she wanted to head for the beauty salon to have her hairy legs waxed. I made a mental note to look out for them later when we met up. But my most pressing concern was where *I* should go.

My favourite part of the store was the designer room on the first floor. My mother had bought my Chanel belt there as my thirteenth birthday present, the first birthday after my father's death. She had known it fitted me because I had tried it on the previous time we had been there together, and she had said I looked '*très chic*' in it. I had had no idea she would buy it for me, though, even when I unwrapped the Harrods bag. I thought it would be an astringent lotion for an oily T-section that we had been looking at on the same day.

But today was not a day for looking at what I couldn't have. Today was a day for casting aside the old and getting on with the new. And even though it had been my decision to visit Harrods, in so doing I was clinging to somewhere I knew. But that was not the way to move forward: no progress was made by standing still. I was in the food hall when I reached my decision. I hadn't meant to go there — I must have been drawn that way by genetic instinct. But nothing would deter me from my plan of action, not even a woman with a silver tray giving out complimentary smoked salmon and caviar blinis.

'Have you tried the orange stuff?' Jason Smart asked, his mouth stuffed with oak-smoked salmon, which had spent a lifetime, no doubt, swimming confidently up gleaming Scottish rivers to reach that destination.

'I haven't time to stop, I'm on my way to a bookshop not far from here,' I explained, for the benefit of Jason as well as the woman with the tray, and I pointed in the direction I believed the small independently owned bookshop to be in.

'Why are you going there?' Jason asked. 'I thought you wanted to come to Harrods.'

'I did once,' I explained, 'but life has moved on since then. That's the whole concept of progress. Head constantly in a forward direction, mentally and physically, while keeping the goal in view.'

'That's what I say too,' Jason replied, with a sincerity I'd never seen in him before.

'Really, Jason?' I said, wondering whether I should take him with me and feed his undeveloped potential with a few good books.

'Yeah. Every time Chelsea are playing away,' he explained. It was for the best, really. I needed to do this alone.

'I'd better go,' I said. 'There'll be a lot to discuss at the bookshop and I want to get back in time to meet Miss Foster.'

It wasn't exactly a lie. Nana had mentioned a small bookshop not far from Harrods. I knew my own book wasn't stocked there because I remembered Nana having said the buyer was offhand with her when she had tried to show it to her.

'Miandol Books?' she had asked. 'I haven't heard of them. Are they new?'

'New and original, like the author,' Nana had replied majestically.

'Not my cup of tea,' the woman had said, handing my book back to Nana, unread.

'I should have guessed that,' Nana had replied, looking her up and down, 'a small independent bookshop like you. I'll stick to Pipers in future.' And with that she had left and headed with more success to Pipers in Piccadilly 'where they know class when they see it'.

Undeterred, I decided that today was the day to have a go myself. Life, as I had made a point of stressing in my Meditation 48, was too short to wait for it to find you. I did not need a two-faced Frenchman to teach me that. After all, where would music have been if Mozart had waited until his fourteenth birthday to start composing? Ten years' creativity worse off, that's where.

I strode into the bookshop with confidence and said to the woman behind the till, whom I recognised instantly from Nana's description of her black-rimmed glasses and frosty glare: 'I'm looking for *The Infinite Wisdom of Harriet Rose, A Collection of Meditations*, but I can't seem to find it. Can you tell me where it is?'

The woman pressed some keys on her computer without even looking at me, and said: 'What's the name of the author?'

'Harriet Rose,' I replied, in a tone that must have left her wishing she hadn't asked. 'That's H-A-R-R—'

'I know how to spell it,' she interrupted, looking at me for the first time.

'Who's the publisher?'

'Miandol Books,' I said clearly, careful not to spell it this time.

'How do you spell that?' she asked, and I wished Nana was there to hear us.

'As it sounds,' I replied.

There was a pause while she tapped a few more keys and read her screen. Finally she said, with a grimace of satisfaction, 'We don't stock it.'

'Really?' I tried to sound surprised. 'But everyone's talking about it.'

'Well, I'm not!' she snapped, adjusting her glasses back up her nose.

'How could you,' I said, with a smile, 'if you don't even have it in stock? Do you know where I might find one?'

She peered impatiently at me. 'You could try Waterstone's.'

I took out my notepad and scribbled 'Waterstone's.' 'Thank you. You couldn't phone them for me, could you? I don't want to walk all that way if they don't have it.'

To my surprise, she picked up her phone and dialled a number. 'Hello, Jean,' she said. 'It's Victoria from My Kind of Books. I have a customer with me who's looking for a book called *The Infinite Wisdom of*— Who did you say it was by?'

'Harriet Rose is the name of the author. Rose like the flower,' I said.

'Harriet Rose. I don't suppose you stock it, do you?' She laughed as she asked and I knew why Nana had disliked her.

'You do?' she said, with surprise, placing her hand over the receiver to ask if I'd like to reserve a copy.

'It would help if Jean could tell me from her screen which other branches of Waterstone's stock it, so I can work out which is nearest to me.' I waited patiently with my pen in my hand and a piece of paper ready to jot down the names of all the branches I knew Nana had sold it to.

'Earls Court may have a copy.'

'Just one?' I asked.

'Six,' she muttered, with reluctance.

'And where else?'

It took her fifteen minutes to reel off, and me to write down, the locations of the fifty-four Waterstone's branches that stocked my book. When she had finished I thanked her for her assistance and suggested that as so many other bookshops stocked it, it might be an idea for My Kind of Books to do so too. It was going so well – I couldn't have planned it better if I'd tried for a week – until suddenly, out of nowhere, I heard a voice shouting across the shop, 'Harriet! Jason said we might find you here. We're all waiting for you outside Harrods! Harriet Rose!'

It was Miss Foster. The woman behind the till smiled at me sarcastically, like a James Bond villain, and I disappeared into the street.

15

It was an unusual time for a rising star. How many celebrities spend their day arguing with the headmistress while their mother, the publicity manager, organises their first television appearance?

I hadn't slept well the night before. I must have sensed somehow what the next day held in store for me. Why did it matter if I arrived fifteen minutes late, when assembly was over? It was nothing new — I'd done it for years and no one had thought to mention it before. I never felt comfortable in a crowd when that crowd was singing morning hymns. Not that I had anything against hymns. It was singing in public that made me uncomfortable. That was why I mimed. No one ever knew — how could they? My lips moved in unison with everyone else's and their noise was too loud to notice whether I added a note to it. It was the same with birthday parties. I hated them too. All that animated hysteria and feigned joviality culminating in 'Happy Birthday To You'.

When Miss Grout called me into her study first thing that morning – or after assembly – I had no idea what she wanted to say. It began quite well: she said, 'Good morning,' and asked me to take a seat. But it went downhill after that.

'There are a few matters I want to discuss with you, Harriet.'

She was consulting notes as she addressed me but I wasn't close enough to her desk to read them upside-down. I pulled my chair a little nearer and tried again. Miss Grout looked up, spotted me and curled her left hand round the top of the page. This was serious.

'First, I must ask you to ensure that you arrive at school on time in future. Our day begins at nine a.m., not nine fifteen, as you well know.'

Somebody must have told her. She wouldn't have noticed if I'd arrived at nine thirty dressed as Elvis Presley and serenaded her with 'Love Me Tender'. There must be more.

'Second, you must try to join in more in class. Your marks are very good, but your teachers' reports suggest that you're quite happy for the rest of the class to speak up while you sit quietly in the background – smiling sometimes, apparently.'

She uttered the last three words as if I had committed the ultimate *faux pas*. To be silent was bad enough, but to smile at the same time bordered on revolutionary. What coup did I have planned, secretly behind my incongruous smile, was what she wanted to know. Was that it? I'd been sent to Grout's study over a smile?

'I speak when I have something to say, Miss Grout.' If she wanted me to speak, then that was what I would do – to please her, of course. 'As a general principle, I don't like crowds. It probably has something to do with being an only child and an only grandchild. I'm not used to fighting for attention. At home I get it automatically. That's

what makes me different from, say, Jason Smart. Jason, as you probably know – or may not – has three brothers, one younger than him
and two older. Jason never stops speaking and not just ordinary
speaking, loud, boisterous speaking, usually accompanied by demon-
strative arm movements. He can't help it – it's what he's used to.
But you don't call him into your room after assembly to ask him why
he talks too much.' I paused, reflected then added a softening, 'Miss
Grout.'

'Well!' she said finally, as if she'd been winded in a rugby tackle.
'Is there anything else you'd like to add before we move on?'

So, there was more. I'd suspected as much from the length of
her notes and the series of question marks and exclamation marks
at the end.

'Just Kant,' I said.

Miss Grout looked flushed as she lifted her gaze from her notes.
'What did you say, Harriet?'

'Kant,' I repeated, louder this time. No one had ever suggested
that Miss Grout was hard of hearing. I tried again: 'Immanuel Kant,
the great German philosopher.'

'Oh, yes, of course.' She seemed relieved, as if she had been rid
of a new difficulty. Probably hadn't heard of Kant.

'He never left Königsberg, the town where he was born. He kept
himself to himself, was not a man for chit-chat, but he produced
on paper some of the most fascinating Critiques the western world
has ever known.'

'So you think you're . . . a great philosopher, do you?' She laughed
as she spoke and lifted her pen, ready for the final battle to begin.
'That brings me nicely to one final little matter, the matter of your
book – your Meditations.'

Did she think I had forgotten what my book was about?

'What about it?' I asked, wondering if, perhaps, she wanted a free copy for the school library.

'There have been reporters outside the school gates.'

'They wrote about me in their newspapers,' I said proudly. 'And I was on the radio.'

'Quite.'

That was it. Just 'Quite', and a lot of scribbling. Then, suddenly, out of nowhere, just as we were beginning to get along, 'What exactly do you think you're trying to achieve, Harriet?'

I hadn't been prepared for that one so I sat silently, and smiled.

'There!' she exclaimed excitedly, pointing an accusing finger towards my mouth. 'That's precisely what I was talking about earlier. Why can't you answer my question?'

But what *was* I trying to achieve? It wasn't a question I'd stopped to ask myself. I should have done. It was important, not just for me but for my readers. This woman was more intelligent than I'd thought.

'That's an interesting question,' I said quietly, as I mused over an answer, for myself as much as Miss Grout. 'I suppose I want to contribute something to the world that will remain when I'm gone.'

'And why would you want to do that?' she asked, as if she had never heard of such a thing.

'Writing books is not as painful as having babies,' I joked, but her face made it clear that she wasn't amused.

'You want to be famous, do you?' Her tone now was one of, 'Aha, it's as I expected!'

It was Miss Marlowe's fault. I knew I shouldn't have admitted in her class that I'd once wanted to be famous. Now none of them would understand my motives at all. 'I want to be remembered –

it's not the same thing. Haven't you ever wanted to be remembered for something that matters, Miss Grout?' I enquired, now that we were having a philosophical discussion. 'Something other than heading a small school in Kensington and giving out penalties?'

Miss Grout put down her pen and crossed her arms over her heavy breasts. 'And you actually think that people will remember Harriet Rose's Meditations for years to come, do you?'

It was clear from her expression that she had not thought about it in that way before. Now we really were making progress. All of a sudden she was seeing her pupil in a new light.

'If I'm able to influence just one individual with my Meditations – perhaps to consider a dilemma from a different perspective, or to reflect on a matter they had not reflected on before, to smile or shed a tear – I shall have truly achieved something important to me. That's what I'm trying to achieve, Miss Grout, to answer your original question more fully.'

She could go back to Miss Marlowe and explain my aims to her, and she, too, would understand.

'Harriet – it's a book of teenage thoughts composed by a teenager and published by her mother and grandmother. Let's put it into perspective!'

'Thank you, Miss Grout,' I said, smiling radiantly at her. At last she was beginning to realise just how much I had already achieved.

No more words were needed between Miss Grout and me: we understood each other and were ready to move on. She didn't need to ask me to leave her room and I didn't need to ask her if I could go. I stood up in silence, nodded once, for courtesy, and went to my classroom. Later that day I left a copy of my Meditations in a Jiffy-bag by her study door. In it I had written:

'To Miss Grout, who understands what I am trying to achieve.' She would like that.

In a way my discussion with Miss Grout could not have taken place at a better time. Like a rehearsal before the main act, it prepared me for my TV performance that evening.

The Face of London was an exciting opportunity created by the *London Live* programme to encourage talented young people to compete for this prestigious title. Publicity had first heard about it on morning television during a pause in a busy schedule for a coffee and a croissant. Like any successful publicist, my mother had got straight on to the telephone and, after a series of irritating conversations with a receptionist who seemed unable to grasp the fact that the programme would be missing out should she fail to put her through to the relevant person, she finally spoke to Bill. It did not take her long to convince him that if they wanted contenders for the Face of London – ambitious, entrepreneurial, self-motivated young people – he should waste no time in interviewing Harriet Rose, the thinking adolescent.

She had faxed Bill a copy of the *Evening Standard* article and he had phoned her to say he would like to film me provisionally for the show. It had to be our greatest coup so far, and all thanks to my ingenious mother and her inimitable powers of persuasion. Once Bill had met us, I wouldn't be 'provisional' for long.

At six thirty p.m. he arrived at our house with his equipment. That gave me just enough time to slip out of my uniform and into a pair of low-cut jeans and a black T-shirt with 'Why' written in white across the chest area. Image was so important in the media. I needed to come across as sharp, intellectually challenging and focused in my first TV appearance to the nation. The 'Why' would achieve that before I even opened my mouth, as we had to explain to Nana. She had never taken to the T-shirt. She said it looked daft, that people would think I didn't understand anything. 'What's the point of "Why" when no one knows what the question is? You'd be better off with "Because" than "Why". At least then people would think you had the answer.'

Thank goodness my mother was on my side. Otherwise I would have been facing the cameras in a red Aran sweater Nana had knitted for me when I was twelve. 'Red's what you want. No one misses red – especially with a nice red band round your lovely hair.'

'"Why" shows an enquiring mind,' my mother explained. 'Harriet has always asked questions, you know that.'

'It's what philosophers do, Nana.'

But it was no use. Nana was not an abstract thinker. 'You should have had a picture of an apple turnover across your front,' she said, as she left my bedroom while my mother and I were arranging the 'Why' to lie flat and in a straight line. If I'd had a bust like Celia Moore in class 4A it wouldn't have had the same impact. My small flat 'Why', very slightly raised at the 'W' and the 'y' was what got the message across – understated, with a quiet hint of greater things to come.

My mother poured wine for Bill and his assistant while they set up the camera and the fluffy microphone. She had the advantage of having spoken to Bill already so they hit it off from the start. I thought she would see through him the moment he made the predictable 'You must be Harriet's sister' remark, but to my surprise she laughed as if she'd never heard it before. I suppose it was the mark of a professional publicity manager.

I asked Nana what she thought of Bill when the two of us were in the kitchen making tea for ourselves.

'Not bad-looking but shifty-eyed,' was her opinion, and I had to agree. But he was our guest and it was our duty to make him feel at home, as my mother pointed out when I refused to come out of the kitchen. Some people might think it was stage fright, but it was more than that. Nana summed it up better than ever I could: 'I don't trust him, Mia. His eyes are too close together.'

'But the two of you can't stay in the kitchen all night. Bill has come all this way to interview Harriet. What am I supposed to say?'

'You seem to be doing quite well without us,' Nana replied. 'You'll think of something.'

But our mutiny was short-lived. More precisely, the time it took my mother to return to Bill's charms, and for Nana and me to silence our fit of laughter.

'He'll hear us!' I implored, as I wiped away tears on the back of my hand. 'I've got to speak to him! I'm still only a provisional!'

'Why?' laughed Nana, pointing towards my T-shirt.

'Because!' I replied, covering the word with my hand.

When I went back to the sitting room, Bill responded with, 'Ah, the author returns!' as I lowered myself on to the sofa to face his camera.

'Are you filming?' I asked suspiciously – I wasn't taking any chances.

'Not yet,' Bill replied, but I wasn't reassured.

'How will I know when you are?' He needed to understand who he was dealing with.

'I'll tell you,' he said, 'and a red light will come on.'

I noticed that he had emptied his glass already, probably in the hope he would get some more.

'More wine, Bill?'

I'd thought my mother had more sense.

105

'Thanks, Mia,' Bill said, holding out his empty glass for her to fill with her favourite Argentinian Chardonnay.

'I'm sticking to tea,' I said to her sternly. And she knew.

'This is Harriet's book,' she said, handing him a copy.

'It's a beautiful cover,' he said. 'Did you design it, Mia?'

'I did, as a matter of fact,' she replied. 'I'm an artist. Red has always been one of my favourite colours to paint with. There's a great deal of depth and warmth to it in the light.'

'Just like the contents of my book.' They needed a gentle reminder.

'That was why we chose it,' my mother agreed.

Bill opened the book and read a few Meditations while my mother and I waited anxiously for his response. 'You have a way with words,' he said, arching his left eyebrow. 'The woman from the *Evening Standard* got you right.' He closed my book and handed it to me, adding: 'She was right about your good looks too, just like your mum.'

I didn't care how provisional our filming session might be, I wouldn't fall for that. My looks weren't why he was there. He wasn't filming me for a modelling competition. I would win the Face of London title for my mind or not at all.

'Shall we get started?' he asked. 'I can see you're anxious.'

'What makes you think that?' I laughed.

'You're a little bit pink.' He pointed to my cheeks, which I'd thought I'd covered nicely with my hair. It wasn't how I'd envisaged my first TV appearance. I'd expected him to bring a stylist and a makeup artist, maybe even Nicky Clarke to do my hair. Instead, my mother had to fetch me her powder, while Nana tried to rearrange my hair behind an Alice band 'so the viewers can see more of your beautiful face'.

In my apprehensive state, I'd forgotten all about the many viewers.

Jean Claude would probably be watching over coffee and *pain au chocolat*. He'd be dunking the pastry in his coffee until the chocolate began to melt, and then he'd look up casually, and see me, all nervous and pink and arranged in an Alice band. 'Do we need all these lights?' I asked Bill's assistant.

'Yep!' he replied, and I knew not to ask any more.

'We're about to film!' Bill shouted, and I stared straight into his camera, imagining Jean Claude was on the other side.

'Try to look a bit happier.' Bill clearly didn't recognise how philosophers look. 'Imagine your mum's cooked you something nice to eat.'

Curiously, this suggestion seemed to work better than picturing Jean Claude, and in no time Bill said we were ready to roll.

He then adopted a more serious expression and encouraged me to talk about myself and my book, as if he was fascinated by my responses. But I knew he wasn't. It was an act for the camera – I could tell from the way he tilted his head to one side when he listened to me. He didn't even ask about my T-shirt, which really gave him away. When we'd finished, he asked if we could do it again, which showed quite obviously that he hadn't been listening in the first place. After half a dozen attempts he said that that should be 'it' and thanked me for making his job so easy. I wasn't sure what he was getting at so I looked at Nana, who shrugged and went to get his jacket.

The programme was to be shown the next evening, between Ken Livingstone and the weather report. At seven p.m. the three of us gathered anxiously round the TV set.

'If they don't use your interview, they want their heads examining,' was Nana's gentle attempt to reassure me. My mother's more subtle approach was to remind me that I had responded perfectly to all of Bill's questions, under the circumstances, but, like me, she couldn't remember what those questions had been. It was sounding more and more sinister – hypnosis could not be ruled out: they might not have been from *London Live* at all. Nana had spotted something odd about Bill's eyes, and neither of us had wanted to come out of the kitchen. We should have asked to see their identity cards.

As the seconds ticked away and there was no mention of the Face of London our fears increased. My mother suggested ringing *London Live* to ask if someone called Bill worked on the programme, but Nana said she wouldn't trust what any of them had to say after this. Then, suddenly, half-way through the programme, there I was, sitting on the sofa like a celebrity out of a magazine. Bill's voice could be heard in the background, asking me what my book was about.

'All sorts of things.'

'Why is it proving so popular?'

'Because there has been nothing else like it in the twenty-first century.'

'That's quite a claim!'

'It's quite a book.'

'So, what in your opinion makes you the Face of London? And you know it's for the viewers to decide.'

I blinked for the first time in the interview and paused for once before I answered. I should have done that before – it made me seem less hostile. But I wasn't hostile. I just didn't like Bill. Would the viewers realise that? 'I want to make a difference. I think I reflect what London has to offer – old and new, classical and modern, Marcus Aurelius and Harriet Rose. London needs change as well as standstill, words as well as silence, Heraclitus and Cratylus . . . Marks & Spencer.'

'Marks & Spencer?' Bill's voice sounded confused away in the distance, like God but without the omniscience.

'Yes, Marks & Spencer,' I repeated, although why, I had no idea whatsoever. But once I'd said it, I'd had to think of something. Several thousand viewers shouldn't be disappointed. 'They're always thinking up new ideas – seafood dips, Greek meze, Indian snacks.' I must have been feeling hungry. 'But however much they try to change, their appeal remains fundamentally the same. Knickers.'

'Knickers?' Bill's voice rose an octave.

'Every self-respecting woman owns a pair of Marks & Spencer's knickers.'

I shouldn't have mentioned knickers on television.

'You shouldn't have mentioned knickers on television,' my mother said.

'Why on earth not?' I asked.

'Because they have nothing to do with your book. You sounded so intelligent, so thought-provoking until you mentioned knickers.'

'Harriet's right, though,' interjected Nana. 'I've got a great pair of Marks & Spencer's knickers. Stomach control. I've had them for years. I bet you couldn't tell.'

My mother and I tried not to look at Nana's stomach, but it was no use once she had made the remark.

'See?' she said, standing side on in a pair of close-fitting burgundy merino-wool trousers. And we had to agree.

'I thought it was just good muscle tone,' my mother laughed.

'Or a secret life at the gym,' I added, picturing Nana in a pair of latex shorts and a boob tube working out on the treadmill.

But Nana seemed to find our comments disappointing. 'Do you really think I would degrade myself by perspiring in public?' she protested.

By the time we had finished the gym issue, we'd missed some of the interview. It wasn't fair. I should have been more important than Nana's stomach.

'At least let's hear the rest of it,' I urged them, turning up the volume with the remote control.

'And where did your inspiration come from for your Meditations?' Bill's voice sounded different on television from real life. I wondered if mine did too, but I had no way of telling. One never heard one's own voice as others did. It was an interesting reflection on personal identity, which I made a mental note to expand upon in my notebook later.

'I drew inspiration for the first section of my book from the people around me. Section One corresponds to a game of chess. That's why there are thirty-two Meditations in that section – one for each piece on the board.'

I hoped the viewers played, otherwise I was in difficulty.

'You're obviously good at chess,' Bill was saying, and the camera was on him now. His head was tilted to one side again.

'My father taught me to play,' I was explaining. 'The book is dedicated to him. He died.'

'It was very brave of you to say that without the hint of a quiver in your voice,' my mother whispered with the hint of a quiver in her voice. I missed Bill's next question as a result. Then I was on the screen again, only closer up this time. You couldn't even see my 'Why'.

'My mother and grandmother chose the title, *The Infinite Wisdom of Harriet Rose*. I always called it my Meditations. They took the words from my Meditation Thirty-three, which is the first in Section Two. That's the more general section, which contains my recent writing. Much of it is what you might describe as metaphysical and epistemological in genre.'

'He won't have a clue what that means,' Nana called. 'I know I don't.'

'Would you like to explain that a little for the viewers?' Bill was asking.

'Why couldn't he just say he didn't understand?' Nana went on.

'They're Meditations about the nature of existence and knowledge.' I looked heavenwards as I spoke, which the cameras focused in on.

I was especially pleased with that shot. It made me seem reflective and intelligent, beyond the petty aspects of the world. I hoped Jean Claude had caught it.

'They deal with concepts such as time, change, life, death, identity, uniqueness, principles concerning the ultimate cause of reality, as well as asking questions about the reliability of our knowledge. Like my T-shirt, the common theme is "Why".'

I must have begun to relax at this point. Bill could hardly get a word in.

'They sound fascinating,' he said, 'and I enjoyed the one you read earlier.'

'The one I read earlier?' I repeated, turning to my mother and Nana, who looked equally confused.

'That must have been the part we missed because of Nana's knickers,' my mother suggested.

Never mind. We had the video recording to fall back on. My mother pressed rewind and we settled down for an entertaining replay. Minor detail was critical for in-depth analysis.

'Quiet!' Publicity said, and I concurred. The sales rep was becoming a little too loquacious for her own good.

'Are you ready now?'

My mother pressed play and we waited in silence on the sofa, ready to hear the interview in full this time. But there was no interview. There was no Bill. There was no *London Live*. There was only a cookery programme.

No one had ever sent me flowers before. I didn't even know that they usually came with a card until my mother asked, 'Who are they from?' and I replied: 'The flower shop on the Fulham Road.'

'But who sent them? Isn't there a card?' My mother was so sophisticated in these matters.

'I expect so – I haven't looked yet,' I said nonchalantly. But where was the card normally placed? There was no obvious sign of one on the Cellophane wrapping. Perhaps it was customary to spear it on a stalk.

'Let's put them in a vase,' my mother said. She was good at arranging flowers. It was part of her artistic nature.

It was a large bouquet of dark red roses – a dozen. Who would send Harriet Rose a dozen red roses? There must have been a mistake. But just then the card fluttered to the floor in a small white envelope with my name on the front, 'Miss Harriet Rose'. My mother and Nana looked on while I tore open the envelope and took out the card:

> Harriet, the English Rose,
> I prefer your words to your silence.
> Cratylus

That was it. No more clues. Just that. I looked to my mother for interpretation. She would explain.

'There are three possibilities. One, you have a fan – someone who saw you on television last night. Possible, but not likely. Two—'

'What do you mean, "not likely"?'

'I mean,' my mother explained – diplomatically, I felt, 'that it would be difficult to track you down so soon, and I doubt your average fan could even spell Cratylus.'

'Who is this Cratylus, anyway?' Nana asked, as she cut a rose stem aggressively down to size.

'An old Greek philosopher,' I explained.

'Then he should be castrated, sending flowers to young girls. What's his telephone number?'

'He's dead, Nana.' I tried not to laugh.

'Dead? I'm not surprised.'

'Or, two,' my mother was growing impatient now, 'someone called Cratylus was watching the show.'

'I knew it!' Nana interrupted again. 'His type don't die that easily.'

'Or, three,' my instincts told me she was saving the most likely possibility to last, 'they're from someone who knows and admires you.'

My mother wasn't only artistic and sophisticated – she was a genius. Why hadn't I thought of that? The reference to 'English', the knowledge of philosophy, the dislike of my silence, the appreciation of my words, it was obvious! Jean Claude had sent the flowers. 'That's what I thought,' I said, into the rose heads, hoping my mother and Nana wouldn't notice my blush. 'What should I do with them?' I asked tentatively.

'It's up to you,' my mother said. 'They're your flowers.'

She was right. They *were* my flowers. It would seem a pity to take it out on the poor innocent roses by throwing them into the bin, which was, of course, my first inclination. Besides, I might have been wrong. Someone else might have sent them, someone worthier than a two-faced Frenchman – no wonder he had two first names. 'I'll keep them while I think about it,' I announced, in a tone that left no doubt the discussion was at an end.

So the bouquet of English roses remained in a pale blue vase on the dining-room table. Harriet Rose's English roses. It occurred to me that I was unlikely to receive any flowers other than roses for the rest of my life. Why couldn't my father have been called Diamond instead? Then I would have received small packages with gift tags reading, 'Harriet Diamond – it has a certain ring to it.' But there it was. It could have been worse. He might have been called Crisp.

I have to say they were the most beautiful red roses I had ever seen. Each one was on the point of opening and the petals felt like silk. They were interspersed with dark green foliage, which made them seem wild but fragile. He must have chosen them himself, especially for me.

Someone like Charlotte would have phoned to thank him at once, and I have to admit that even I wondered about it – but out of politeness rather than an overwhelming devotion to networking. What pleased me most about the gift was that Jean Claude, or someone equally discerning, had been influenced by what I had said in my interview.

When the petals began to fall, I would keep one and press it in a copy of my *Infinite Wisdom*. It was my way of saying, 'Well done, Harriet. Encore!' The first chapter in what was destined to be a fascinating existence was complete. Did I really believe that? Maybe not, but it made the present far more exciting.

When I saw from my bedroom window a second bouquet arrive, I threw on a white towelling robe to hide my Mickey Mouse nightdress and ran downstairs to the front door. My mother had already got there. It was a larger bouquet than the first, a selection of red, orange and yellow flowers of varying shapes and sizes held together by a big red bow. I was impressed. Jean Claude had style. And he was not a man to be deterred without a fight. It was beginning to look as if a simple 'Thank you' was inevitable. I knew where to look for the card this time.

'I'd better check the card to see who they're from,' I said with the *savoir-faire* of a prima donna as I tore open the little white envelope: 'It was good to meet you. Thank you for your warm hospitality. Bill.'

Bill? Why was Bill sending me flowers? The only hospitality I had shown him was to pass him tea from Nana's tray when he'd finished his wine.

'That was kind of him,' my mother said, as she took the card from my hand, 'but they're not as nice as yours.' She walked away, clutching the bouquet, as I searched the floor for the little white envelope.

'Mrs Mia Rose': a man had sent my mother flowers.

I helped her arrange them in three large vases. On closer inspection, I discovered there were no roses, only an array of cheaper, unsophisticated flowers, like tulips and gladioli. It should have been obvious they were not from Jean Claude. No one but a prat like Bill would send gladioli. In fact, it was quite a relief to discover they were not for me. We carried the three vases into the sitting room and positioned them as unobtrusively as possible. But it was difficult. Our sitting room, which until then had been elegant and refined, now looked like Dame Edna's dressing room. My dozen red roses stood poised in the background like a regiment of soldiers about to break up a street riot. I didn't know where to look.

Nana felt the same. 'What's all this?' she gasped, when she walked into the sitting room. 'Has someone died?'

'Bill sent us flowers,' my mother told her.

'Not us,' I corrected. 'You. He sent you flowers.'

'Well, he meant them for all of us.'

Did she think we were stupid?

'Beware of Greeks bearing gifts,' Nana said.

'Bill's not Greek, Nana. That was Cratylus.' Nana had not had the benefit of a classical education.

'You want to watch out for that one,' she said to my mother, and I wondered whether it would be safer if Nana took over publicity.

'They're to thank her for her warm hospitality.' It was important that Nana was fully informed.

'I told you not to offer him a glass of wine. Tea and biscuits are all his type understand.'

Nana had a point. Chardonnay had clearly given Bill the wrong impression.

No one had bothered to think of the impact all this would have on me. A conversation about the dangers in encouraging a shifty-eyed TV producer with negligent offers of Chardonnay was hardly what one expected to hear between one's mother and grandmother first thing in the morning. Fourteen was a difficult age in the most ordinary of households – it was only a year to the day since I'd got over the shock of my first period and having to cope with winged sanitary pads without proper instructions. Did my family have no sensitivity to my feelings at all? Where would it all end? My mother going out on dates while Nana and I waited up for her to come home at a reasonable hour? I shouldn't have to put up with this. It was demeaning to her maternal status. I would have to say something. I turned determinedly to face my mother and said, 'Don't you think you should be making my breakfast?'

She understood. I could tell by the way she put marmalade on my toast without asking if I'd rather have peanut butter. No more words were needed between us. Cratylus had wiggled his little finger again and normality had been restored.

The winner of the Face of London competition was to be announced at seven p.m. on Thursday evening. As my mother had recorded the wrong channel, we didn't know what number to call to cast our votes. Bill could have told us, but Nana and I thought it a bad idea to contact him again. At school the day after the programme a total of four people had told me they had voted for me – Celia Moore, who was in the form above me and tended to be more sensible than most, Jason Smart, his older brother Philip, and Mr Shaw, the science teacher. His vote surprised me the most. He was probably trying to steer me towards the arts.

Celia said that she had liked my T-shirt and thought I'd answered the questions brilliantly. 'You were really cool' were her exact words. I liked Celia Moore. I would give her a signed copy of my book. At least she would understand it. No one else at school had even mentioned that they'd seen me on television, although I knew many of them had by the way they whispered and sniggered when I walked past them.

My mother said that was a good sign – it meant that I must have been superb – but Nana said I should go up to them next time and ask if they'd like a signed photograph. I thought long and hard about it and decided I favoured my mother's response very slightly, although I would bear Nana's in mind for an emergency.

Vote wise, it wasn't looking promising, though. Even the solo singer who used to be in a classical boy band would get more than four votes from the rest of the band members. Of course there was Bill. He would probably vote for me just to see my mother again. The more I thought about it, Bill was my best bet. I expect that was why my mother had offered him the wine in the first place. She was no average publicity manager. Look at what she had already achieved, newspaper articles, radio and TV, surely it was only a matter of time before I met the great man himself, Parky. Nana would enjoy that. She'd always had a soft spot for Parky, even though he hadn't come to my launch party. But first things first. There was the small matter of the Face of London competition and the £10,000 award that would go towards furthering the winner's enterprise.

How would I spend the money if I were to win? a researcher called Jackie wanted to know, when she rang me the night before the results were to be announced. It was a difficult question to answer with a mouth full of Four Seasons pizza and an anchovy bone to dislodge. Jackie asked if she had called at a bad time but, like a true professional, I told her I'd just finished a Four Seasons and her timing couldn't have been better.

'Oh, I love Vivaldi!' she exclaimed.

'I haven't tried that one,' I replied.

What would I do with £10,000? I was tempted to say I'd donate the money to charity, but I didn't want to sound like a Miss World contestant, so I said, 'I don't want to think about it in case I don't win.' Which was true. Nana called it tempting fate, like having planned what we would do when my father got better.

Jackie wished me luck with the results. 'Fingers crossed,' she said, and she was about to go when I asked her for the voting number.

'Do you mean you haven't voted yet?' She sounded surprised. What should I read into that? Did I have so many votes that she thought we must have been voting, or was the reason for my lack of votes suddenly very clear? But before I had time to ask her how many I had so far, she was gone.

At least we now had a number to ring, which was something. My mother dialled first, then Nana, and I voted last. We had decided that one vote each would be enough. I didn't want to seem over-keen and, besides, if I was going to win, I would do so fairly, democratically, objectively.

I took Thursday off school, nausea. It was true in a way – every time I thought about seven p.m. and *London Live* I felt sick. Nana made me some nice chicken broth for lunch, but after one spoonful I had to give up. 'You must be feeling bad,' she said, as she took away my soup bowl. 'Why don't you go and lie down for a while? We'll give you a call when it comes on.'

When it comes on! Why had she had to go and say 'when it comes on'? That was what I was trying to forget. 'I can't lie down, Nana,' I snapped. 'I'm too nervous.'

'Then do some writing,' my mother suggested. 'I haven't seen you write anything since your book was published. Isn't it time you started your next one?'

Funnily enough, it hadn't occurred to me that I might have other books published. It was as if I had become *The Infinite Wisdom of Harriet Rose*. What else could I write? My autobiography? I was too young for that. Perhaps a novel. I had heard there was money to be made in fiction. I sat on my bed and tried to think of an interesting plot, but all I could come up with was a story about a fourteen-year-old girl, whose father had died, brought up by her mother and grandmother in an understated house in Kensington, who had her book published and became an overnight success to the delight of a good-looking Frenchman who had been pursuing her ever since she had mistaken him for a dolphin. It would never work. Why didn't I face it? I was just another talentless teenager. I didn't need *London Live* viewers' votes to tell me I was a failure. I knew it already.

I replaced my pen in its loop at the side of my notebook and went downstairs where Nana was preparing tea and apple turnovers. 'You'll feel better after you've had one of these,' she said, pushing a plate into my hand. How could I refuse Nana's home-baked apple turnover? It would be like telling the Father at Holy Innocents I didn't believe in God. I have to admit that after my second one I did begin to feel a lot better. I even found myself joking with my mother about the contestants on *The Weakest Link*. Before I knew it, seven o'clock had arrived, which meant the start of *London Live*. We had all checked the video this time and Nana had been ordered not to say anything until the programme was over.

'It sounds a daft idea to me – the three of us sitting on the sofa not speaking, like the three monkeys,' she complained. My mother told her to think of herself more as the wise old owl who lived in the oak. That seemed to appeal to her sense of self-image and she didn't say another word after that.

Jackie had told us correctly. The results were not on until just before the end of the programme, when a brief clip was shown from the interviews of the six contestants. I was on second, after a group of self-trained line-dancers from East Sheen who had financed themselves round the Americas by losing a combined total of fifteen stones on the Atkins diet.

'Look at the one on the right! She's got legs like tree-trunks!' Nana whispered loudly, as if that didn't count as speaking.

'Sssh!' my mother implored. 'Harriet's coming on next.'

It was a clip of me reading from my Meditations, which we had missed the last time: '"It is a populous place filled with noise and words and laughter, ever changing as its walls expand to encompass new ideas and beliefs. I know this place as I have dwelled within its boundaries all my life, watched as it succeeded, failed and began again. I have seen it through the many changes of life and death, tragedy and joy. I know this place from inside-out and all ways. For this place that I describe, it is my mind."'

When I looked round, my mother and Nana were crying. It was a confusing moment. I'd thought it had gone quite well until then. 'I did my best,' I said, in an attempt to alleviate their despair. 'And if they don't like it, well, so bloody what? There are plenty of others in the world who will.'

Somehow I had managed to change their tears to laughter. We were ready for the battle to begin.

'Perhaps one more vote each would be acceptable?' my mother suggested, looking tentatively at me.

'I don't suppose it would do any harm,' I agreed. Then we all tapped the number into our mobile phones, and pressed repeat for the next five minutes until it was announced that the lines were closed.

'What happens next?' Nana's generation wasn't accustomed to television voting. In her day, they'd relied on a clapometer.

'They count up the votes,' my mother explained.

'We could be here for hours!' she said with horror at the prospect of sitting quietly on the sofa for the rest of the evening when she could have been in the kitchen making supper.

'It'll only take them a minute,' I said.

'A minute? And you seriously think you can believe a result like that? Not even that woman on the other channel in the afternoon could add up that quickly. It's a fix!'

'Now we have what you've all been waiting for – the results of our Face of London competition.' As the woman spoke, she opened an envelope that contained the name of the winner.

'It would have taken them that long just to write down the name and stick it in the envelope,' Nana went on. 'Do they think we're daft?'

The woman looked down, read the name to herself, grinned and said nothing. I had seen it too many times: it was a tactic they all used to heighten excitement. But it wouldn't work on me. I was no media puppet to be manipulated in this way.

Perhaps Nana's cynicism was beginning to rub off on me, but I'd had enough. I stood up to leave the room.

'Harriet!'

'Yes?' I asked. 'What?' I had decided to abandon 'Why?' in favour of 'What?' It got to the point more quickly.

'I didn't say a word,' my mother said, looking at Nana who, for once, was sitting silently in the corner like a wise old owl. We turned to face the grinning woman on *London Live*.

'Congratulations, Harriet! A very worthy winner! We look forward to presenting you with your prize.'

The *Kensington and Chelsea Messenger* was the first to arrive that night. I recognised the reporter from outside the school gates, so it seemed appropriate to let him in. 'But don't offer him wine,' I told my mother, as she opened the front door.

We had only just sat down when the bell rang again. *Pimlico Press* was turned away, along with the *Hammersmith Daily* – my mother told them she'd never heard of them, which, of course, was untrue: we had pasted their unfavourable reviews into our red leather album. She must have forgotten amid all the excitement.

What we hadn't expected was that the nationals would arrive. First the *Mail*, followed swiftly by the *Sun*, the *Mirror*, the *Express*, the *Telegraph*, *The Times* and the *Independent*. There were far too many to invite into our sitting room so my mother greeted them at the door and asked them to wait, saying, 'I'll have a word with Harriet and see if she'll speak to you.'

It was important how I answered the questions of the reporter from the *Kensington and Chelsea Messenger*, and not just because the newspaper would be delivered to Jean Claude. The reporter had impressed me from the moment he had greeted me outside my school gates and written such a favourable article about me. He asked his questions politely, in a manner that drew from me a measured response. If he thought I looked nervous, for instance, he would offer me a piece of chewing-gum, and when I declined it, as naturally I did, he would say that was no problem and put it back in his pocket.

Had I expected to win? No. What would I do with the money? I'll think of something. What were my plans for the future? To carry on writing and selling my books. Did I see London as encouraging new talent? I did now. How would I change it? I'm a philosopher, not a politician.

The trouble began on the front porch in an atmosphere that could only be described as frenzied. I counted sixteen men and women, some with cameras, others with notepads, all competing for my attention with questions I had already answered.

'Did you expect to win?' a woman asked.

'Yes,' I replied.

'What will you do with the money?' a man enquired.

'Spend it.'

'Do you see London as encouraging new talent?'

'Not particularly.'

'How would you change it?'

'I would replace all politicians with philosophers.'

Two hours later, when the *Guardian* arrived and the others had gone, I was bombarded yet again with the very same questions. The repetition was too much for anyone, except perhaps an accountant or an insurance broker, to bear. By now, my plans for the future were to leave school and pay for my own private tutor, hire a chauffeur, travel the country doing book signings, present the prime minister with his own signed copy at Downing Street, and put up for Parliament myself.

'Which party?'

'I haven't decided yet.'

'What would you change?'

'The world.'

'Had you expected to win?'

'It's just the beginning.'

My mother and Nana had left me to it and gone to bed. I could hear Nana snoring when I finally closed the front door. It was the reality I needed. My life was changing all around me, but fundamentally it remained the same – it was my Meditation 37. I went to my room and tried to sleep, but the questions they'd asked wouldn't go away. My head was filled with 'what' and 'how' and 'when'. Eventually I switched on my bedside light, got out my notebook and wrote:

Why is 'why' so important to me,
And why not 'who', 'what', 'where' or 'when'?
Why can't I be like the others I see
Who don't seek the motives of men?

I've searched for the truth
Through all of my youth,
But the answer I still cannot find.
Should I ask 'why' no more,
Close my eyes, shut the door?
Not while reason lives on in my mind.

Before I could switch off my light, I heard it again – the doorbell. A reporter, no doubt, who had been a little slower to pick up on the story. It was too much. Even good-looking fourteen year olds needed a bit of beauty sleep.

I ran down the stairs and peered through the peephole, but it was too dark to make out the reporter. I would have opened the door as far as the security chain allowed but as I was in my red cotton night-shirt and matching bedsocks I left it closed. He would have to go away. It would teach him to act faster next time.

I watched as he climbed on to a moped he had left underneath the street-lamp. I could see him clearly now. He was dressed in a black and white striped rugby shirt and navy blue jeans, and his black hair was still visible when he had pulled on his crash helmet. That was when I realised: it was not a reporter who was riding away down the street, it was Jean Claude.

The next day the papers were full of me. I even made some front pages. 'Harriet Rose the English Rose' was a popular phrase with the tabloids, while the *Independent* favoured, 'A new talent with an ancient message, the Face of London brings a new depth to the word "British".' The *Mail* said I had 'star quality mixed with high standards, which augured well for the future of London's young people'. The *Mirror* thought, 'The people of London have not just voted with their eyes and ears but also with their brains.' *The Times* saw me as 'an eclectic mix of confidence and uncertainty, wisdom and naïveté'. They had probably been influenced by the 'Why?' on my T-shirt. Strangely, the *Guardian*, who had arrived last, described me as 'a precocious teenager who suffers from delusions of grandeur' but, as my mother was always saying to Nana and me, who listens to the minority?

For once my mother was wrong. The *Guardian* appeared to be

the only paper anyone read at school. I had no idea it was so popular, even among over-privileged children like Charlotte Goldman. I expected at least that her father would have read in *The Times* of my 'confidence and uncertainty, wisdom and naïveté', but no: all I heard the next day was 'precocious Harriet with delusions of grandeur' being whispered or shouted over and over again. I began to wonder whether I had dreamed the other articles until finally, towards the end of the day, Celia Moore came up to me and said, 'Well done, Harriet. I thought you'd win. You were much better than the others.'

'Thanks, Celia,' I said. 'Did you really think so?'

'Definitely,' she replied, as if she genuinely meant it. 'You must have been so pleased, especially when you read the article in *The Times*.'

'It was rather good, wasn't it?' I replied loudly – some of the others were walking past.

I knew Celia Moore wouldn't feel threatened. How could she with a pair of breasts the size of hers? I almost burst into tears. Was this how my high standards 'augured well for the future of London's young people'? Why did there have to be more Charlotte Goldmans in the world than Celia Moores? But if the rest of the school could believe a minority, then so could I: Celia Moore was right. I was much better than the rest. I had deserved to win.

Was this all there was to being famous? A subject for others to gossip about? My life would never be the same again. Whether I liked it or not, I would have to get used to being famous and the fact that it made me stand out from the crowd.

But the *Guardian*'s words rang in my ears for the rest of the day and into the evening. That night I decided to look up 'precocious' in my pocket dictionary so that there would be no confusion over the precise insult being aimed at me. It said: 'Precocious: prematurely developed or advanced in some faculty or tendency'!

So I looked up 'faculty' to make sure which part of me was supposed to be prematurely developed.

'Faculty: physical or mental capacity.'

I got out my black notebook and wrote the following Meditation:

I never use words that I do not understand.
It helps to avoid misunderstandings.
Like calling someone 'precocious' when the word they should
    be using is 'reflective'.
Or thinking someone is 'over-confident'
when they have to count to ten to stop themselves blushing.
Or 'advanced' because they prefer good literature to glossy
    magazines.
Or saying that they are 'prematurely developed' when they
    don't yet wear a bra.
I shall be myself, however you describe me.
A maverick, unafraid to stand out from the crowd.
And so bloody what if you do not understand me?
What matters is that there are those I love and respect in the
    world who do.

They were sending a car to pick me up and take me to the *London
Live* studios to be presented with my cheque the following afternoon,
which, fortunately, was a Saturday. Jackie had said I would be filmed
live and that I should smile a lot and look happy. I asked if she'd been
speaking to Bill and she replied that she knew how daunting television cameras could be when you weren't used to them. I said so
could people, but she just laughed, as if I'd meant to say something
funny.

My mother and Nana were coming with me. We had wondered
about leaving Nana behind, but she insisted that my mother needed
a chaperon. 'My mother?' I said. 'This is to do with me, not my
mother. It's my presentation. Surely I'm the one who needs a chaperon.' I think I must have been pre-menstrual. Normally I would
have recognised straight away that Nana was worrying about Bill.

As it was, it took a furtive wink from Nana when my mother wasn't looking for me to catch up. Nana was quick like that. Being a sales rep had made her even quicker. I wished I felt quick. But I didn't. I felt like a slightly bloated teenager with sore nipples and an excruciating desire for chocolate, and cheese and onion crisps.

I had wanted to wear my winning black 'Why' T-shirt again, for continuity, but my mother said I should put on something else. 'There are so many different aspects to your character, Harriet,' she explained. 'Why not show the sweet, feminine side this time?'

'Do you mean I didn't look sweet and feminine last time?' I asked. Objectivity has always been important to me.

'You couldn't help but look sweet and feminine,' she replied, with a smile.

'Then why did you say "this time"?'

'Because last time you were concentrating quite rightly on getting across the questioning, searching, reflective side of your nature. And you've succeeded in doing that. So I thought this time you might want to highlight your beauty, your innocence, your grace.'

I should have known not to question a publicity mogul like my mother. Of course she was right – I wasn't only a thinking adolescent. My physical side was important too – even René Descartes had realised he had to solve the mind *and* body problem. 'What about my white linen shorts and a white T-shirt with my floral chiffon blouse over the top?' I suggested.

'Perfect!' my mother exclaimed. 'And I've bought you a little present to wear with them. It's to say congratulations, Harriet, from me – and your father.' She handed me a small package wrapped in silver paper with a matching ribbon tied round it.

There was a small box inside, the type that suggests size isn't everything.

'You shouldn't have done that,' I protested, unwrapping it hastily. 'Not when you've already spent so much on my book.'

But when I opened the box I was glad she had. The lid opened like an oyster shell to reveal a small platinum necklace with a St Christopher medallion hanging from it. For a moment I have to confess that I forgot all about my request for no presents. 'It's beautiful,' I cried, holding it up to read the inscription on the back.

'Beautiful like you,' my mother said.

I read the inscription out loud. It said: '"Someone to watch over you."' And that was exactly what I wanted. My mother fastened it round my neck while I held up my hair. 'Do you think it clashes with my worry beads?' I asked her — she would know.

'I can't see that you have much need for worry beads at the moment,' she replied. But I kept them on, just in case.

'Don't we look smart?' said Nana, as we climbed into the back of a black stretch limousine. And she was right. We did. My mother had chosen a lemon silk dress with a transparent silk overcoat through which I could see her beautifully tanned arms. And Nana was in her favourite oyster grey trouser suit with a double-breasted jacket, and a crisp white cotton blouse underneath that had taken her half an hour to iron that morning.

'What are you going to say?' my mother asked, as the three of us sat in a row in the back of the limousine.

'I haven't decided yet,' I replied snappily. I knew as I said it that she was only trying to be encouraging but I couldn't help it. It didn't matter, though — she knew it was because I was nervous.

That was why she tried again: 'They'll probably ask how you'll spend the money.'

'Obviously!' I said, but I hadn't thought about that. I should have done. Jackie had even mentioned it before I'd won. But I was a writer – creative and moody – not a publicity manager. So I asked, 'How do you think I should answer that?'

'What would you like to do with ten thousand pounds?'

It may sound silly but I hadn't appreciated just how much money I'd won until then. She shouldn't have come out with it like that. I felt even more nervous now.

'Why don't you buy yourself a nice helicopter? You'd like that.'

'You couldn't buy a helicopter with ten thousand pounds, Nana.'

'Well, I could put the rest to it. I've still got a few thousand left over from the sale of my house.'

'It's a lovely thought,' my mother replied diplomatically, 'but I think a helicopter might be a little dangerous for Harriet, and we've got nowhere to keep it.'

'You're probably right,' Nana said reflectively.

'And, anyway,' my mother went on, 'I think the idea is that Harriet spends the money on something that will further her talent. Something that will promote the book, for instance, like an advert in a newspaper or a magazine – or a TV commercial, perhaps.'

'I've got an idea!' I interjected. That shut them up. They turned towards me, one on either side, their faces gleaming with eager antici-pation.

'What is it, Harriet?'

I knew my mother would be first to ask. It was part of her nature to be impatient. That was why she always read the end of a book first to see what happened. If I were ever to write a novel, which no doubt someone would persuade me to do one day, I would make sure the end came at the beginning, just so it didn't spoil my mother's enjoyment.

'Why don't I give the money to Miss Grout?'

'Miss Grout?' my mother repeated. 'You mean *your* Miss Grout with the who-do-you-think-you-are eyes and the you-may-be-young-and-beautiful-but-I'm-the-one-with-the-power mouth?'

I could see my idea hadn't gone down as well as I'd hoped. 'I didn't mean I'd give it to her to spend on herself,' I elaborated.

'Well, I'm glad to hear you're not thinking of throwing it away,' said Nana. 'She'd need to spend a lot more than ten thousand pounds before you saw an improvement in her.'

'What I had in mind,' I went on, raising my voice a little so that they knew it was time for them to listen, 'was a donation to the school, a feature for the entrance, something that drew the eye as soon as you stepped past the gates, a symbol of learning and culture.'

'Like what?' my mother asked quizzically – she always believed in getting straight to the point.

'Like a statue of Harriet Rose, of course. Nothing too grand. Maybe sitting with my book in my hand and an expression of contemplation about my face.'

I must say, I hadn't expected laughter when I showed them the expression I had in mind. I think it must have been nerves – we were approaching the TV studios.

'It sounds too good for them,' was my mother's only comment as we climbed out of the limousine like pop stars arriving to give a concert.

'You're probably right,' I agreed. I would have to think of something else.

We were met at reception by Victor Darling himself, which impressed me. I had expected him to send out an assistant. But, no, there he was, all made up in a designer suit and foundation. 'You must be Harriet Rose,' he said, holding out an elegant, well-manicured hand. 'The Face of London. And what a pretty face too!'

Was he trying to patronise me? 'Hello,' I replied, shaking the hand. 'This is my mother and grandmother.' I felt safer once I'd said that, as if I was part of an army rather than a solitary corporal.

'I'm pleased to meet you,' Victor said politely to them both, but I was sure he looked longer at my mother – Bill must have been talking about her. 'Why don't we all go into the Green Room and have a little chat?'

I was happy with that suggestion – at least he wasn't trying to separate us – so I smiled, just a small smile, the sort that doesn't show your teeth, and followed him down a long corridor with lots of doors off it until we reached a brightly lit room with spongy sofas and armchairs. It was like an airport waiting area.

'Wine? Pepsi? Orange juice?' he asked.

'Nothing for me!' I replied abruptly. I had decided in advance that I would have to be careful what I said. No drinks for me in the Green Room to make me talk more. Water would do, straight out of the tap and into my mouth before it could be tampered with.

'Are you sure, Harriet?' my mother asked. 'You don't want to be thirsty – your throat will dry up and you won't be able to speak.'

'Certain,' I said, nudging her hard. I shouldn't have had to: she should have thought to protect me without having to be prompted.

'Mrs Rose? Wine for you?'

I gave her a look just in time.

'Er, no, thank you, Victor. Maybe later.'

'And . . . ?'

'Call me Olivia.' Nana smiled sweetly, which meant she must like him. My spirits lifted. 'Do you have sarsaparilla? I haven't had that for years.'

'I don't think we do, Olivia, but I can find out.'

'No, no, I'll just have a nice cool glass of tap water.'

I'd known I could rely on Nana.

To break the silence I asked, 'Bill isn't here?'

'Bill? No, he's our roving interviewer.'

'Roving?' said Nana. 'He's got the eyes for it.'

Victor Darling laughed loudly, which made me think that Nana and I had been right to be concerned about Bill all along.

'I expect you watch the show?' Victor asked. I didn't answer – I could see it was a rhetorical question.

'There's really nothing for you to be nervous about.'

I wondered how he knew I was nervous, until I realised I had tight hold of my mother's arm. But I didn't let go.

'It'll just be a little chat, nothing more than that, about your life, your interests and who you are. You're an intelligent girl – you know the sort of thing.'

But did I? The last time I'd been asked to talk about myself and my interests in public could hardly have been described as a success – Charlotte Goldman reduced to tears and Miss Marlowe trying to force me into an unnecessary apology just because a few misplaced words had slipped out of my mouth.

'Maybe we could practise a little now?' I suggested to Victor, who thought that was an 'excellent idea'. Encouraged, I let go of my mother's arm and uncrossed my legs.

'Why don't you kick off by telling us about your family,' Victor suggested.

It was just the sort of prompt I could have done with in class. But Miss Marlowe was no Victor Darling, even if she did have his brown moustache. 'I'm an only child,' I said quietly, sensing an air of sweetness and femininity coming over me, 'and my mother and father were both only children too. *Enfants uniques*, my mother calls us. Which makes me an only grandchild too.'

Out of the corner of my eye I could see Nana grinning proudly at me.

'My mother and Nana are my only living relatives. My father died just over a year ago and Grandpa died not long before that. My other grandparents were dead before I was born. We used to have a pet dog, but she died too.'

Victor moved uneasily in his chair as if he wasn't sure of this angle all of a sudden. 'But you've probably got a boyfriend you'd like to talk about?' he ventured hopefully.

But did I have a boyfriend? It was a complex question to answer on the spot without the opportunity for quiet reflection on the concept of 'boyfriend'. Certainly I had believed, rightly or wrongly, that I had the beginnings of one – a dinner invitation, flowers, a telephone call, not to mention a familiar hand on my knee. But was that really what a 'boyfriend' was all about? Surely there must be more to it than that. A further dimension of proximity? A mutual fusing? And for all I knew, Charlotte Goldman had already found the fuse.

'Not really,' I responded hesitantly, and I could tell Victor was unimpressed by my answer.

'She has lots of admirers, though,' my mother made a point of explaining, nudging me with her elbow as if she was trying to jump-start me.

'I'm not surprised,' agreed Victor, 'a good-looking girl like you.'

Was he trying to be flirtatious? I wasn't putting up with that, however popular Victor Darling might be. 'I'm really more interested in my writing than in boyfriends at the moment,' I said, tilting my face just a little to the side so he could see my seriousness in full profile.

'Ah, yes, your writing.' Victor nodded as he spoke and I could see I had managed to steer our conversation around an intellectual bend for the better. 'Tell me something about that.'

I had never liked talking about my writing – it was one of the reasons why I had buried my Meditations in my Emma Hope shoebox. Not that I didn't appreciate the immense opportunity that the present of the book had bestowed on me. And I couldn't honestly say I disliked my new-found celebrity status. But to actually talk about it to a total stranger, who might then broadcast what I'd said to an entire capital, was a very different matter altogether.

'I believe in the importance of inner contemplation,' I said, studying my bare knees for some reason as I spoke, 'an ordering of the mind, a search for what matters, an investigation into the complexities of being.'

Although I stopped speaking at that point, my mind continued along the path it had begun – how best to define my Meditations, whether it was wise to mention the *Meditations of Marcus Aurelius* or whether that would lose Victor entirely, whether Descartes' *Meditations* might prove a more accessible alternative. But I had little time for such reflections – Victor Darling was talking again: 'I've just had a brilliant idea!' he was saying. 'Instead of Harriet on her own, why don't we film you all together – mother, Nana and Harriet, the three generations. How about that?'

To my amazement, Nana removed her grey and white velvet hat and began to rearrange her curls with the tips of her fingers, saying, 'How do you want me, Victor? Happy or serious?' I couldn't think why she was enjoying herself so much.

'Listen to Nana over there!' Victor replied. 'What about Mother?'

'We'd only spoil it,' my mother had the good sense to say. 'It's a kind suggestion, Victor, but Nana and I are just here to give Harriet moral support, aren't we, Harriet?'

As she spoke my name, my mother stared sternly at me, opening her eyes to their full capacity in an expression that only I would understand. It meant 'For goodness' sake, Harriet, don't just sit there as if you'd rather be at home in your pyjamas tucked up in bed with a good book – speak to the man, capture his attention!' It was just the look I needed.

'Victor!' I said, a little louder and more animated than before. 'Isn't Harriet Rose enough for you?'

He looked at me as if he'd suddenly noticed who I was. 'Convince me!' he replied challengingly.

I took a deep breath and said, 'I can't stand people who don't mean what they say.' It was the first thing that came into my head. But, as my mother always told me, it's the way you say it. 'And there is someone I quite like, but I'm unconvinced by his Bermuda shorts – you can see up them.' I seemed inadvertently to have hit a Victor funny-bone. 'And I was put off him at my book launch by the attention he paid to a fluffy airhead dressed like a raspberry fool.'

Victor was a new man. 'Stop it, Harriet! Enough! You'll make me cry and Makeup will have to do my foundation again!'

'When you cry you open the floodgates of the soul,' I said. I was on a roll. It wasn't even one of my Meditations. I'd just made it up.

'God, what a talented daughter you have!' Victor said to my mother, as he stood up and led me towards Makeup for some powder, 'to stop you shining under the lights, darling'!

It couldn't have been going better. I'd forgotten all about the programme and my nerves until he added, 'You can do your hair there too.'

Do my hair? How was I supposed to do my hair? I never did my hair. Either it stayed loose, or I tied it up when I was going for a swim or washing my face. I looked hard at my mother for reassurance.

'She has such a lot of hair to do – I'd better help her,' she said, while Nana lifted some in her cupped hand, saying, 'Just feel the weight of it!'

Debbie, the makeup girl, said I needed a touch of foundation on my nose and forehead to make me 'nice and even'. Nana pointed out that I was nice and even naturally, but Debbie didn't appear to hear her. Swiftly she applied the makeup with a damp sponge, which Nana confirmed with her was new, while I watched what she was doing in the mirror. No one had ever done my makeup before. I didn't really like it. I wished that it was over. It was making my eyes water. And I didn't like Debbie either.

'What did you say your name was?' she asked, in a squeaky, unintelligent voice. 'Hilary, wasn't it?'

'Harriet,' my mother answered for me. 'Harriet Rose. You were introduced – you must have been helping yourself to Victor's wine.' Then my mother laughed as if she was joking. But she wasn't. She didn't like Debbie either.

'You've tried to write a book or something?'

'I've written a book, yes,' I said, watching in the mirror what I looked like when I spoke.

'I'm writing a book, too,' Debbie replied. 'It's a tragedy.'

'Quite,' my mother said.

Nana pulled a face and sat down next to me as Debbie went to see if she could find a new brush for the powder. 'Dozy bitch!' Nana laughed. 'She couldn't even write her own name.'

When Debbie had finished my makeup and my mother had done

142

my hair, Victor Darling came back to take us to the studio. 'You look lovely, Harriet,' he said, right in front of Debbie.

'We were a little bit shiny, weren't we?' Debbie squeaked.

'Like a diamond!' Nana replied, and Debbie disappeared into a cloud of hairspray and nail-polish fumes.

The studio was hot and bright and scary. The cameras were much larger than Bill's and they moved round the floor on small wheels like Daleks. The director was called Phil. He was younger than I'd expected. I liked Phil. He tried to make me feel relaxed and he smelled of a nice spicy aftershave. 'We'll practise a few times, Harriet, until you're comfortable,' he said.

'It might take some time,' I replied. 'How long have you got?'

It wasn't exactly flirting, I was trying to make myself feel comfortable.

'You'll be fine,' he reassured me. 'Just be yourself.'

Be yourself? That was my Meditation 41. He must have read it. 'I am myself,' I said, with a knowing smile that Phil would recognise. '"Nothing can change me, I am myself. You can legislate, defy, manipulate, but whatever lies ahead . . ."' I left a pause for Phil to complete the quotation, but he didn't. Instead he looked at a cameraman – and frowned.

I could feel myself going bright red and shiny – I feared Phil would send for Debbie, so I did what I'd taught myself to do when I felt myself going red: I closed my eyes and counted to ten.

'Are you all right?' I heard Phil say, but I couldn't reply because I'd only got to six.

'Someone get Harriet a chair, for God's sake. She's going to faint!'

I got to ten and opened my eyes. I was surrounded by three concerned cameramen, Phil, my mother, Nana and a woman I hadn't seen before. I closed my eyes again.

They led me to Victor's sofa, the one he sits on every evening. But it wasn't seven o'clock, it was ten to seven. In ten minutes' time we'd be going live, and I hadn't even practised what I was going to say. 'I'm fine, really!' I said, but Phil insisted that I finish a full glass of sparkling water, and I didn't like sparkling water. The bubbles made me feel dizzy and I already felt dizzy.

Someone was speaking to me. I could hear their voice in the distance. I had to concentrate. It might be important. Instructions. Directions. The cheque.

'What did you say?' I asked, as calmly as I could.

'That we're almost ready now.' It was Phil.

'Just tell me what to do,' I said, trying to sound strong and confident, 'and where to do it.'

'All you have to do is go over there to the wings, then turn around and walk back across the studio floor towards Victor – you know Victor, don't you?'

Of course I knew Victor. Just because I had recited one of my Meditations to Phil through a simple misunderstanding, that did not give him the right to be condescending. 'Yes, of course,' I replied, a little abruptly.

'Then Victor will congratulate you on winning the Face of London competition.'

'I know what I've won!' I laughed. Phil's attitude was beginning to get on my nerves, and his aftershave was making me feel nauseous.

'He'll give you the cheque and ask you what you're going to do with all that money.'

'Fine!' I said enthusiastically. 'Let's do it!'

So they counted down to one while Victor Darling stared into the camera without moving an eyelash and I stood in the wings, my mother and Nana squeezing my arms and giving me encouraging looks. Then I could hear his voice, and Harriet Rose, and the Face of London, and fourteen years old, and her book. It was time. Someone pushed me gently from behind. This was my moment.

I walked slowly across the floor, careful not to slip, towards Victor Darling who was standing, holding out his right hand and clutching a cheque in the other. My cheque. For £10,000. Live on television. Transmitted to the whole capital of England. The Queen was probably watching, with Prince Philip and their corgis. I stopped when I reached the outstretched hand and shook it. So far so good.

'Congratulations, Harriet, a worthy winner.'

It was just as Phil had described. Then we sat down on the sofa, just as he'd said we would, only closer than I'd expected.

'And you know what I'm going to ask you now, don't you?'

If he mentioned boyfriends again I was walking off the set. 'No. What?' I asked, staring him defiantly in the eye.

'Well, you are a very talented, beautiful young lady, Harriet. It would be nice to get to know you a little better.'

The nerve of the man! They must all be the same, these roving journalists. 'I don't date older men,' I replied sternly, casting a glance into the wings where Nana gave me an approving nod.

Victor laughed and pretended to look embarrassed, as if I'd mis-understood the question, and said, 'Then you'll be relieved to hear that I was going to ask you to read one of your winning Meditations to us – as long as that doesn't count as a date!'

I gave him the benefit of the doubt and smiled. He passed me a copy of my Meditations and I prayed it would open at a suitable one – one that my father would have been proud of.

'Meditation Thirty-five,' I said, and began to read:

'I once lost a race when I'd won it.
It taught me that life's seldom fair.
I watched while they made losers winners,
Pretending that I didn't care.

'I've tasted the beauty of winning.
I've savoured the joy of success.
I've relished the failure of rivals.
I've longed for perfection, no less.

'But now when they make me a winner
I hesitate as they applaud.
For winning can sometimes be losing.
Perfection is often best flawed.

'So tell me I've won, but with caution.
Remind me of others who failed.
And we'll all wait for that final curtain
To teach us what winning entailed.'

I closed my book so that Victor would know I'd finished. I was glad I'd reached the end, not because I didn't like what I'd written but because I was afraid that my voice had begun to quiver. I'd so wanted it to sound right. All the time I'd been speaking I had been thinking about my sack race and my father, and what winning this competition really meant to me and my publishing team. The book could not have opened at a more appropriate page even if a helping hand had guided me there.

Phil had zoomed in so close to my face that I feared they expected me to say something more. But I'd said all I had to say, and I'd never been good at small talk. Fortunately Victor came to my rescue: 'It seems almost inappropriate to congratulate you on winning after that – it sort of takes the glory out of presenting you with your cheque.'

'I'm sorry,' I replied, with concern. 'I can read another, if you like – there are some funny ones later on.'

'No, no,' Victor said. 'That was beautiful – a lesson to us all.'

I hoped he wasn't being sarcastic. I don't think he was because he squeezed my arm gently as he spoke.

'And what are you going to do with your prize money? Will you let us into the secret?'

But what was I going to do with it? We hadn't decided. I had to say something, but what did I want to do with all that money? What did it really mean to me? It was a prize for a book I'd written, but which would never have left my bedside drawer if it hadn't been for my publishing team, Miandol Books. My mother and Nana. The three generations, as Victor had called us when he had suggested they were filmed too. And what had I said? Had I encouraged the idea? Had I grasped the opportunity to show the two people dearer to me than anyone else in the whole world how much they meant to me? What sort of daughter and granddaughter was I, for all my thoughtful Meditations? One who was so caught up in her own importance that she had neglected those who mattered most in her life. But she wouldn't do it again.

'I'm going to spend it on my publishers – Miandol Books. You met them earlier, my mother and Nana. Is it all right if they join us?' Before he could answer, I was beckoning them to join us on the sofa. My mother seemed hesitant until Nana took her arm and led her on to the set. Victor Darling was the perfect host and stood up to greet them as they approached. It was a long enough sofa for all of us, especially after Victor had persuaded Nana to put her big black shopping-bag on the floor. How was he to know that it housed half a dozen copies of my Meditations in case we met anyone 'important' while we were there, like Melvyn Bragg or Michael Parkinson? Not that Victor wasn't important in his own shiny way, but sales reps are like that, always looking for a new outlet for their formidable powers of persuasion.

'Welcome, welcome, Mia and Olivia – mother and Nana of our budding star,' Victor was saying, and it surprised me to find he was so astute.

'It was my mother and Nana who published my *Infinite Wisdom*,' I explained proudly. 'They are Miandol Books – short for Mia and Olivia.' I was sure I saw my mother blush when I said that, but it might have been the strong lights.

Not Nana, though. Nana was in her element. 'You're a clever man, Victor Darling, to have the good sense to spot the talent of my beautiful granddaughter,' she was saying, smiling playfully with her eyes.

'Well, I have to put my hands up,' he said, with his hands in the air, as if we needed a demonstration, 'and admit that I didn't actually choose Harriet myself. It was the British voting public who did that.'

'But you would have done, I bet, given half a chance,' she pressed him. 'Don't tell me you didn't have a good laugh at those line-dancers with the fat legs from—'

Before she could finish her sentence, Victor interrupted with: 'And I understand you're the sales rep, Nana, and you, Mia, are in charge of marketing and publicity.'

'That's right,' my mother said, and I was relieved to hear her voice, 'although we've both had easy jobs – the book speaks for itself. It's beautiful. A true reflection of an innocent yet wise mind.'

I wished she hadn't said 'innocent'. What if Jean Claude was watching? It made me sound like Alice in Wonderland. I rearranged my floral chiffon blouse over my T-shirt so that it fell seductively off one shoulder, and said: 'I've always been interested in philosophy, particularly Descartes and his *Meditations*. In a way, I suppose, my book is a tribute to him.' I turned to look straight into the camera that was looming towards me as I spoke. That should do the trick.

'And you were saying you'd like to spend the prize money on your publishing team,' Victor said, by way of a prompt – he was probably running out of time. 'Any thoughts, Nana? Ideas?'

I wished he'd asked my mother or me first.

'I've always fancied the idea of a nice helicopter,' Nana suggested.

'Where can you buy a helicopter for ten thousand pounds?' laughed Victor. 'Tell me and I'll buy one myself!'

He shouldn't have laughed like that. It was rude of him. Viewers might think Nana had said something silly.

'I think Nana had in mind a helicopter trip,' I said. 'Maybe to the country, or something like that.'

'Perhaps to a country-house hotel?' my mother joined in. 'Something stately in a parkland setting.'

'It would have to have a good restaurant,' added Nana, licking her lips.

'Nothing less than a gourmet one.' My mother laughed. 'Michelin-starred, of course.'

'Only the best for Harriet and her team,' agreed Nana.

'A swimming-pool would be nice,' mused my mother.

'As long as it was indoors,' was Nana's proviso. 'There are a lot of mosquitoes around at this time of year.'

'Absolutely!' agreed Publicity. 'Perhaps a health club with a sauna and Jacuzzi and a steam room.'

'I wouldn't mind one of those treatments they do on your feet,' enthused Nana.

'Reflexology, I think you mean,' my mother replied.

'No. I was thinking of chiropody – I've got a bit of hard skin on the soles of my feet.'

'Have you ever wondered what it would be like to fly through the sky like a bird until you come to a place where the sun always shines and champagne is served chilled in silver goblets with long stems?'

I'd just wanted to hear the sound of my own voice so I knew I was still alive. It was supposed to be *my* interview after all. I was the award-winning Face of London, not Nana or my mother. I had created the much acclaimed Meditations, and not without a great deal of hard work and dedication and research into the methods of other writers of philosophy. Surely I was entitled to some say in what I chose to do with my prize money?

Victor was looking quizzically at me and I sensed it was time for a weather report. 'I'm afraid we'll have to interrupt your plans there, girls,' he said.

Girls? I hated it when people said that. It sounded so patronising.

'But whatever you choose to do, I'm sure you'll have a fabulous time. And well done once again, Harriet.'

The cameras pulled back from our faces to focus on Victor while my mother, Nana and I were instructed to leave the sofa by a woman at the periphery, who seemed, nevertheless, to think she was very much in control.

'I thought that went well,' whispered Nana, as we were led away.

'It might have been an idea to let me have a little more say in what I do with what is *my* money after all,' I suggested, pointing to my name on the somewhat crumpled cheque in my hand. I could see from their faces that they hadn't thought of it like that until then.

Their excitement had carried them away, as it was sometimes prone to do. And what was wrong with that in the great scheme of things anyway? It showed they were vibrant, enthusiastic women, who knew how to enjoy themselves, even in the face of adversity. Hadn't we all suffered enough? Didn't we owe it to ourselves to let our magnificent heads of hair down, even for just a weekend?

'But I loved your ideas all the same!' I added. And their faces lit up again.

The following Monday was just as exciting. The telephone didn't stop ringing with orders from shops that the sales rep hadn't even approached but whose owners had seen me on *London Live*. And there were re-orders from shops that had already sold out and needed more. Nana took the calls. We always knew when it was a book order because her voice changed and she said, 'Yes, this is Miandol Books – Olivia speaking.' Then she would throw a tea-towel at us, or whatever else she had in her hand at the time, to order us out of the room. Of course we always listened at the door – in case she needed to ask us something – but she never did. She was formidable. If my mother or I answered the telephone to a book buyer they never wanted to speak to us – they always asked for Olivia.

There was only one drawback to having Nana in sales – her counting. It was appalling, not just her adding up on the invoices, which my mother and I secretly corrected when she was in bed, but the number of books being ordered. We had discovered it by chance that morning. Nana was showing off about the number of books she had sold, and we totalled up the precise number. To our amazement, we found that she had sold more than a thousand from a one-thousand-copy run.

'Where did you think the other books were coming from?' I asked, adding up the numbers on my pocket calculator in case I'd made a mistake. But I hadn't. I excelled at mental arithmetic. It was my forte after English, philosophy and the mind-body problem.

'I don't know what all the fuss is about,' Nana said casually. 'It's nice to know they want it.'

'We'll have to get more printed,' my mother said, trying to calm the atmosphere.

'What are we going to tell the buyers?' I asked. 'The phone hasn't stopped ringing for the last hour.'

'Nana will think of something, won't you?' my mother said hopefully, turning to Nana, who was busy cleaning a window.

Nana always cleaned windows when she was worried about something. And the force she was applying to the sitting-room panes made me fear that there was more she hadn't told us. 'How many books do we have left to send out?' I asked.

Nana picked up a second duster and started polishing with two hands.

'Nana?' I repeated in case she hadn't heard me, but she had.

'None,' Nana mumbled, into her sparklingly clean window pane.

'None?' I repeated.

Nana stopped cleaning and turned to face me head on. 'I've already sent out every book we had left!' she said, proud like a lioness protecting her young.

'Why didn't you tell us? You shouldn't have kept taking orders when we'd run out. It will take weeks to reprint,' my mother said.

'I couldn't speak to all those nice people on the telephone, then let them down, not when they wanted to buy Harriet's beautiful book with her name all over it and her lovely photograph.'

'Let's get this right. You've already dispatched the eight hundred or so books remaining after the launch and school sales. That means, including this morning's sales, we're approximately nine hundred copies short!'

Nana laughed mischievously. 'I know – I'm terrible, aren't I?'

'Nana! It will cost thousands of pounds to print all those copies, even though there are orders for them. Where did you think the money would come from to pay for them?'

'Well, what's money for if it's not to be spent?' was Nana's philosophical response.

'We'll have to order them straight away,' my mother decided.

It sounded like a sensible idea, until Nana said sheepishly, 'I've already done that.'

It transpired that she had ordered a further thousand copies of my beautiful book. We called an emergency board meeting. I was elected accounts executive and Nana was put in charge of customer relations. It took her thirty-five telephone calls of flattery and spin to satisfy the buyers that there had been a slight delay but their books would be with them shortly. So, we had no books to sell. That was the bottom line.

'Only our own copies,' my mother confirmed.

'And I wouldn't sell mine for the world,' Nana added, tears welling in her eyes, as she focused her mind on just what she had done.

'And you promise there are no more orders you haven't told us about?'

'I swear on the soul of Fred Astaire.'

'Then we should be working out the total we've raised so far,' Publicity pointed out, which seemed to cheer up Sales no end.

I got out my pocket calculator again and did a few sums.

When I passed them my calculations, there was a collective sharp intake of breath. Then Nana got out a hankie and we wiped our eyes. We had a right to be proud of ourselves.

'This calls for champagne!' my mother said.

She ran back from the kitchen with a bottle and three glasses. 'Let's drink a toast,' she said. 'To Harriet.'

'No, to Daddy,' I replied.

We raised our glasses as Nana said, '"I know not where you are, but I shall love you from afar" – Meditation thirty-four, isn't it?'

'I didn't know you'd actually read my book, Nana,' I said, with surprise.

'Read it? I could recite every Meditation by heart if you asked me to!' And we could tell from her eyes that she meant it.

But then a shadow came over her face and we knew she was thinking of the copies she had ordered without telling us. Dear Nana, always so determined, so impetuous, so proud.

'It doesn't matter, Nana,' I said reassuringly. 'Really it doesn't.' But it mattered to Nana. She felt she had let me down. She would need several apple turnovers to help her get over that.

'I've an idea,' I said suddenly. 'I don't know why I didn't think of it before. We can put my prize money towards the reprint. Call it a second edition. All the best books have them. And it will make the first edition even more collectable. People will be fighting for them on the Internet.'

'But you liked the idea of spending the prize on a luxury break, a holiday, something special you'd never forget.'

'I'll get it back eventually when the invoices are paid,' I answered heroically. 'We can go on our holiday then.'

But my mother remained uncertain, and Nana said she'd already started to pack.

'Then you'll just have to unpack,' I answered.

The argument would have continued for hours if the telephone hadn't rung.

'That'll be another order,' my mother said, running to answer it. 'I'll get it this time.'

I could tell by her voice that it wasn't an order – I could hear relief in it rather than the anxiety I'd anticipated. And she kept saying, 'Wonderful' and 'Marvellous'. That made me rule out Jean Claude – with him, she would have been more likely to use words like 'unavailable' and 'inopportune'.

Nana and I listened from the sofa, hoping for a clue, but none came. Eventually, she replaced the receiver and said, 'That was Jackie from the TV studios.'

'From the way you were talking, it sounded like they were impressed by us,' I said.

'I'm sure they were,' she replied, 'but that wasn't why she was ringing.'

'Don't tell me they want us on again?' Nana suggested, trying not to look too excited.

'She was ringing to say that someone had seen us on the show and contacted the programme about us.'

'There! I told you we were good!' Nana exclaimed. 'Who was it? A film director – Steven Spielberg?'

'Someone called Christopher Small.'

'I haven't heard of that one,' Nana said, continuing her hopeful train of thought.

'He's a hotelier,' my mother explained, which came as a cruel blow to Nana, although I found it far more encouraging.

'He doesn't happen to own a stately hotel set in parkland with an indoor swimming-pool and a gourmet restaurant, does he?' I asked.

'Two Michelin stars,' my mother replied excitedly, 'and we won't have to pay a penny. He and his wife Fiona want us to stay there as their guests this weekend. All they ask for in return is a few photo-shoots with my stunningly beautiful and intelligent daughter to use as publicity for the hotel. The Face of London comes to the country, accompanied by her publishing team. They've even asked if I'll help them with a few publicity ideas! How about that? What do you say, Harriet?'

'Will they send a helicopter to pick us up?' I asked.

'We have to provide our own transport,' my mother replied.

'Then that's what we'll do,' I said, an idea forming. 'Leave it to me.'

22

'I saw you on television with your mother and grandmother on Saturday night.' Whenever Charlotte Goldman smirked, she never looked you in the eye. 'It must have been *so* embarrassing.'

'Embarrassing?' I asked, raising my right eyebrow to emphasise my surprise. 'Why on earth would I have been embarrassed?'

'I just meant I think you're really brave having them on TV like that, then announcing you're taking them on holiday with you.'

'You still go on holiday with your grandmother?' Jason excelled at regurgitating what other people had said as if he'd thought of it himself – he was hoping to be a lawyer.

'Why shouldn't I? I love being with my grandmother. She's more fun than you are!'

At one time I would have ignored Jason's remark, but now I'd resolved to tell it how it was. Why not? So what if they didn't like me for it? I was here to learn, not to make friends with under-achievers like Jason Smart.

'Don't be so nasty to Harriet. She can't help it if she's got nobody else to go on holiday with.'

She was so obvious – did none of the others see how obvious Charlotte Goldman was?

'You're so bloody obvious, Charlotte!' I said, turning to confront her. Cowards hate direct confrontation – it reminds them of every-thing they're not (Meditation 52).

'I didn't mean anything by it – I was just trying to be nice, that was all.' As she spoke she let her voice quiver and looked round to gauge the others' reactions.

'How is Charlotte obvious, anyway?' asked Jason, seizing the oppor-tunity to divert attention from his own remark.

'Work it out for yourself, Jason. It shouldn't be that difficult, even for you.'

'You think just because you've been on television and radio and in the papers and everything that you're famous,' Jason went on, his voice becoming louder and louder as he expressed what he believed to be his very good point.

'Isn't that what it is to be famous? Being on television and radio and in the newspapers?' I asked.

'Well, yeah, but . . .'

'But you don't like it being me. Is that your problem?' I asked. I could feel the blood rushing to my head. I hoped no one would notice and think I was embarrassed. I wasn't embarrassed. I was angry. 'And your problem too, Charlotte Goldman?'

'She must be pre-menstrual.' Charlotte sniggered into her desk.

She was right. I was pre-menstrual. But how did she know? It was eerie. 'And you must be a witch!' I replied, as Madame du Bois entered the room to give us our French lesson.

Once a week we were instructed to write an essay in French on a subject of our choosing, as long as it was French-related, and someone was invited to read theirs aloud to the rest of the class. Before Charlotte had come to our school, Madame du Bois would invite me regularly to read my essays. Now, however, Madame preferred to ask her. My mother described it as an excess of patriotism, but Nana said the loss was Madame's.

There was something about the back of Charlotte's head that irritated me, especially when she nodded it as she was doing now. The nodding meant that she was thinking hard about her answer, forming cleverly constructed French phrases to describe her French-related experience. I could imagine what she was writing: my eventful trip to Harriet's mother's health club, meeting the French Jean Claude. All told in her way, of course – clumsy Harriet and her exaggerated diving exercise, poor Harriet with her bleeding lip, gracious Jean Claude taking pity on Harriet and asking her to tag along on a date with him and his fellow countrywoman.

Soon she would be invited to read her essay to the rest of the class. Madame du Bois would then congratulate her on her eloquence and wide vocabulary while the rest of us tried to piece together what she had been saying. It was not that it was particularly difficult to translate into English, rather that she spoke so quickly, running her words together as if she was selling vegetables at a French market. I wished Madame du Bois would remember the rest of us sometimes. Charlotte Goldman seemed to have a monopoly on all things French.

'Charlotte,' Madame du Bois called, as we put down our pens in anticipation. '*Vous êtes prête?*'

But I was '*prête*' too. In fact I had been '*prête*' for some considerable time. Suddenly Miss Grout's words flooded back to me: 'You're quite happy for the rest of the class to speak up while you sit quietly in the background, smiling sometimes, apparently.'

'Madame du Bois!' I spoke with the voice of a person who had been held back for far too long. '*Je suis prête aussi.*'

I sensed thirty pairs of confused eyes scrutinising me for signs of sunstroke or a bump on the head. Could they have heard Harriet Rose volunteering to speak in class in another language when someone else had already been chosen? Harriet Rose, whose response to 'Would you like to introduce yourself to the new pupils?' was 'No, not really.'

Madame du Bois invited me to proceed, with an expression of reluctance and disbelief. It was exactly the absence of encouragement I needed. I got to my feet and threw myself into the delivery of my well-crafted French essay – how it had been my birthday, how I had invited the half-French Charlotte to accompany me to my mother's health club, how an inadequately displayed out-of-order sign had led to my accident, how a Frenchman, Jean Claude, had come to my rescue, how the three of us had dined at a French restaurant, how I had ended the evening by inviting Jean Claude to my launch party at the London Portrait Academy, how he had telephoned me subsequently on several occasions. I thought that that was an appropriate place to end my discourse, purely to heighten the literary effect. I had learned as a professional writer that what one leaves out can sometimes be more important than what one puts in. Yet it was all there. Not even Charlotte could have expressed herself more eloquently.

When I had finished I sat down. I did not seek applause, but I had hoped that my efforts would not go unrewarded, at least by Madame du Bois. I had given these people my heart. I had sat in a class, which included Charlotte Goldman, and confessed to a *liaison dangereuse* with a Frenchman whom she was in the process of endeavouring to ensnare. What on earth more could I have done?

'Well, that was all very interesting, Harriet,' Madame du Bois said finally, 'but you were supposed to be writing an essay on Descartes' solution to the mind-body problem. Weren't you listening at the beginning of the class? It's Monday. French philosophy day.'

The irony was that I knew all about Descartes' mind-body problem – it was my own I was having difficulty with.

'Bad luck, Harriet,' Charlotte whispered, as she walked past me at the end of the class. Then, as I was searching for a suitable response, she added, 'I didn't realise Jean Claude had actually telephoned you – you should have told me.'

She had a way of pronouncing 'Jean Claude' as if she'd been practising it in front of her bedroom mirror.

'Why would I have told you?' I enquired in all innocence.

'You're right – I suppose you wouldn't,' she said, with a shrug of her shoulders, 'but you'd think he might have mentioned it.'

However much I subscribed to the word 'why' I wasn't going to use it now. So I said: 'Perhaps he thought it was none of your business.'

She seemed taken aback by the abruptness of my reply, unprepared for its directness in her world of put-downs and back-stabbing. For a moment I thought she was going to resort to the tears tactic again, but if she was she had second thoughts when she saw that none of the others was around and said instead: 'I think that's up to Jean Claude to decide, don't you?'

'You're right,' I replied, echoing her words to me moments before. 'I suppose it is.' I shrugged my shoulders and walked on, then added, 'Just like it was up to Jean Claude to decide to send me a dozen red roses.'

As soon as I'd said it I wished I hadn't. I shouldn't have let an airhead like her irritate me. But even God got irritated sometimes – why else would there have been a power cut on prize day right in the middle of Felicity Wainwright's nauseating acceptance speech? What if Jean Claude hadn't sent me the red roses? What if there was someone else who preferred my words to my silence? Someone who had read one of the Cratylus articles about me in the local newspapers, maybe even the *Kensington and Chelsea Messenger* reporter. He had offered me some of his chewing-gum, after all.

I didn't want to be at school any more. They hadn't liked me since I'd become famous. I couldn't pretend for, as I'd stressed in Meditation 36, 'There is no point in self-delusion because self-delusion is really no delusion at all.'

It was a subject I needed to discuss with my mother, and what better time than the following morning when she brought me breakfast in bed because I wasn't feeling well enough to go to school?

'I don't want to go back to school.'

'Why not?'

'They don't like me now I'm famous.'

'"If you can meet with Triumph and Disaster and treat those two impostors just the same . . ."'

The words sounded familiar, but as it was first thing in the morning I couldn't put my finger on which Meditation they were from. So I took a guess and completed the quotation with 'Then you'll have much more fun.'

It sounded right, but I couldn't be sure until my mother replied, '"You'll be a Man, my son."'

My son? I thought she knew my work better than that. I wouldn't correct her though. Even Shakespeare was misquoted sometimes. So I said nothing and got on with my breakfast.

'Croissants and hot chocolate – your favourites!' she said proudly.

But the croissant tasted French to me. And I didn't want to be reminded of the French. In fact, I wanted more than anything to forget about them. 'Do you see anything wrong with you and Nana coming on holiday with me?'

'Just as long as you promise you won't make us go to bed too early,' she replied, with a smile. 'Why do you ask?'

'It was something Charlotte Goldman said to me yesterday,' I explained, as my mother opened my bedroom curtains.

'Do you mean she actually managed to put together a whole sentence?' She laughed.

After that I felt a lot better, and before long I was happily dunking my croissant in my hot chocolate, French-style.

My mother sat down on the edge of my bed. I could tell from her expression that she was waiting for me to say more. But I couldn't decide how to explain what I was thinking. So I said nothing. Eventually she broke the silence: 'You know, you'll have to get used to mixed reviews if you're going to be a famous writer. No one is liked by everyone. After all, you wouldn't expect Mickey Mouse to appreciate Dostoevsky, now, would you?'

My mother had a way of putting everything into the right perspective. I decided there and then never to wear my Mickey Mouse nightshirt again. In fact, I might wash and iron it and give it to Charlotte Goldman as a Christmas present.

I had ordered the taxi to pick us up at four p.m. on Friday. We had done our packing the night before. Nana's case was the heaviest. She said it was because she needed larger clothes and more of them. She was the tallest of the three of us, at least for the time being, and she seemed to feel the cold more than we did. 'There's nothing worse,' she explained, 'than seeing daft old women wandering around with their flesh exposed.'

My mother thought she'd better check inside Nana's case 'to make sure you haven't forgotten anything'. I don't know where my mother thought we'd put it if she had. By the time we had removed the tins of biscuits, fruit loaf and Earl Grey tea, the case was a lot lighter.

'Why have you packed so many handkerchiefs, Nana?' I asked, as my mother removed another pile.

'You need them in the country to swipe all the flies and other insects you get there,' she said, replacing six or seven. Her desire for handkerchiefs was nothing new. They had always been essential to Nana – large white cotton ones with a blue O in the corner. No one could leave the house without her asking, 'Have you got a hankie?' And if the answer was: 'No,' we had to wait until she'd fetched one. I never used them. They remained stuck up my sleeve where she had put them. But it reassured her to know that the handkerchief was there – just in case.

'Give me some, Nana,' I said, grabbing a handful. 'I'll take them in my bag.'

'I hope you haven't forgotten your hatpin,' Nana said, as she passed me her hankies. Nana wouldn't let me go anywhere without a hatpin. 'Don't forget your hatpin!' she always said, and her eyes would leave me in no doubt as to what I was supposed to do with it and where it was to go should the dreaded emergency ever arise. It would take a brave member of the opposite sex to outmanoeuvre Nana's hatpin. She never divulged whether it had ever been used for anything other than holding up the brown floppy brim of the hat she had removed it from when I was ten or eleven, but I under-stood from my mother that she had been entrusted with a similar one when she was about my age. I had once asked her whether it was an old Scottish custom to carry a hatpin with you at all times, but Nana had taken on an unusually stern and fiery look and said, 'Don't be daft, Harriet!' And I knew not to ask her again.

But I wasn't daft – I knew when to avoid Nana's wrath, so I said, 'I've already packed it.'

Although my case was lighter than Nana's, it had taken longer to pack. My mother, of course, had helped me. It was crucial that I was prepared for whatever photo-shoot Christopher and Fiona

Small had in mind. You never knew who might see the photographs. Before long, Harriet Rose might even become a brand name. So we carefully selected a variety of swimming costumes and bikinis, and my mother lent me some of her sarongs. We thought that would cover the pool shots. And we put in a couple of pairs of jeans and shorts for the more casual teenage look for around the grounds. Trainers, of course, were an essential accessory, and would come in handy if they wanted me on the tennis court. With my white visor worn back to front, of course. Then we had to cover the possibility of evening dress in the Michelin-starred restaurant. Nothing too mature, just my black and red launch-party outfit and a long white dress, cut off one shoulder, which my father had said made me look like a Greek goddess. My mother suggested I take a couple of her pashminas too – they would add colour to the photographs and transform a casual outfit into a more formal one, if necessary. My mother, I was sure, could have been a stylist or fashion designer if she had wanted to – she knew all about the clever touches so important to people like me in the spotlight. And that just about covered it – apart from a selection of T-shirts and my red and blue sequined Emma Hope shoes. That left only the question of what to wear for full impact on arrival. It was an easy decision – I didn't need my mother's help with that. I chose my best faded hipster jeans with silver sequins round the pockets, a simple white T-shirt and the silver and black Chanel chain belt.

'Perfect!' my mother exclaimed, when she saw me coming downstairs. 'I couldn't have chosen better.' Then she fetched me a pale blue pashmina in case it grew cooler later on. I had no idea what she had packed for herself as she had done it so quickly, but I knew I could rely on her good taste. And that was that. We were ready for

Tegfold Hall Hotel. I only hoped that Tegfold Hall Hotel was ready for us.

I insisted on answering the door to the taxi-driver. It was important to me that the travel arrangements were mine alone.

'How long will it take us to get there?' my mother asked our driver, when we had been travelling for about fifteen minutes.

'About two minutes,' the driver replied. 'It's just round the corner.'

'Round the corner?' cried my mother in disbelief. 'They told me the hotel was in the heart of the countryside, surrounded by undulating hills and frolicking sheep. You don't see many of those in this part of London!'

'I knew there'd be a catch,' Nana exclaimed, narrowing her eyes in suspicion. 'Driver, turn round! We're going home.'

'Take no notice,' I called to him. 'We're getting out here.'

'Don't be silly, Harriet,' my mother entreated. 'We're not staying in a hotel here. It's not what we were promised. Don't you see? It's a con!'

'Well, make your bleeding minds up,' the driver growled, over his left shoulder. 'I can't wait here all day.'

I needed to take control. The situation was getting out of hand. I hadn't anticipated this kind of confusion. 'This isn't the hotel, you idiots,' I explained tenderly. 'It's a heliport. We're flying to the hotel in our own private helicopter. I've arranged everything. Now, hurry up and get out. They'll be waiting for us.'

It was hard to tell which of us was most excited. When I was booking the surprise, I had expected it would be me. But, judging by their faces, I might have been wrong.

'So that's who you were speaking to all that time on the telephone when you ordered me out of the room,' laughed my mother. 'I thought it must have been Jean Claude.'

'He should be so lucky,' interjected Nana, 'after the way he's behaved with that little raspberry ripple.'

'Harriet wouldn't be so stupid,' my mother added, as we headed for the heliport.

'Of course not!' I replied – unconvincingly, I feared. It wasn't exactly a lie. I hadn't actually planned to ring him to apologise for not having opened the door to him in my nightshirt, I'd just wondered about it – until I'd remembered I didn't know his telephone number. 'Anyway,' I said, 'let's think about more important matters. We're not going to let a misguided Frenchman spoil our special holiday.' I felt better when I'd said that – as if I'd drawn a line under my signature – and now I needed their undivided attention for the next part of my surprise. 'There's our helicopter!' I shouted, perhaps a little loudly. 'Over there! The one with my photograph on the tail boom!'

My mother was the first to spot it. Nana said she couldn't see for the tears of joy in her eyes.

'It's the photograph from my book,' I explained. 'I got them to enlarge it for me and print *The Infinite Wisdom of Harriet Rose* underneath. You'll see the big black letters when we get closer.'

And there it was, proudly displayed under the sack-race photograph of my face. *The Infinite Wisdom of Harriet Rose* for all to see, even when airborne, as we soon were after the pilot had settled us in.

There was only one thing missing for the moment to be complete, and that was the presence of my father, which not even I could do anything about. Yes, my prize money had provided me with an opportunity to create for us all an experience we would cherish for ever, but as I'd stressed in Meditation 60: 'The value of money should never be confused with the value of experience. And although it is true that money very often provides the opportunity for experience, it is only experience itself that has intrinsic value – unless you're a coin-collector. And they don't count.' I knew I had *London Live* and the British voting public to thank for this opportunity, but it was being part of a family such as mine that made the moment worthwhile. And that was something all the money in the world couldn't buy.

As we swept over the Thames and the streets of London I knew that my mother was also wishing my father could have been there. It was just the sort of adventure he would have loved, but he'd never had the opportunity. Not that his had been an uneventful life – far from it. As my mother often pointed out to those who expressed sadness at the brevity of his life, it was the quality of his existence which made it worthwhile, not the quantity. Everything he did, he did with energy and enthusiasm – even getting up in the morning or mowing the lawn. And if he had an obstacle to overcome, his way of tackling it never made it seem like an obstacle to anyone else. That was one of the characteristics that made him so successful professionally. I'm certain that his determination would have helped him succeed in whatever career he had chosen. As it happened, he had been a vet.

He had begun his career in Edinburgh where he had met and married my mother. Over the years they had lived in several different parts of Britain – they shared the desire for change in every aspect of life except that of being together. And the longer they spent together, the closer they became. I had witnessed that for myself so I didn't need to hear it from others, although I did. It wasn't that they never argued – of course they did. Both of them were fiery, spirited Celts. How could it have been otherwise? But the arguments never lasted long, and never touched the fibre of their bond.

As the years passed, and my father's veterinary practice grew, neither of them allowed financial success to tarnish the principles they had taught me: not to measure a gift by its financial worth but by the spirit in which it had been given and the thought that had gone into the choosing of it; always to search for intrinsic worth rather than retail value; the importance of who we were rather than what we had. And so forth. He might have gone, but his lessons continued to guide me, even as I sat in my own private helicopter, heading for a country-house hotel, paid for with my own money. I knew why those things were important to the three of us just then, even if others might misjudge us or envy us or wish to bring us down. I felt for the St Christopher round my neck. 'Someone to watch over you.' Could it be that my father had sent me a sign after all?

I had not expected it to be so noisy in the helicopter. Fortunately Nana had some tissues in her blazer pocket, which she suggested we stuff into our ears.

'How will we be able to talk to each other?' I asked. Even as a philosopher, I had the odd moment of practicality.

'We can use sign language,' Nana said, stuffing an ear. Once her mind was made up, there was no point in trying to dissuade her. So we all packed our ears with her tissues and set about our new form of communication. I went first – I had to. My mother and Nana were engaged in a fit of the giggles. I held an imaginary champagne glass in my left hand and used the right one to simulate pouring champagne into it. Then I pointed to an actual silver champagne bucket hidden discreetly in the front beside the pilot. My mother understood immediately and leant forward to reach for the champagne bottle and three flutes. But I held up two fingers to let her know the champagne was just for her and Nana – I had requested

freshly squeezed orange juice for myself, remembering my
Meditation 63:

> Let not fame
> Go to your head
> Like pink champagne.

I wasn't taking any chances.

Fortunately my mother understood my two-fingered gesture –
although Nana mimicked it with misplaced hilarity.

The journey would last approximately forty-five minutes, I had
been told when I made the booking. And what a booking it was!
Anyone would have thought they'd never had a fourteen year old
book a helicopter flight before. If it hadn't been for the fact that the
supervisor had seen me on *London Live* and knew how much money
I'd won, they wouldn't have accepted the booking at all. As it was,
I had to convince him that I was *the* Harriet Rose by reciting one of
my Meditations to him, which he entirely misunderstood and found
extremely amusing. But that was why he was a helicopter booker,
not a professional writer.

From the air, the streets of London were almost indistinguish-
able. I searched for the occasional landmark – such as the Albert
Hall and South Kensington – but to no avail. I couldn't even work
out where my school was, or if we had passed it. It wasn't that I
cared who saw me flying through the sky with my face and book
title prominently displayed on the tail boom of my private helicopter. Indeed, had Jean Claude happened to be sauntering through
South Kensington on his way home, pondering the hidden meaning
of one of my Meditations, and looked up to see me and my book
hovering over his head like a guiding star, it really wouldn't have

mattered very much to me at all. And if he chose to read more into the experience than a mere coincidence of events, well, that was entirely up to him.

The champagne bubbles seemed to lull my mother and Nana into a state of peaceful euphoria: before we had reached the half-way point, they were fast asleep. I used the opportunity to jot down a few reflections on the paradoxical nature of anticipation – the closer we got to our destination, the longer I wanted the journey to last.

It was the pilot who alerted me to the proximity of Tegfold Hall Hotel, pointing a forefinger to the land below us. I had been aware for some time of the absence of man-made intrusion, hills and valleys, woodland and fields, stretching below me like a giant canvas in every shade of green. Then suddenly, in the midst of it all, a building emerged, nestling into its surroundings – hidden yet visible, natural yet created, inviting yet forbidding, a beginning yet an end.

We were descending, metal bird that we were, seeking out our destination with mechanical accuracy. I nudged my mother and Nana: I didn't want them to miss our arrival. Down, down we fell to earth, attracting the attention of hotel guests, like pins to a magnet. Which celebrity was about to arrive? Wasn't that her photograph on the helicopter? Would she be staying at the hotel? Might they strike up a conversation with her? Would they get an autograph – a photo-graph of themselves with her even? I could sense their excitement from the air. A mother and her young daughter were waving at us. An elderly gentleman was shielding his eyes with his right hand. A golden retriever was barking and running in circles as he sensed the atmosphere of expectancy around him. A young couple was striding purposefully towards the landing pad, in matching navy Barbours and green wellies, their speed increasing as they drew closer. Our pilot instructed us to stay where we were until the rotor-blades had stopped turning, which gave us the time we needed to rearrange our clothes and brush our hair.

'I put my camera in here somewhere,' said Nana, rummaging in her big black shopping-bag. 'I couldn't find any flash cubes, though, so I'll have to take snaps of you outside.'

'It might be better to stick to my digital camera,' my mother suggested, diplomatically, as the pilot helped her out first. I should have been first – the crowd might have thought she was the celebrity, as I pointed out to her quietly from behind.

'I'll get back in, then,' she said, removing her arm from the steadying hand of the pilot.

'It's too late now!' I pushed her out again. 'Stop making a fuss. You're drawing the wrong kind of attention to us.'

It wasn't the arrival I had anticipated but, as I'd said in Meditation 38: 'Anticipation means you don't have enough to do.' Of course I'd elaborated on the principle in my book, but that was the gist of it.

'Hello! You must be Harriet Rose.' It was the woman I'd seen from the air in the wellingtons. 'I recognise you from your tail boom. I'm Fiona Small.'

'Welcome to Tegfold Hall Hotel. I'm Christopher Small and I recognise you from *London Live*. You're even prettier in the flesh.'

Somehow, I felt more empathy with the man than I did with his wife. Impressions are like that – quick to form but, in my experience, the more reliable for it. 'How do you do?' I said, smiling politely at them both. 'May I introduce my mother and grandmother?'

'You look just like you did on television,' Fiona said to the three of us.

'I expect we do,' I replied. 'It was only shot six days ago.'

Fiona laughed as if I'd meant to be funny.

The pilot waved goodbye to us and promised to return at nine thirty on Monday morning. That way, I would be at school by eleven and have missed only an hour of PE and a music lesson, which Miss Grout had said was fine as long as I made sure I got plenty of exercise at Tegfold Hall and listened to some music. Fiona assured me that both activities would be possible as there was an indoor and an outdoor swimming-pool and a harpist always played during afternoon tea. I would hardly know I wasn't at school.

As Fiona strode across the field in her mud-splattered wellingtons, I wished I hadn't worn my blue suede pumps with the satin bows.

'I hope you've brought some sensible walking-shoes with you,' she remarked, looking down at my feet.

'Of course!' I laughed. But had I? I ran through the shoe selection my mother and I had so carefully chosen – the blue and red sequined slip-ons, the white and silver leather trainers with tasselled laces, the black leather sandals with a detachable ankle strap. It wasn't looking promising. I might have to borrow Nana's brown lace-up brogues, the ones she always complained of 'walking in at the sides'.

Fiona didn't take off her wellingtons when we reached the hotel. Instead she walked through the grand portico entrance and across the black and white marble-floored hall, which was the size of a ballroom, oblivious of the pale brown trail she was leaving behind her. I liked that about Fiona. She wasn't a woman to get worked up about small matters of personal grooming. She knew a touch of dirt here and there had never done anyone any harm. She was a confident, relaxed, slightly shabby countrywoman, who wouldn't give a toss for the superficialities of steam pressing or Shake 'n' Vac. And judging by her ragged windswept hair, an afternoon session with a pair of Mayfair scissors was not a pastime to which she subscribed either. People could say what they liked about country-folk, but there was something about them that I found appealing. I removed my pale blue pashmina from my shoulders and took my sunglasses from the top of my head where they were holding back my hair.

'You'll probably want to freshen up,' Fiona suggested, 'after your journey.'

'Not particularly,' I said casually, sensing an air of countryness overtaking me. 'It doesn't seem worth the bother.'

Just then, Christopher ambled up to us with Nana and my mother, one on each side, and his boisterous golden retriever, the one I'd spotted from the air. He raced towards me as if he'd never seen a well-dressed female before – the dog that is, not Christopher. I hadn't expected that his front paws would reach right up to my new white T-shirt when he jumped up on his hind legs. In London, dogs tended to be smaller and better behaved.

'Jack! Get down!' Christopher called, but Jack seemed not to hear. I made a mental note to avoid Jack during my photo-shoot.

'When we saw you all on *London Live*, I said to Chris, "We *have* to get the three of them down here. It would be such fun." And here you are!'

Fiona probably spoke so loudly because she was used to communi-cating across such enormous rooms. The drawing room, which was visible through oak-panelled double doors, was bigger than our entire downstairs. It was magnificent, with pale blue striped wall-paper and an elegant fireplace with an ornately carved surround and heavy, sweeping yellow silk drapes that flowed on to the parquet floor.

'Ben will take your luggage upstairs.' Ben was a rather large, spotty boy not much older than me who was standing behind Christopher.

'Such fun!' Fiona said again, as if to remind us that we were supposed to be enjoying ourselves. She didn't need to remind us: we would have been enjoying ourselves, if only the woman would let us.

Ben was ordered to take us to our rooms. Mine was the Churchill Suite on the first floor, my mother's was the Disraeli next door and Nana had Wilson in the attic.

'You can swap with me if you like,' my mother said to Nana, when she saw the size of Nana's room compared to ours. Not that there was anything wrong with the Wilson. In fact it was quite a cosy room with its pink and green floral curtains and matching quilt, the views over the herb garden at the rear. It was just that compared to my Churchill with its black-and-white art deco design and king-size four-poster bed and separate vast sitting room area bedecked with book-shelves from floor to ceiling on every wall, it seemed a touch on the small side.

'You could share the Disraeli with me,' my mother went on. 'It's big enough for a family of eight.'

'I'm quite content with my little Wilson up here, thanks all the same,' Nana replied. But we could tell by her face she didn't mean it.

The Smalls had left an itinerary on my bed. It was printed on headed paper with a sketch of the hotel in the top-right corner. It read:

Diana Janney

Day 1: Friday

5.30 p.m.   Arrival

6.00 p.m.   Harriet and Fiona to discuss possible photo-shoot
opportunities for *Gleam*

6.30 p.m.   Afternoon tea in the lounge

8.00 p.m.   Dinner in Gladstone's restaurant

Day 2: Saturday

10.30 a.m. to 1.00 p.m.   Harriet's photo-shoot in *Gleam*

1.00 p.m. to 2.00 p.m.   Light lunch

2.00 p.m. onwards   To be confirmed

Day 3: Sunday

[The weekend was beginning to sound longer than I was used to.]

11.00 a.m. to 12.30 p.m.   Interview with Harriet for *Heart of
the Country* magazine

2.00 p.m.   Book signing in the library

6.00 p.m.   Residents' cocktail party followed by buffet supper
beside the pool

Day 4: Monday

9.30 a.m.   Departure

I read my itinerary with astonishment. I had not anticipated anything
as widely circulated as *Gleam* – Fiona was more switched-on than I'd
given her credit for. However, I'd never heard of *Heart of the Country*.
It was probably new.

I looked at my watch. I had ten minutes to prepare for my meeting
with Fiona to discuss the photographs in *Gleam*. There was only one
thing to do: call Publicity.

'I'm going to be photographed for *Gleam* magazine,' I said, trying not to sound too excited. 'Fiona's running through it with me in ten minutes. Any ideas?'

'They'll be looking for a story,' my mother warned. 'Don't say anything about Jean Claude or your swimming accident.'

I hadn't thought of that. Suddenly I was going off the whole idea.

'It's a great opportunity, though,' my mother went on, sensing her protective instinct might have gone a little too far. 'The Smalls will expect you to mention the hotel and how much you're enjoying your stay here. I think you should also focus on your book — what it's about, who influenced you.'

'Obviously I'll mention my publishing team,' I suggested.

'I wouldn't,' my mother disagreed. 'They'd expect to meet us and you can't predict what Nana will say.'

'You're probably right,' I agreed — but could I predict what I would say? I was beginning to wonder.

I met my mother and Nana as arranged outside my room.

'Six o'clock, that makes it teatime,' Nana said, as we descended Tegfold Hall's magnificent staircase one family portrait at a time.

We were met at the foot by Fiona. She had changed out of her jeans and wellingtons into a pair of well-cut black trousers and a cream silk sleeveless blouse that she wore with the collar turned up. 'Hello, Harriet. You got my itinerary? Mia, I hope you'll come too. We might need your input. There's someone I'd like you to meet.' It was probably the *Gleam* journalist or photographer to discuss the layout for tomorrow.

That left a redundant sales rep with an appetite for afternoon tea. 'I'll be in the drawing room when she's finished with you,' Nana shouted happily after us.

Fiona led us along a series of winding corridors, her black leather court shoes clicking as she went. I wished I hadn't chosen my trainers – the squelching of rubber soles on marble didn't give the right impression. I'd only worn them to make Fiona feel at ease.

We arrived at an inner courtyard on the other side of which I saw a conservatory-style entrance to the hotel's leisure club. The first thing I noticed about it was its name, written in large red letters right across the conservatory glass window. It was called Gleam.

'Pop off your shoes, both of you, and slip into these.' She handed us each a pair of white cotton slippers, then put on her own. 'This is where we have our relaxation breaks,' she explained, with pride – it was obviously her idea. 'Yoga and pilates weekends are popular at the moment, as I'm sure you know.' But we didn't. We weren't the type for Pilates. We'd rather have been with Nana, stuffing ourselves with cream cakes and scones.

'That was what gave me the brilliant idea of getting you down here when I caught the end of your presentation.'

I noticed my mother's face in one of the club's many mirrors – she was as confused as I was.

'This is Steve, our relaxation expert. He'll explain more.'

Steve was short and muscular and dressed as if he was auditioning for *Star Trek*. 'We want to attract more guests to our Gleam treatment weekends,' he explained.

'Get lots of press coverage – you know the sort of thing, Mia,' Fiona said.

My mother hesitated. 'I have to confess, although I belong to a health club, I really only go there for the swimming. I know very little about relaxation techniques.'

'That's where Harriet comes in.' It was Fiona again. 'I thought she could read her Meditations beside the pool, maybe help the guests with their chants, give them their own mantra, generally teach them the art of meditation. The press would love it – "Harriet Rose and her award-winning Meditations". What do you say, Harriet?'

Nana was on her second chocolate éclair when we found her. She was wiping clotted cream from the corners of her mouth with a big white napkin, whilst pretending to be enchanted by the gentle murmur of plucked strings emanating from a female harpist in the corner of the drawing room. 'I thought you were never coming back!' Nana whispered angrily, through an enraptured smile still fixed encouragingly on the harpist. 'If it hadn't been for my little friend over there, I'd have looked a right idiot sitting here on my own all this time in a hotel lounge. Men have been swarming round me.'

My mother and I looked about anxiously, but the only man we could see had his head buried in a copy of the *Financial Times* and a mobile phone pressed to his right ear.

'Swarming, they've been!' she confirmed, and we thought it best not to disagree.

'We'd have been here sooner,' I said, 'if it hadn't been for Steve.'

'Who?' asked Nana.

'The hotel's relaxation instructor.' My mother took over. 'He wanted Harriet to show him a few of her techniques.' We laughed.

Nana looked at us in bewilderment. 'Don't be so daft,' she said loudly. 'Pull yourselves together and tell me what you're talking about.'

'Fiona seems to have formed the impression,' my mother explained, 'that Harriet's book is some sort of manual on how to meditate. She hoped that Harriet would instruct the hotel guests on their breathing techniques and how to put themselves into a meditative trance!'

'With lots of press coverage, of course,' I added. 'Don't forget that.' Then my mother and I began to laugh again.

'I don't see what's so funny,' Nana exclaimed. 'I hope you gave her something to meditate about.'

The harpist was playing slightly louder now, and the man with the mobile phone had put down his newspaper and was staring at us. He was older than I'd thought, with thick grey hair and a matching moustache that had caught a few specks of raspberry jam with its corners.

'I knew there was something wrong with that woman's judgement as soon as I saw the room she'd given me,' Nana was saying. 'Let's get back to London before she asks us to sit cross-legged on the floor.' She got to her feet in such a hurry that she dropped her napkin. I could hear the harpist break into a rendition of 'Yesterday' in the background, played rather faster than I was used to hearing it, and with a certain urgency about it that she had managed cleverly to capture in the expression on her face.

'Calm down!' my mother urged. 'We've explained to Fiona her mistake. She understands exactly what philosophical meditations are now. I've given her a copy of Harriet's *Infinite Wisdom* to read overnight. The local press are still coming in the morning, but I've managed to persuade her that the library would be a more suitable backdrop for Harriet and her book rather than the Gleam health club. She got the message. Publicity has seen to that. Everything's going to be fine.'

There was nothing like a fresh pot of Earl Grey tea to calm Nana down, and before long she, too, had seen the funny side.

'Why don't we all go and change for dinner?' my mother

suggested. 'Then we can work up an appetite with a walk in the grounds.'

As the three of us got up to go, I heard a voice in the background whisper, 'Goodbye, Olivia.' It was the man with the grey hair and moustache.

I had expected to sleep well after a five-course gourmet dinner in Gladstone's restaurant. It wasn't just the number of dishes that had been exhausting, but the number of decisions I'd had to make: still or sparkling water, gazpacho or bouillabaisse, Coquilles St Jacques Provençal or scampi *à la maison*, followed by either *filet de boeuf* with a red wine reduction and truffle *jus* or grilled sea bass served with lemon risotto. And, as well as a choice of sorbets to clear the palate, there was the question of pudding, which appeared to be a speciality of the celebrated pastry chef – *crêpes* Suzette or *pot au chocolat* with Cointreau or raspberry soufflé or *tarte tatin*. And with each new course, there was the question of how I would like it and whether I wanted anything with it. I even had a selection of breads to choose from: onion, sun-dried tomato, olive, herb or walnut. Then, just when I thought the decision-making process must surely have been exhausted, I was offered coffee – filter, cappuccino, espresso or Irish. I felt as if I'd gone from hotel guest to prime minister in the course of two hours.

The maid had turned down the covers on my king-size four-poster, and left a mint on the pillow, as if the *petits fours* with our coffee hadn't been enough. My mother was only next door, as she reminded me when I telephoned her to make sure she'd remembered to floss her teeth. But somehow, as soon as I switched off my bedside light (which wasn't easy to do as the switch, I eventually worked out, was confusingly on the wall) I knew I'd be awake half the night.

It was so much darker here than it was in London, especially once the shutters had been closed. At home, I was used to street-lights and car headlamps. It was no use. I'd have to get up and do something. Lying awake only concentrated my mind on matters I would rather forget, like the last time I'd seen my father alive and the first time I'd seen him dead, and all the holidays we'd shared together and all the days without him that lay ahead. He should have been next door now in his stripy pyjamas, chatting and laughing with my mother, knocking three times on the wall when he switched off their light.

He should have been there in the morning to give me a wake-up call before he went downstairs to read a newspaper on the lawn while my mother and I got ready for breakfast. He should have been suggesting tennis after breakfast and getting angry and swearing whenever his serve went out. He should have been checking the bill as we prepared to leave and frowning when he realised they'd got it right.

I jumped out of bed and threw open the shutters to let in some light. There was a big full moon right outside my window. It looked just like a face if you squinted and released your imagination. It did not take long for the face to come into focus – the narrow gleaming eyes, the long nose with wide nostrils, the dimple in the chin just under the wide smiling mouth. It was all there if you looked hard enough and knew what you were looking for. My father might not have been on the other side of the wall, but he was still watching over me. Of that I suddenly felt certain.

I sat down at the writing desk under the window and picked up a pen with 'Tegfold Hall Hotel' written on it. It was what he had wanted me to do, after all. Hadn't he delighted in my writing? 'Dear Daddy,' I wrote on the hotel's paper. 'Are we here this time without you, or did you stay to watch us, as if we were actors on a stage, performing lines you know already, applauding us at the end of every scene? Are you the spotlight as we take a bow? Are you the prompter when we forget our lines? Was it written that your exit be so soon?'

I stopped writing. Once I had finished, I didn't know what to do with the piece of paper. It looked so tragic all alone in the centre of the desk, surrounded by pretty postcards of the hotel and a 'places of interest' brochure. He wouldn't have wanted to be remembered like that, a tragic piece of history in the midst of a continuing now. He *was* the continuing now, he *was* the 'things to do'. And so was I. I tore up the piece of paper and threw it into a wastepaper basket at the side of the desk. Then I picked up the pen again, selected the prettiest postcard of the hotel and wrote:

> Jean Claude
> I have found la vie en Rose –
> have you?

Breakfast was served in an informal dining room that overlooked the gardens and the tennis court. There were more guests staying at the hotel than I'd realised. A table had been prepared for us in the corner by the window. When I saw the three chairs, I thought for a moment I was with my parents again and left the chair in the middle empty for my father.

'Is this where you want me?' Nana said, smiling warmly towards me as she lowered herself into it. And she was right. I did want her there. It was just that my father should have been there too.

I didn't think they would notice my silence – I'd never liked talking at breakfast: I needed time to plan the day ahead.

'Are you all right, Harriet?' my mother was the first to enquire once my scrambled eggs and smoked salmon had arrived. I'd never had scrambled eggs with smoked salmon before – that was why I'd chosen it. I wanted everything to be different from other holidays. That way, I wouldn't keep remembering who was missing.

'Of course I am,' I snapped. 'Why wouldn't I be?'

'I thought you would choose the full English like me,' Nana suggested, breaking into the yolk of her egg.

'I used to,' I replied, 'but I prefer this now.' Somehow I hadn't expected the salmon to be cold, especially when the eggs were warm. 'They've forgotten to cook the salmon!' I exclaimed, looking around for our waiter.

'It's probably a foreign chef,' Nana suggested. 'Why don't you swap it for mine?'

I have to admit I was wondering about it until my mother explained: 'It's supposed to be cold. I'll have it if you don't want it, take mine.'

But there was no way I was going to start a new day with a bowl of muesli and a live yoghurt, however cold the salmon was, so I said, 'I was only joking – I know it's supposed to be served cold.' And I attempted a laugh that didn't fool either of them.

'Are you sure there's nothing else bothering you?' my mother persisted, which only made me feel worse. I'd so wanted this holiday to be special for us all, which was why I'd booked the helicopter to take us there. A surprise present from my prize money. My way of saying, 'Thank you both for all you've done for me.' And I knew why they'd done it, all of it – the book, the launch party, the media coverage, the competition. It was their way of saying, 'You can still do it, Harriet. Life goes on. You may have lost your father, and you know we miss him terribly, but you still have the two of us. And together we'll triumph in the face of adversity, because that's the type of women we are – strong, confident, determined, talented . . . modest women, who will carry on, whatever Fate may throw in their way.'

But the trouble was, I didn't feel like that just then. I wasn't as confident as Nana. I wasn't as strong as my mother. I felt afraid of what life might hold for me without a father to rely on. Yes, I had the two of them. But what if they went too?

As I looked at my mother savouring her coffee and Nana munching the corner of a brioche, which she had to admit was better than the fruit loaf she had tried to smuggle with her, it hit me that, in all likelihood, one of us would go first. 'Go', of course, being the unsentimental, practical way of referring to the one thing feared by everyone: death. It had already crept up and taken one of my family by surprise. Who was to say it wouldn't take another — any time, soon, today, tomorrow, the following week? As the oldest, Nana would be expected to go first, and I shuddered at the thought.

'You can't be cold sitting here!' my mother said. She always noticed me, even when I thought she was preoccupied with something else important, like food.

'No, I'm fine,' I replied.

But I wasn't fine. I was far from fine.

What if Nana wasn't next? What if it was my mother? There was something impossible about the concept, like trying to imagine swimming without water. I must make a note of that thought — it would make a very good Meditation. If my mother went first, that would be the end of me too. I would be orphaned. I was too young for that — who would help me decide what to wear? Who would protect me from harm and tell me what to say to Pink Panthers like Charlotte Goldman? Who would laugh at funny situations with me? Who would share my thoughts? Who would I buy cards for on Mother's Day and surprise with a Mother's Day lunch when she thought she was going shopping at Waitrose? Who would advise me on how to deal with Jean Claude?

'You're looking pale this morning, Harriet. Are you *sure* you're all right?'

'Yes! I told you I was! Don't keep on!' I snapped angrily. It wasn't fair of her to give me so much to worry about.

Perhaps we were nothing more than creations of God's imagination, ready to go when He stopped thinking about us. Perhaps if we didn't give Him reason to stop thinking about us, we'd carry on. I'd have to broach the subject subtly with the others, warn them somehow without it being too obvious what I was worrying about.

'I'm sure there is something worrying you, Harriet. What is it?' my mother asked.

Here was the opportunity I'd been looking for – and so soon. 'I think we should all go together, when we're ready to go, not before. No one should dictate when the time is right but us.'

'Has that waiter been complaining that we're taking too long?' Nana asked, looking around her.

'I think Harriet's talking about death,' my mother explained.

'Oh, is that all?' Nana said. 'I thought it was something serious.'

The local press were gathered in the library when I walked in for my photo-shoot later that morning. There must have been half a dozen, each clutching a long-lens camera. I had seen this scene before – I knew what to expect: the look of curiosity about the eyes, the scrutinising of the face they had come to see, the eagerness to capture *the* shot that no one else would manage to get. But, as I was to realise, these press weren't the same as London press. These local press had other things on their minds.

'Isn't he a beauty?' an older member of the local press was saying as I entered the room.

'Don't you just love his eyes?' another was agreeing.

I coughed to let them know I'd arrived. It shouldn't have been necessary, but it was.

'And he's got very strong legs,' a third agreed. 'He must get a lot of exercise.'

I learned a lot about the local press that day. If you try to compete with a golden retriever you'll only end up disappointed.

'Hello,' I said. 'You must be the local press. Sorry to keep you waiting.'

'Have you met Jack? I expect you have,' a man by the fireplace asked me, without taking his eyes off his four-legged friend. 'What a character!'

But I was a character too. I'd even worn my cream Panama hat so they would realise that.

The older man creaked to his feet and finally addressed me: 'Take your hat off, love, and we'll make a start.'

I removed the Panama hat it had taken my mother and me so long to position at just the right tilt. As I did so, a mound of the hair we'd carefully piled up inside it fell to my shoulders in a state of disarming disarray.

'Has anyone got a comb for her?' the man asked, removing his lens cap.

'It doesn't matter,' I replied defiantly. 'I'll run my fingers through it.'

It must have been that very act which caused so much excitement in Jack. He wanted me to run my fingers through his coat too. Within seconds, he was at my feet, rubbing his long wet nose against my cream linen trousers and tugging at the ankle strap of my black leather sandal.

'He's a naughty little fella!' cried a portly man beside the window, whom I hadn't noticed until then. 'He just wants to play. Throw something for him!'

Then the local press debated what they should throw for Jack, while I tried to detach him from his curious position around my left ankle.

I think it was my idea to throw a copy of my book – first, because it was the only thing, other than my Panama hat, that I had in my hand, and second, because I felt the time had come for the local press to remember exactly why they were there. And, in a sense, the throwing of my Meditations did have the desired effect. Jack left my ankle and raced across the heavily polished parquet floor in search of the book. It was the ripping of it to shreds that I hadn't anticipated. To be fair to the local press, neither had they. But it was no use doing what they did and attempting to piece together the soggy pages. For as I'd said in Meditation 64, which, ironically, was stuck to Jack's wet tongue, 'Our mistakes in life are like rips in a sheet of paper – once they have been made, the paper will never read the same again, however much you try to conceal them.'

'What a shame!' said the portly man, who had been by the window but who was now stooping beside the remnants of my Meditations. 'Your poor old book – I hope you've got another.'

Did these men not realise whom they were stooping beside? Had they no understanding of the relevance of the title, which now read, *The nite do* of *Harri ose*.

'I've already sold more than a thousand copies,' I explained, as politely as I could under the circumstances. 'Surely that's why you're all here today – to photograph me with my book?'

'No one said anything to me about a book,' one member of the local press replied. 'Anyone mention a book to you, Larry?'

Larry shook his ruddy head, which caused a cascade effect down several chins, and said, 'All I was told to do was to get some shots of the Hall as a promotion for the Smalls. I thought you must be the model.'

Flattering as it was that Larry had mistaken me for a fashion model, I had hoped, wrongly it seemed, that there was something in my bearing of an author. Larry did seem, however, to take a sudden interest in the book cover, the remains of which he was now holding. 'So you must be Harri Ose,' he said.

'Harriet Rose, actually,' I replied. 'You're holding my collection of Meditations.'

'Well, Jack seems to have enjoyed them, whatever they are. He likes to get his teeth into a good book, don't you, Jack?'

The six men seemed to find Larry's last remark extremely amusing – even Jack looked up from his chewing to see what all the noise was about. Poor innocent beast – oblivious of the jocularity his playful act had inadvertently caused in what was supposed to be the higher species, after all.

'I'm ready when you are,' I felt an urge to point out. 'I don't suppose it matters too much if my book isn't in the shots, just so long as you mention it in your articles.'

Larry, as the oldest, appeared to be some sort of spokesman for the rest. 'I don't know about that,' he muttered, scratching his chin with a box of film. 'We've got to go by our brief, you see. Otherwise everyone would be wanting free publicity.'

When I'd been led by a poorly drafted itinerary to expect an interview by the celebrated *Gleam* magazine I had never envisaged the alternative could be as extreme as this. 'I think you should know that I'm here at the invitation of Mr and Mrs Small, who saw me being presented with an award on *London Live* for my book. I'm the Face of London winner.'

'Oh, I see,' Larry said, with a sigh. 'You're from London,' as if that suddenly explained everything.

'The Smalls thought it would be good promotion for their

hotel if you were to photograph me staying here after my win. The library seemed to us all to be the obvious place to start.'

As I spoke, I let my gaze wander along the bookshelves crammed with old and new classics. That was all I'd ever wanted for my book, a little gap on the shelf between Racine and Rossetti in the evolution of the written word. I shouldn't have had to explain my presence to these men of the press: I had a right to be here.

'Sit yourself down over there, Harriet, at the desk,' a younger man in a knitted sweater advised, pointing with his camera lens to a mahogany carver chair that stood in front of an antique kneehole desk, 'then turn round to face us.'

At last, I thought, the photo-shoot was to begin. I walked elegantly towards the desk, careful to avoid Jack, who was now asleep in the centre of the room, exhausted by the excitement of the event. I lowered myself gracefully on to the black leather seat and turned casually to face the flashing of six long-lens cameras.

'That's it, love!' Larry called. 'Give us a smile!'

I tried unsuccessfully to follow his instructions. I'd never been able to smile on demand. Somehow it seemed contrary to the very concept of smiling, which should, in my opinion, be an involuntary natural response to an uplifting or enjoyable moment.

And yet I felt confident that as the photo-shoot progressed the act would come more easily to me, like learning to swim by mastering the waves. After all, this was only the first of the four outfits my mother had ironed and left on the bed upstairs for my changes. Even fashion models needed time, no doubt, to warm up.

'Smashing, Harriet,' I heard Larry call, from somewhere behind the flashing lights. 'Thanks, love.'

Encouraged by Larry's gratitude, I felt prompted to make a suggestion: 'Perhaps I could read a book? It doesn't have to be mine.'

'You read a book if you want to,' Larry replied. 'We've finished with you now.'

I turned to collect my Panama hat, which a member of the press had placed on a bust of a Roman emperor by the window.

'Don't you think it suits him?' one of them laughed, as if status counted for nothing.

As I removed my hat from the finely chiselled face to reveal his thoughtful intelligent eyes, I just hoped it wasn't Marcus Aurelius.

'I expect you'll be heading back to London now?' Larry asked, as he zipped up his anorak.

'Our helicopter's coming to pick us up on Monday morning,' I couldn't help saying – I'd paid five thousand pounds for it, after all. It would have been a pity to miss the opportunity.

'Did you hear that, Ted? She's only getting a helicopter back to London!'

'The book must be doing all right,' Ted suggested.

It was the opening I'd been waiting for.

'The first edition has already sold out,' I said with a contented smile. 'A second run is being printed as we speak to satisfy demand. I expect you'll see it before long down here in your local book-shops, once word gets round – my face and the book title covered the entire tail boom of the helicopter.' Then I tapped my right temple with my forefinger, hoping that was the correct side for the brain, and said: 'You have to be smart in the publishing industry. It's no use just sitting back and hoping your book will sell.'

I hadn't intended to say quite so much. The words must have been building up inside me, like bubbles in a champagne bottle. By the time I'd finished, the local press were ready to go, jackets on and silver camera boxes in their hands.

'Good for you, love,' said Larry, as he walked past me, patting the top of my head with his free hand. 'We're lucky you could spare us the time.'

Harriet Rose, I said to myself, you haven't lost your touch.

Gleam's brochure suggested it was an invigorating experience to alternate between the hot and cold tubs, but Nana said it was asking for a dose of flu. After a morning of Jack and long lenses, however, I was prepared to risk it even if Nana wasn't.

'You two stay in the pool, then, if you don't like the sound of it,' I said, as I walked towards the hot tub. 'I'm in need of invigoration.'

There was no one in the club but us, or we'd never have persuaded Nana to go in. As it was, I had to stand by the door to the changing room on guard while my mother helped her change into her swimsuit.

I had never seen Nana in a swimsuit before – I hadn't even known she had one until she showed me the black and silver striped all-in-one with a white pleated skirt and a matching white flower on the strap. 'I've only worn it once,' she said, stroking it affectionately, as if it were a long-lost friend. 'Grandpa bought it for me to wear to the beach with Auntie Evelyn and Uncle Johnny in 1985. I remember because it was our silver wedding anniversary.'

She didn't often reminisce about my grandfather. I think it was too painful for her to think about him, so the occasion must have been very important to her indeed.

'I wore a big floppy straw hat with it. Auntie Evelyn said I looked like Lauren Bacall, but Grandpa said I was much better-looking than her. I didn't know I'd kept it,' she went on. 'I hope it still fits.'

It did, perfectly. I told her so when she and my mother walked with me towards the pool.

'Don't we look lovely?' Nana said, to my mother and me, and we had to agree.

By the time she reached the pool's edge, Nana had had second thoughts. It was too much to expect a woman in her seventies to swim for the first time, she said. She might have a heart-attack in the water, with no ambulance to call and wait an hour for. Her ankles could swell and her joints stick, and she wasn't going to rely on a pair of swimming-pool attendants to carry her in the breaststroke position to dry land. 'I'm not going in there,' she added, 'you don't know who's been in before you. I'm not taking any chances at my age.'

'It's only a swimming-pool, Nana,' I implored. But it was no use. Nana's mind was made up.

'I'll sit here on this comfortable-looking lounger,' she said, 'and read a newspaper.'

'But we've come here to swim,' my mother insisted. 'Harriet wanted it to be special, all of us swimming together for the first time. Come on, show us your backstroke!'

'I've told you, I'm not going in and that's final,' Nana snapped. I don't think she'd slept well in the Wilson.

'Well, if you're not going in, sod it! Neither am I!' my mother exclaimed, with a furtive wink at me.

Then she sat down on a lounger facing Nana and crossed her arms. The two of them stared at each other like a pair of boxers in their corners, silently scrutinising each other's faces for a sign of weakening. Two pairs of striking blue eyes and a battle of fiery wills which I had seen in combat many times before. It was hard to tell who would win. It was a close-run contest. I slightly favoured my mother, only because I knew how patient she could be when she was determined about something. I recognised the signs – the tightening of the lips, the fixing of the gaze, the flaring of the nostrils. I had seen her lock herself away in her studio for hours on end when she had a portrait to finish that she wasn't happy with. Even if it was just a minor detail, she wouldn't stop until it was right. When she had a commission she would work on a canvas for weeks, then wipe it out and start again if necessary.

Surprisingly, then, she was the first to move. She uncrossed her arms, reached for a cocktail stick that had been abandoned in an empty glass and brandished it in the air, like a sword, as she announced to Nana: 'This calls for a duel!' It worked. Nana saw the funny side, and the two of them got into the pool, roaring with laughter.

Although it was described as a hot tub, in fact the water was lukewarm. I lay back, resting my head against its wooden surround, and reflecting on the empirical importance of contrast: without the hot tub, the cold one wouldn't feel so cold, and once I'd been in the cold tub, this very same hot tub would suddenly seem hotter, whilst all the while remaining just the same. Which in turn made me ask myself the following question: if I hadn't expected to be photographed for *Gleam* magazine, would the photo-shoot with the local press have seemed so drab? And similarly, once I had experienced the drabness of the local press photo-shoot, would my interview the next day with the obviously more sophisticated *Heart of the Country* magazine seem all the more fulfilling?

Once I had begun on this journey of philosophical enquiry the road seemed endless: had I not been blessed, for instance, with a questioning, intellectual mind, would the superficial meanderings of Charlotte Goldman have seemed quite so trite? Were it not for the dull predictability of the likes of Jason Smart, would the cultivated philosophical sophistication of Jean Claude seem just as acute? If it hadn't been for the tragic loss of my father, would the happiness of my mother and Nana mean so much to me?

As I climbed out of the hot tub and into the cold one, I promised myself one thing: if ever I found myself brought down by the cold-tubness of life again, I would remember how warm the hot tub had subsequently felt.

'So, do you feel invigorated?' my mother asked, as I joined her and Nana beside the pool where they were sipping non-alcoholic cocktails, compliments of the Smalls.

'Ready for anything,' I laughed, reaching for my glass. It was a throw-away remark, I hadn't meant it literally. But fate is like that, as I'd said in Meditation 65: 'It listens to your every word then sits back and watches as it puts those words to the test.'

My test was 'Sonia Worthington', as she introduced herself to us on her arrival at the pool. We hadn't asked for an introduction, but Sonia had insisted upon it – it was her way of finding out who we were.

'We saw you arriving in your helicopter yesterday . . .' she said, studying our faces to pick out the celebrity. By 'We' she seemed to be referring to herself and a girl of about ten or eleven who was now hiding behind her mother's back. It was an easy manoeuvre: the back was clad in several layers of pleated black overskirts and housed in a red rubber ring. '. . . and recognised your face. But we couldn't place it.'

'You probably saw my last film,' my mother replied, with a laugh.

Unfortunately Sonia didn't share my mother's sense of humour. 'I thought you looked like an actress,' she replied excitedly. 'You've got that air of aloofness about you.' Sonia lowered herself and her rubber ring on to the edge of the pool where she sat dangling her feet in the water.

'Actually, it's my daughter who's the celebrity,' my mother confessed.

'How do you do?' I said politely, offering Sonia my hand. My right hand, the one with which I had written my successful book. 'I'm Harriet Rose.'

Sonia turned for assistance to her daughter, who was standing beside her now. 'Harriet Rose, Sophie!' she shouted, her voice echoing across the pool as if Sophie was in the next village. 'Who's she?'

Sophie shrugged her little white shoulders and jumped in.

'That's a lot of splashing for a little thing like you,' Nana called, as she wiped water off her irritated face. But Sophie had disappeared beneath the surface and was heading like a tadpole for the deep end.

'I don't suppose I could have your autograph, Harriet?'

It was the first time I had heard those words and I would never forget them. The trouble was that although there happened to be a biro on our side table Sonia had nothing for me to write on.

'I'll tell you what,' Sonia said finally, 'why don't you autograph my rubber ring?'

Not wanting to miss the chance to sign my very first autograph, I agreed to her somewhat bizarre request and wrote a flamboyant 'Harriet Rose' round the red rubber ring. It was quite a large ring, so I even managed to fit in 'With all good wishes'. Naturally Sonia was delighted, and, secretly, so was I.

'It's coming back to me now,' she said, staring into my eyes with a hint of recognition. 'You're the winner of that competition on the television, aren't you?'

My first autograph and my first fan. It was a moment to savour.

'That's me!' I said, throwing my hair over my shoulders so she could see more of my face.

'I'd have voted for you if I hadn't been baking a cake.'

'Well, she won anyway,' my mother said comfortingly.

'And she deserved to, whatever those nasty judges said about her.'

I looked at my mother and Nana, who were as confused as I was.

'I'll buy your record, Harriet,' Sonia said. 'You've got a lovely voice.'

'You've made a mistake,' my mother was swift to explain. 'Harriet's not a singer. She's the author of *The Infinite Wisdom of Harriet Rose*. She's the Face of London.'

I hadn't thought of myself as 'the' author before. 'An' author had been wonderful enough for me. My mother's words put the whole Sonia experience into perspective. I didn't care who Sonia thought I was, even if it was a singer in a talent contest. What mattered was that *I* knew who I was, and so did my mother and Nana. I was 'the' author, *the* Harriet Rose.

'Oh, what a shame!' Sonia sighed, and disappeared up the swimming-pool in search of Sophie, having abandoned her red rubber ring beside us.

That night I had a dream. I didn't normally remember my dreams, but this one was very vivid. I dreamed I was drowning in a giant tub of ice-cold water. 'Help!' I cried. 'It is I, Harriet Rose. *The* Harriet Rose, acclaimed author and philosopher and winner of the Face of London competition.'

But no one heard me. I could feel the cold water washing over my head, releasing it from the beige Panama hat that was keeping my hair up.

'Over here! I'm drowning!' I called in despair, but I didn't need to. Jack had already spotted me and was in the tub, swimming frantically towards me with a big red rubber ring between his teeth. In seconds he had thrown the ring over my head and was dragging me towards the wooden perimeter of the tub.

'You've got very strong legs, Jack,' I remarked, as he pulled me to safety. 'You must get a lot of exercise.'

'When I'm not busy reading,' Jack replied. 'I like a good book.'

Just then a helicopter swooped down and a figure leaned from the open door, holding out a hand to pull me to safety. It was a woman in a black and silver swimsuit and a turban hat. 'Here! Have this!' she said once I was safely inside the helicopter, handing me an apple turnover. 'You'll feel better in no time.'

Then we were flying over the familiar streets of London. Higher and higher we went, until we were approaching a red-brick building. A crowd was pointing up at me, waving and mouthing words I couldn't make out. We hovered in the air, then started our descent – it was a female pilot with auburn hair and the aloofness of an actress about her. 'I learned how to fly in my last film,' she shouted, as she landed our helicopter. 'You probably saw it – *Mamma Mia Has Landed*.'

But neither of us had heard of that one, so I said, 'Was it a musical? If you tell me the words, I'd love to sing it to you. I have a wonderful singing voice.'

'Read us one of your Meditations,' implored a woman with who-do-you-think-you-are eyes as we reached the ground.

'I can't, they've sold out,' I replied, as I bounded out of the helicopter, like a golden retriever.

'You can have my copy,' said a good-looking Frenchman with two faces. 'I was given it last night by the Pink Panther.'

I woke with a start, half expecting to find the Pink Panther by my bedside. It was Sunday morning, our last day in our peaceful country retreat. Soon I would be back in the cut-and-thrust buzz that was London, fighting for success against the odds, battling for an opportunity to be heard against a background of noisy traffic and sharply clipped vowels.

'Do we have to go back to London?' I asked my mother, as she arranged my hair in diamanté combs, ready for my magazine interview. 'Can't we stay here with these wonderfully low-key country people?'

'You love London, really.' She tugged at a strand of my hair. 'You'd miss the excitement of high-profile parties at the London Portrait Academy and dates in French bistros with the likes of Jean Claude.'

'Just the one date,' I corrected her. It was important that she kept it in perspective. 'And we weren't even on our own.'

'Well, as good as,' my mother laughed. 'I was talking about the substance.'

She had a point, but did Jean Claude see Charlotte Goldman in that way?

'I sent him a postcard of the hotel on Friday when we arrived,' I confessed. 'It seemed only fair when he'd called at our house and I hadn't opened the door to him.'

'I can't remember why you didn't answer it,' she said distractedly. My mother was unpredictable like that – I'd expected at least a re-action to the postcard-sending.

'I had on my red nightshirt and matching bedsocks at the time,' I reminded her. 'I thought it was just another of the *paparazzi* wanting to photograph me after my win.'

'I don't know why you still wear that nightshirt and bedsocks.' She frowned.

'They were a Christmas present from my father,' I replied.

I saw her expression changing from bemusement to sorrow and wished I hadn't said that. But I had. There was nothing I could do about it except change the subject.

'Why do you think he called?' I asked.

'Who?' she asked, and I knew she was lost in her own thoughts.

'Jean Claude, of course,' I snapped, partly because she'd made me talk about the Christmas present.

'He was probably just passing,' she suggested half-heartedly, as if Jean Claude was of no concern to her, 'on his way home.'

'But we live in a cul-de-sac,' I had to point out. 'How could he be "just passing" a house in a cul-de-sac?'

'Well, perhaps he'd been out for the evening somewhere nearby,' she suggested, without a thought for how that would make me feel.

'Who with?' I asked, reddening. 'He's new to London. He only knows me and . . . He only knows me.'

'I was forgetting,' my mother said apologetically.

Fortunately for her, we were interrupted by something being pushed under my bedroom door. My mother was first to get to it.

'It's a copy of the *Morning Post*,' she said, 'one of the local papers.'

We carried the newspaper to my king-size four-poster and spread it out on the cream satin bedspread. My mother turned the pages as I scanned the headings.

The article about me was half-way through, sandwiched between 'LOCAL CHEF CHOSEN TO COOK ON LUXURY LINER' and 'BEAUTY QUEEN RUNNER-UP CRIES: IT SHOULD HAVE BEEN ME'. Considering their lack of effort, I had to admit the picture wasn't bad. In fact, had it not been for Jack's tail across my feet it would have been very good indeed. It had a natural, country quality to it, as my mother pointed out. The gentle force of innocence captured in a frame. And Larry had obviously put a great deal of effort into the headline too: 'LONDON AUTHOR PAYS FLYING VISIT TO TEGFOLD HALL WITH SMALLS'.

Fourteen-year-old author Harriet Ose flew into Tegfold Hall Hotel this weekend in a private helicopter at the invitation of

207

well-known proprietors Christopher and Fiona Small. The pretty, blonde schoolgirl (pictured above) explained: 'The Smalls saw me being presented with my cheque on *London Live* as the winner of the Face of London competition and they invited me and my family to stay with them for the weekend.' Harriet won the prize for her book, *The Infinite Wisdom of Harriet Ose*.

'He did well to piece all that together and only drop an R,' I remarked, then read on:

The book is a collection of Dedications that Harriet put together herself. She has already sold over a thousand copies of the first edition and a second print run is imminent.

'"A collection of Dedications"!' my mother exclaimed. 'It sounds like a Tribute-to-Elvis album.'

Fiona Small herself, the well-known proprietor, knocked on my bedroom door just as we'd finished checking Larry's article for any more mistakes. I said goodbye to my mother, and Fiona led me to her drawing room where my interview for *Heart of the Country* was to take place.

'I popped a copy of the *Morning Post* under your door – did you see it?' she enquired, as we walked side by side along the corridors, clicking in unison – I had worn my blue and red sequined shoes, with small but well-formed heels, this time.

'Thank you, I did,' I replied.

'I thought it was a beautiful picture of you,' she said, with which, naturally, I agreed, 'although it's a pity it didn't show more of the hotel than the back of a chair, much as I like that chair.' And she laughed a nervous laugh as if there was more she wanted to say. 'We were wondering if you could talk *Heart of the Country* into a few more shots – perhaps outside showing the front of the hotel with its name on the pillars.'

'I'll do my best,' I said. 'Leave it to me.' I could see that during the course of a couple of days poor Fiona had grown to rely on me.

'Good luck,' she whispered, then was gone.

Isabel Longhurst was seated in a pale blue high-backed armchair with her feet on a matching footstool when I walked into the room.

'Don't get up!' I called across the room to her as I approached, but she wasn't attempting to.

'You must be Harriet Rose,' she said, addressing my shoes.

I felt like saying, 'The left one's Harriet and the right one's Rose,' but I realised I wasn't a natural comic, as my mother had reminded me before my interview. I was better at being serious and philosophical.

'And you must be *Heart of the Country*,' I said.

'Isabel Longhurst,' she said, as if she was announcing herself at a débutantes' ball.

I arranged my white cotton dress carefully round me on the sofa as I sat down – it was important that it didn't crease before the photographs had been taken.

'Charming,' Isabel said. Just that. Nothing else. She was busy writing on her wide-lined notepad. As she wasn't the type of woman to be disturbed, I said nothing either.

Eventually, she was ready to begin. 'So, Harriet, tell me something about the book you've written – *The Infinite Wisdom of Harriet Rose*.' Isabel left a slight pause between each word as she read my title from her notes. 'Describe it to me in your own words. Take your time.' Then she smiled, looked down at my shoes again and rubbed her black and white pen between finger and thumb.

I was silent for a while. I didn't want to rush my answer. My mother had expressly warned me not to do that. Finally I said: 'Why?'

Isabel looked up from my feet to my eyes and said: 'Well, because my readers will need to know whether it's worth reading.'

It was the first time I'd seen her eyes. They were small and brown, and darted from side to side when she was thinking hard about something.

'Why?' I said again.

'Because there are lots of books to choose from and *Heart of the Country* likes to review those that stand out from the rest.'

As Isabel crossed her right leg over the left, the folds of her long floral skirt swayed round her ankles, revealing black leather ankle boots with stiletto heels.

'Why?' I said again.

'To give readers a book to enjoy and tell their friends about.'

I leaned forward on the edge of the sofa and tried again: 'Why?'

'Because it's important that people choose a book that will put a smile on their face or a tear in their eye or a thought in their mind.'

'Why?'

Isabel didn't even pause this time before she answered: 'It shows we're alive.'

'Why?' I could barely keep up with the pace myself.

'Because it reminds us of experiences we've had ourselves, of people we've loved, of people we've loathed, of our achievements, our failures, our goals, our fears.'

'Why?'

'Because it's a well-written book – and that's the type of book that *Heart of the Country* wants to identify with.'

Isabel uncrossed her legs and pushed the footstool away from her with the sole of her boot. 'So, in a word, Harriet, how would you describe *The Infinite Wisdom of Harriet Rose?*'

'Why,' I said again – my mother had told me not to be intimidated. 'That's what I've been trying to tell you for the last five minutes. My collection of Meditations is about wanting to know "why".'

'Why what?' Isabel enquired, and I admired her journalistic tenacity.

'Why writers see things differently from non-writers, why I couldn't contemplate a life that didn't include my mother or Nana, why winning can sometimes be losing and perfection is often best flawed, why my father had to die, why I don't think about things the way the rest of my contemporaries do, why I can't be as outgoing or sophisticated as my mother, or as persuasive and determined as my grandmother, or as clever as I sometimes appear, why girls like Celia Moore with large breasts don't feel as threatened by other people's success as flatter-chested airheads like Charlotte Goldman.'

I couldn't think of any more whys just then, so I stopped.

'That's a lot of whys,' Isabel Longhurst said, with a smile. She hadn't smiled before. She should have. It softened her face and warmed her eyes.

'There are a lot of pages,' I replied.

'And are there answers in those pages?' she asked, as if she was genuinely interested.

'Only for those who look for them,' I said.

'Then I shall look for them.'

'Then I'm sure you'll find them,' I replied.

We talked for a long while about my mother and Nana and my father after that. I even mentioned a little about Jean Claude. She asked me if I had a copy of my Meditations with me and I explained that Jack had half eaten the last one. Then I showed her Larry's photograph and article in the *Morning Post* and she said she could do a great deal better than that. So she accompanied me outside, took out her digital camera and told me how to look and where to stand. She even agreed to take a photograph of me beside the pillars with 'Tegfold Hall Hotel' visible in the background. Then she said she was sorry to say it was time for her to leave now. And she promised to send me a copy of the magazine. And then she was gone, like a mighty floral sandstorm. *Heart of the Country*, a well-named magazine.

I think it was Nana who pointed out the minor hitch with the book-signing aspect of Fiona's itinerary – we had no books left. The second print run was due to be delivered the following week at the earliest. I had organised it myself as I was paying for it with the rest of my prize money.

'Fiona will understand,' my mother said, over a sandwich by the pool – we hadn't time for anything more: the interview with Isabel Longhurst had overrun by nearly an hour and the book-signing was scheduled for two p.m. which left only half an hour for lunch.

'Perhaps we could take the names of those people who want to buy a copy and send them when they arrive,' Publicity suggested.

'But how will they know what it's like?' I pointed out. 'There's only my half-eaten copy left.'

'You can still see your beautiful face on the back, though,' Sales reminded me. 'That would be enough to sell thousands, if you ask me.'

But I lacked Nana's confidence – it was probably my age.

'I've an idea!' Publicity exclaimed, and at once I felt encouraged. 'You could do a recitation – you don't need the book for that because you know most of your Meditations by heart.'

It was the perfect solution, and only my mother would have thought of it. 'Better still,' she was on a roll, I could sense it, 'why don't we suggest to Fiona that she combines her buffet supper and cocktails by the pool at seven this evening with the recitation? All the hotel guests will be about, and you could do your reading by the pool. It would be like *An Audience with Harriet Rose*. What do you think?'

Before I had a chance to reply, my mother added, 'And as Nana suggested, we'll take the names and addresses of anyone who wants to order a copy.' The art of being a good publicist was to keep everyone happy. That was why my mother had been chosen for the role rather than Nana or me.

Now we had only to inform Fiona of the change.

'Your father was right,' my mother said, when I emerged from the bathroom in my white Grecian dress. 'You look truly beautiful.'

'I can't wait to see her standing by the pool,' Nana added, feeling for her white cotton hankie up the sleeve of her blue silk dress. 'I wish her grandpa was here for this!'

Encouraged by their comments, I followed them down the sweeping mahogany staircase, careful not to trip on the flowing hem of my mother's sleek black velvet evening dress with folds of silk in the train. 'The perfect finale to a perfect weekend,' I said, as we walked gracefully across the black and white marble floor, which complemented us like a matching accessory.

The Infinite Wisdom of Harriet Rose

In an attempt to emulate my mother's creative flair, Fiona had arranged a selection of ornate candles round the pool, which gave off a beautiful aroma of frankincense. Instantly I was transported back to the confessional box in Holy Innocents Church. 'Concentrate your mind on all your talents.' The Father's words echoed in my head like a prophecy. 'Then you will begin to see that he is still with you.'

I was about to make my way towards Fiona, who was chatting to a distinguished-looking man in a cream linen suit, when my mother stopped me. 'Before you start,' she whispered, 'I think you need this.' She picked a big white rose from a bush beside us and placed the stem neatly behind my left ear. 'A beautiful white rose,' she said softly. 'The perfect final touch.'

Fiona had scattered antique tapestry cushions along the edges of the pool and the diving-board. The guests were gathered on either side of the pool, laughing and chatting and sipping champagne served on silver trays by waiters in black tie. In minutes their conversation would abate to be replaced by an expectant hush.

I fingered the rose stem behind my ear to make sure it was firmly in place. Then I threw off my white velvet slip-ons and walked heroically along the diving-board, careful not to trip over the tapestry cushions. I could hear Fiona's voice in the background urging the guests to be silent, announcing that a recitation was about to take place, initiating a triumph of applause. They were ready for me to begin.

'I'm unable to read to you this evening from my book of Meditations, *The Infinite Wisdom of Harriet Rose*, because the last copy was eaten by Jack yesterday at a press conference. And for those of you who don't know, Jack isn't a member of the press but Fiona and Christopher's golden retriever.' I was taken aback when they actually laughed – it had taken so long to happen that I didn't know how

215

to respond. I decided to join in. Only mine sounded more pronounced than theirs and it went on longer.

'I'm going to start by answering what you're bound to be asking – what are my beliefs and who is Harriet Rose? Not just the author of *The Infinite Wisdom of Harriet Rose*, of which you will no doubt have heard, but the person behind the Meditations. I shall finish by reading just one Meditation, which isn't in my collection as it's new. So new in fact that I only wrote it this afternoon.'

I saw my mother and Nana exchange a glance. The moon was lighting their faces like spotlight. I'd surprised them, just as I'd planned.

'Heraclitus famously said that we cannot step into the same river twice. Everything, that is, is in constant change. Nothing remains the same. By the time I have reached the end of my talk to you, I shall be a different person from the one who began it. And you, my audience, will have altered too. Each of us is aware of our own evolution, yet each of us searches for those aspects of ourselves that never change, that make us who we are, above and beyond our state of flux.

'Over there, beside the gentleman with the silver tray, my mother is listening to every word I say. Next to her, my grandmother is doing the same. Daughter, mother, grandmother, three links in the continuum without a break. My mother, a mother to me but a daughter to my grandmother. Two very different perspectives contained within the same unique individual. As our roles change, what is it that remains the same?

'I wrote a book, a collection of my Meditations begun when I was twelve years old. It contains two very different sections – the first, a dedication to those people who have influenced my life for good and bad. The second, a more general set of reflections on the life I observe outside me and within. Section Two would not have been possible without Section One, and Section Two in turn has led to the

Meditation I shall read to you this evening. As it isn't part of my collection, it isn't numbered. Therefore I have called it: "On Metamorphosis".'

In my hands, which were shaking only slightly, I held the piece of hotel writing-paper covered on both sides with my words written clearly in black biro.

'On metamorphosis, you see, is where I am today. Growing physically, mentally, spiritually all the time. Ever changing, yet ever staying the same. Otherwise you could not look at me and say: "There goes Harriet Rose, author of *The Infinite Wisdom of Harriet Rose* — I know her." I am not just a set of distinct Harriet Roses all gathered into one, like a bouquet, I am a unique, identifiable individual. How do I know? Because I understand what matters to me, has done, will do, always. Not just what, but who. Two of them here tonight, others who have gone. Gone but still here. All part of the continuum that is Harriet Rose.

'Everything in constant change — yesterday, today, tomorrow, birth, life, death — yet remaining the same. Where will you be tomorrow, ladies and gentlemen? You cannot step into the same river twice. Who will you be tomorrow, ladies and gentlemen? Only you can say.'

I had reached the end of the first part of my talk, so I paused before the second part of the continuum.

'I was once asked in class by my teacher to stand up and address my fellow classmates about myself. I described those aspects that mattered to me, the things that made me who I am. Then I sat down and began to realise that my answer was not what my teacher had had in mind. I listened as the others described their favourite pastimes, their parents' occupations, the ages of their siblings, where they lived. But did that really tell me who they were?

Diana Janney

'My new Meditation, "On Metamorphosis" , is the second version of my answer to that very same question, but visited this time from a new perspective. I hope, when you have heard it, you feel I have answered the question "Who am I?" to your satisfaction.'

I took a deep breath, then began: '"On Metamorphosis".

'I wrote a collection of Meditations because reflection is
    important to me.
It was published by my mother and Nana because I am
    important to them.
The book became successful but that was not what mattered
    to me.
The three of us strove together and that was what mattered
    to me.
I talk about my writing now, I never did before.
I don't mind speaking in public now, I always did before.
I want to make a difference, I want people to think.
Because thinking makes us people, and people make us think.
I once believed in always, before my father died.
I still believe in always, since my father died.
I began my *Infinite Wisdom* with a dedication to my father.

I end this Meditation with a dedication to my mother . . .
Is there someone who is missing when I pick up my pen,
    when I talk of what
I've lost, when I dwell so much on 'then'?
Is there someone I've forgotten when I think of what to say,
    when I write my
Meditations, when I talk of yesterday?
It's not that I've forgotten, for that could never be.

It's just so hard to tell you how much you mean to me.
So I wrote this Meditation especially for you –
My mother, whom I value for everything you do.'

I folded the piece of paper in half, held it by the crease and dropped it gently on to the water, which was as still as the silence around me. I watched it as it floated on the surface like a Panama hat.

'Thank you all for listening to "On Metamorphosis",' I said quietly – I didn't want to interrupt the silence.

But someone did. And she did so with applause and cheers enough for a whole audience. It was my mother. Nana couldn't join in – she was too busy with her hankie. Then the rest of the audience applauded too – I even heard a man at the back calling for an encore. But I hadn't prepared an encore, so I waited quietly until Fiona took over.

'I'm sure everyone was entranced by Harriet's recitation,' she said, smiling graciously at me. 'I know I was.'

'Hear hear!' Christopher shouted.

'If you would like to order copies of Harriet's *Infinite Wisdom* please do give your names and addresses to Harriet's publishing team over there – Mia and Olivia. They'll post them to you once the second print run has arrived. I hope you have all enjoyed your evening and your stay at Tegfold Hall Hotel and will come back again soon.' Then Fiona looked towards me, where I had joined my mother and Nana, and said: 'And, of course, that includes the three of you.'

30

I had left an hour to pack, which may sound a long time but there were so many drawers and wardrobes and shelves to check, not to mention all the hotel soaps and bath gels and shampoos I had to fit into my travel bag. I knew my mother and Nana were waiting for me downstairs because they had knocked on my door on the way past to tell me.

I was almost ready to leave. I just wanted to savour one final solitary moment in my Churchill suite, the place where I had created my new Meditation. In retrospect, I wished I'd kept it instead of allowing it to sink to the depths of a hotel swimming-pool. But such is the essence of a creative nature. As is an artistic dislike of being disturbed. Which was why when the telephone rang I let it do so several times before I answered it. I knew I'd overrun departure time. But surely when I was paying nearly five thousand pounds for a return helicopter trip, I had the right to keep the pilot waiting just a little while.

'I'll be down in a minute,' I snapped. I didn't care which of them it was. 'I'm collecting my thoughts.'

'That could take a long time when there are so many of them,' said a deep, virile voice at the other end of the telephone.

'Jean Claude?' I whispered, partly because I was having difficulty getting my words out, and partly to mask my snappiness when I'd answered the phone.

'Hello, Harriet. I rang to see if you could help me.'

If he asked for Charlotte Goldman's telephone number I was hanging up.

'With what?' I picked up a pencil to make me feel more confident.

'I'm looking for *la vie en Rose*,' he said, in a way that made me think he'd been practising it. 'Where do I find it?'

It wasn't fair. He'd had time to plan what he would say – probably nearly two hours if the post was reliable at his college in South Kensington. 'So you got my card,' I said – it was more of a thought, really.

'It's very difficult to get to speak to you, no doubt like all celebrities. I tried telephoning your house several times, but your grandmother seemed a little – how you say? – displeased.'

I wished she'd kept her candyfloss comments to herself. After all, she had no proof of what he'd been up to, just because he'd left at the same time as Charlotte Goldman and read my Meditations to her.

'Then I rang at your door after you'd won your special award but no one answered.'

'I have to be careful,' I explained. 'There are so many press and fans around.' Well, what were Sonia and Sophie Worthington if they weren't fans?

'And I sent you some flowers, but I don't know if you got them.'

So I'd been right. Jean Claude was Cratylus. There was a God after all.

'Were yours the red roses?' I asked casually. I just wanted confirmation. Precision is important to philosophers.

'Perhaps the "Cratylus" confused you?'

'I couldn't think who would prefer my words to my silence.' I laughed, remembering, perhaps a little too accurately, the words on his card. 'Thank you for the flowers,' I said.

'Thank you for the postcard,' he replied. Then both of us were silent and I was afraid he might have hung up.

'Actually, my helicopter's waiting for me,' I was inspired from somewhere to say. 'I'm about to leave.'

It was the prompt he needed. 'I would like to see you again,' he said, in a tone that Jason Smart couldn't have mastered in a million years.

'When did you have in mind?' I asked, as if I had a diary to consult.

'How about two minutes?' he replied. 'I'm downstairs in Reception.'

I weighed up the possibility that he was joking but there was something about the way he'd said it that made me think he was telling the truth. But I had to be sure before I went to the trouble of unpacking and changing into my sequined jeans and Chanel belt. 'But why would you be at Tegfold Hall?' I asked. 'Shouldn't you be at college?'

'I have a study period this morning,' he explained, 'and I thought maybe we could study together.'

'You mean you came nearly seventy miles just to see *me*?' As soon as I'd said it, I knew I shouldn't have sounded so surprised.

'I'm impulsive,' he said, 'and I checked with the hotel the time of your departure before I caught my train.'

I wished he'd stopped at 'impulsive' – he was beginning to sound a touch too keen. Or perhaps not. It was too early to say.

'Tell me how else I was going to see you again.'

He had a point. I had been somewhat elusive. But wasn't that how a woman was supposed to be? I was about to give him a few suggestions – perhaps he could have serenaded me outside school, thrown pebbles at my bedroom window late at night – when another voice did it for me: 'For goodness' sake, put the boy out of his misery and let him see you,' Nana shouted down the telephone, 'or we'll be standing here all day.'

I decided I didn't have time to change out of my older, more comfortable jeans and baggy T-shirt – I couldn't take a chance on what Nana might say to Jean Claude downstairs.

As I descended the Tegfold Hall staircase for the last time, with the grace of Scarlett O'Hara, I paused as I reached the half-landing beside a portrait described as *Sir Peregrine Small*, who looked uncannily like William Shakespeare. When Jean Claude spotted me, he bounded up the stairs two at a time to greet me French-style, with kisses on both cheeks, and help me with my travelling bag. A Jason Smart would have suggested we sat on it and slide down.

'Sir Peregrine Small looks uncannily like William Shakespeare,' said Jean Claude, as he reached me.

'I thought the same,' I replied. He went down the stairs in front of me, as a man should do in case a lady falls, which gave me an opportunity to examine his outfit. A good dress sense was too important for me not to. And I had to admit to being impressed by Jean Claude's – a blue cashmere sweater thrown loosely round his shoulders, the sleeves tied at the front. And he moved like a sportsman who'd just won a match.

'Nana and I will be waiting for you in the helicopter,' my mother had the good sense to say, linking Nana's arm and pulling her away before she had time to ask him if he'd read any good books to anyone lately.

'It's a beautiful hotel,' Jean Claude remarked, observing the grandeur of the hall. 'I've never been in the English countryside before.'

'It's not all like this,' I explained – I didn't want him to be disappointed. 'I was invited here as a guest of the owners, the Smalls.'

Just then, as if proving that timing was everything, Fiona and Christopher Small appeared. 'I'm glad we caught you before you left,' Fiona said, placing a friendly arm round my shoulders. 'I just wanted to say how much we've enjoyed your stay with us, especially your Meditation last night – everyone was talking about it.'

'I'm glad you liked it – I'll send you a copy of the book when the new print run arrives,' I said. 'May I introduce you to a friend of mine – Jean Claude . . . ?' I remembered, as I had when I sent the card to his college, that I didn't know his surname.

'Jean Claude du Bois,' he said, holding out his hand as I thanked the Smalls for their hospitality.

'Du Bois,' I said, as we crunched across the gravel driveway. 'That must be a common name in France – it's the name of my French teacher.'

'That's right,' Jean Claude replied. 'She's my mother.'

I stopped in my tracks. Madame du Bois, for goodness' sake! Our Madame du Bois, with the enigmatic smile and twinsets.

'My mother says you are a very good student,' he went on – perhaps it wasn't as dire as I'd thought.

'I used to be,' I said quietly, 'before Charlotte Goldman arrived – you remember her?'

'Ah, yes, Charlotte,' he said, with a smile, 'but she's half French, so she will of course be good at the language.'

'Even if she is useless at everything else,' I added – he might as well have the full picture. We were approaching the helicopter. The pilot was standing beside the door, waiting for me. When he saw us, he waved and smiled.

'Oh, there's Anthony!' I said, with perhaps a touch too much feigned enthusiasm. 'I'm glad it's him again – he's wonderful, the perfect pilot.'

The perfect pilot stamped out the butt of his hand-rolled cigarette with a black rubber boot and opened the helicopter door for my pending arrival. Unless I slowed my pace across the lawn, that left me approximately thirty seconds to think of an engaging exit line.

'I seem to have caught my heel in the grass,' I said, coming to a sudden standstill.

'How have you managed that in trainers?' Jean Claude asked, stooping to examine my foot.

'It must be sticky grass,' I muttered – I couldn't go without finding out how much Madame du Bois had said. 'I expect your mother told you about my mistake in class?' I undid the lace of my left trainer casually, then did it up again.

'I don't think so. What mistake was that?'

'When I told her all about my accident at the swimming-pool on the evening you and I met instead of explaining Descartes' mind-body problem.'

'Oh, *that* mistake,' he said. 'She did mention something about it.'

The bitch! I knew it!

'It was a joke, really,' I added, standing up again. A joke! Confessing an entire evening's thoughts and adventures with a good-looking Frenchman in front of the whole class to his mother! Some joke!

For a moment he said nothing as we stood on the beautifully manicured, if curiously sticky, lawn. I was fearing the worst when he said, 'I can help you with the mind-body problem if you like.'

Now, as everyone knows, except perhaps Charlotte Goldman, Descartes' mind-body problem explores the arguments for proving that the mind, the soul, is distinct from the body. It formed quite a challenging philosophical dilemma. But at that moment, my dilemma was of a very different nature although, I have to admit, just as challenging. Was Jean Claude volunteering to help me grapple with a philosophical theory or did he have some more practical grappling in mind? It was an interesting duality, but one on which René Descartes had chosen to stay silent.

'Perhaps once you're back in London, we could . . .' He had an interesting way of starting a sentence then leaving me to finish it – it was probably a French thing.

'Yes, we could,' I replied, with a hint of a smile, leaving a suitable pause for him to fill in the more practical arrangements. But he didn't. He said nothing. And we'd reached the helicopter.

'If you like,' I said, 'you can share our helicopter to London and we can discuss Descartes on the way – if you don't mind shouting?'

I don't know why I hadn't thought of it before. It must have been the country air – it slows you down.

Anthony helped me into the helicopter with a large, steadying hand, which I clasped with enforced familiarity as I said: 'Thank you,

Anthony. This is a friend of mine from London – I hope there's room for him?'

Anthony nodded and Jean Claude climbed in after me.

'Hello again, madame,' he said to my mother, who didn't seem in the least surprised to see him. 'We met briefly in the hotel's entrance hall.'

My mother smiled and they shook hands. Then he turned to Nana, who was peering at him over her handbag, which was drawn to her chest like a breastplate. 'Madame!' he called from his side of the heli-copter – I thought I should keep them as far apart as possible. 'I am Jean Claude du Bois, Harriet's friend.'

'Harriet's and who else's?' were Nana's opening words, which were hopefully drowned by the noise of the helicopter starting up. I'd been right: Anthony *was* the perfect pilot. Nana got out the cotton-wool balls she had brought from her hotel bedroom and offered them to my mother and me as if they were boiled sweets.

'Would you like some for your ears?' my mother asked Jean Claude, more as an explanation I felt.

'Jean Claude and I are going to talk,' I explained, 'about Descartes' *Meditations*.'

'What?' exclaimed Nana, in a pitch of which her cotton-wool balls rendered her blissfully unaware. 'Meditations? Has someone been copying your book?'

'Descartes is a French philosopher, Nana,' I explained loudly as we took off.

'Then it doesn't take a genius to work out who told him about your Meditations,' Nana shouted back, casting a suspicious eye over a confused Jean Claude.

I thought it might be best if he and I postponed our philosoph-ical discourse until we were back in London, and Jean Claude happily agreed. I passed him a pair of Nana's cotton-wool balls and the four of us continued our forty-five-minute journey to London in silence.

From my seat by the window, the English countryside sped past me. Or did I speed past it? It was just the sort of philosophical question I liked to get my teeth into. Minute by minute, was I leaving the countryside behind or was it leaving me? And what did a minute mean? A measure by which to assess how long I had been in a timeless country location, or a country location ever changing with time? And what was time? Did it need change in order to exist? Such thoughts whirled in my mind like the helicopter blades overhead, only not as noisily.

In no time, so to speak, we had reached London. The contrast it made with what I had left behind was surprisingly stark. But, as my cold-tub experience had taught me, contrast was an important aspect of our empirical observations. London wasn't intrinsically noisy and over-populated, it was noisier and more populated than the English countryside I had left. And didn't that in turn tell me something about myself, that I wasn't intrinsically shapely, but shapelier than Charlotte Goldman and flat by comparison with Celia Moore? And what of the 'I', the voluptuous, shapely 'I' into which I would undoubtedly grow before long? I had only to look at my mother to be certain of that. Was there something of that 'I' already in 'me' now? And, if so, what did it tell us about the concept of time?

'Are we nearly there?' Nana's booming voice interrupted my thoughts. 'This pilot seems to be taking his time.'

It wasn't the philosophical answer I'd been searching for. Ironically, though, it did have its purpose – Jean Claude awoke with a start just as we were about to fly over my school.

I looked at my watch. It was ten fifteen. Class 3B would be about to start PE. If Alice managed to hurl the ball into the air with the vigour for which she was notorious, they would be staring up at the sky as we flew overhead. They couldn't fail to see my photo beaming down at them, with *The Infinite Wisdom of Harriet Rose* beneath it, like an angelic caption to be ignored at their peril. If they were very observant indeed, and I suspected that they would be, mine would not be the only angelic face their peering eyes would see. And I didn't mean Nana or my mother, angelic though they undoubtedly were.

'Jean Claude,' I said, removing my cotton-wool balls from my ears and gesturing to him to do the same, 'why don't you change seats with me so that you get a better view of London?'

'That's very kind of you,' he said, as I pushed him into position by the window.

'Not at all,' I replied, sitting back with a contented grin.

'Isn't that your school down there?' he asked, pressing his forehead and wavy dark hair nicely against the window pane.

'Do you know? I think you're right,' I said, leaning over to join him. 'That looks like my class waving up at us in their funny little white shorts.'

We were flying so low I could see Jason's acne.

'Those are the boys on the sports field,' I said, as Jason leaped in the air, his lips forming into an excited 'Harriet Rose', 'and those are the girls, stopping their game of netball to run in our direction.'

I counted fourteen of them, staring up into the sky as if they'd spotted a UFO, which, in a way, we were until they saw my name and picture and Jean Claude's face pressed close to mine at the window.

'They seem pleased to see you,' he remarked. 'You must be very popular.'

'As I said in my Meditation sixty-nine,' I replied, '"Popularity is like a dose of flu. The faster it comes on, the sooner it tends to disappear."'

'I'd never thought of it like that before,' Jean Claude reflected, as we left 3B behind to get on with their games, a ruddy array of varying degrees of astonishment.

We landed at the scheduled time, which left me half an hour to return to the school it had taken me seconds in the helicopter to leave. I had planned in advance that part of my prize would be spent on a special car to take me and my family home before my mother drove me to school. I had wanted the surprise to be one for just the three of us, as I explained to Jean Claude.

'*Oui, oui*, I understand,' he replied. 'I have another forty-five minutes until my first lesson of the day so I shall walk.'

I had noticed he had an endearing way of pronouncing the 'u' in 'minutes' as if it was a double 'o'. 'Only forty-five minoots?' I said. 'You must walk very quickly.' Then I remembered the speed at which he had been moving through the swimming-pool when we first met.

'In France, where I live with my father and stepmother, I walk three miles to school and back each day. It gives me time to admire the countryside and, how you say?, collect my thoughts.'

We had so much in common, Jean Claude and I – the love of our own solitary company, philosophical reflection and an appreciation of the simple, unsophisticated pleasures in life.

'Well, goodbye, then,' I said, as I climbed into the back of the vintage Rolls-Royce I'd organised, where Nana and my mother were waiting on the black leather back seat, which matched their designer sunglasses perfectly.

'I shall phone you this evening,' he called after me, 'to arrange when we meet for our Descartes discussion.'

'I think I'll be in, therefore I shall be.' It was a joke that only a fellow philosopher would understand. Jean Claude did. I left him standing on the street corner with a smile on his face, just the way I liked to see him. How different, I thought as I watched him disappear, from the dolphin I'd first seen.

The Kensington streets seemed drab and dreary after the grandeur of Tegfold Hall Hotel. I wanted a concierge to carry our bags to our rooms, I wanted a harpist to welcome us into the drawing room.

'Home, sweet home,' Nana said, as we stepped over a pile of post into the hall. 'I'll put the kettle on and make us a nice cup of tea.'

My mother carried the bags upstairs and I gathered up the post in case there was any for me.

It was the first time since my father's death that we had come back from holiday to an empty house. Once or twice my mother and I had gone away without him so we were used to that, but when we came back, he would meet us at the airport with a flask of hot tea in winter and a bottle of chilled mineral water in summer and drive us home with tears in his eyes because we were back. And they weren't dramatic tears either. They were proper adult tears – and we had only been away for the weekend. Then, when we got home, we ate dinner that he had prepared, and he listened as we amused him with stories of our travels.

But that was then. It was different now. Those days were gone, like him. The house seemed like an empty shell instead of a home. The hall was dark and the sitting room smelt of dead gladioli. I ran to the piano and carried the remainder of Bill's flowers to the dustbin outside the kitchen door.

I went upstairs and checked that the silver-framed photograph of our last holiday together was still under my pillow where I had left it. Then I replaced it on my bedside table before anyone could see that I'd hidden it.

By the time I had unpacked my clothes, my mother had come to tell me that we should be leaving for school. I didn't hear her at first – I was too distracted by memories the silver-framed photograph had recalled. Why hadn't she just called up the stairs as she normally did?

'Wait for me in the car,' I said. 'I'll be down in a minute.'

'Don't take too long,' she whispered gently. 'You wouldn't want to miss French!'

I'd told her on the way home about Maman du Bois. She thought it was a good thing Jean Claude's mother was someone I knew, even if I had inadvertently told her more about myself than I should have. 'She'll admire your honesty, your openness,' she reassured me. 'They're appealing traits of your personality, and pretty unusual, I would imagine. You shouldn't be embarrassed by them.'

Of course, my mother was right as usual, which was why I

decided to wear my non-regulation black cardigan over my uniform that morning, the one with 'I am' written in silver capitals on the back.

'You'd better not let Miss Grout see you in that,' my mother warned, as I climbed into the car. But I was who I was, open and honest and not embarrassed by it, so I left it on.

I had anticipated the class reaction when I walked through the door – my mother and I had even discussed it on the way there. I was ready for them. 'Here she comes, the superstar,' I heard someone call as I walked towards my desk. 'Are you sure you can be bothered with school? Don't you have interviews you should be doing?'

I got out my French exercise book, just as we'd planned, ignoring them completely until they had something sensible to say.

'Parky was in here looking for you earlier,' another shouted. 'He said could you ring him about Saturday.'

I didn't flicker.

'Harriet,' called another, 'you couldn't tell me in your infinite wisdom which lesson comes next?'

'French,' I said, still reading my exercise book.

'Where have you been anyway?'

I'd been waiting for Charlotte's question. 'I've been staying in an enormous villa with a swimming-pool the size of this school with Jean Claude, his father and stepmother – they keep it for summer holidays,' was what I wanted to say. But I couldn't lie, so instead I said, 'I spent the weekend at a country-house hotel as the guest of the owners.' They didn't need to know any more than that, not unless they pushed me.

'So were you, like, staying with that bloke in the helicopter?'

At least Jason had got to the point. I could handle that.

'No,' I replied, watching Charlotte's face as I spoke. 'He came to the hotel this morning looking for me.'

'Did you have another book-signing party to get him there?' she said, through a smirk.

'I'd forgotten until you said that,' I replied, 'that you gatecrashed my last one.'

'How do you know Jean Claude didn't invite me to go to your book launch with him?' she asked, her cheeks reddening.

I hadn't thought of that. He might have invited her after our dinner at the bistro. How was I to know what contact they'd had? He'd said he was impulsive. Perhaps Nana was right about him, after all.

'Who is he, anyway, that nerd in the helicopter?' Jason thought he should ask.

'He's not a nerd, he's a friend of mine. We have a lot in common.'

'What – does he think he's a superstar too?' laughed Miles Brown – I'd expected him to be jealous.

'I'm sure Jean Claude could be a superstar if he wanted,' I replied sternly. 'He's got the looks for it, unlike you, Miles Brown.'

I was aware that Madame du Bois had entered the room as I was reducing Miles to size but it didn't stop me. I'd had enough of these people and their petty resentments.

'Harriet!' Of course Madame du Bois would have something to say about my outburst. Join in if you want to, I thought, as she fingered her pearls. I'm ready for you too.

But she didn't. Instead she smiled compassionately and asked me to begin the lesson by reading some Ionesco. It was clear that I'd underestimated Madame. In her day she had probably been teased herself for her looks and intelligence. There was a certain *bon chic-ness* about her, now I came to think about it. I studied Madame throughout the half-hour class and by the end I was seeing her in a totally new light. Why hadn't I noticed before the understated elegance of her navy and yellow cardigan with gold buttons, the suave sophistication of her dark brown bob, the demure poise as she wrote on the blackboard. There was much to be learned from this quietly stylish woman – she must have recognised something of herself in me.

'*Merci, madame,*' I called impulsively, as she passed my desk to leave the room.

'*Je vous en prie,*' she replied, with a smile of empathy. '*À demain.*'

'*À demain*'. It stayed with me for the rest of the day. So much more poignant than 'See you tomorrow'. '*À demain*' focused the mind and the mouth on the next day's proximity, especially when pronounced quickly in the French way. '*À demain*' sounded almost like, 'Attention!' to be followed by a silent '*Je suis arrivée!*'

I decided there and then, as I walked down the overcrowded corridor, that I would abandon 'See you tomorrow'. From now on, it was '*À demain*' for me.

When Miss Grout handed me a letter as I passed her in the corridor, I assumed it was about my 'I am' cardigan. I left it on, though – I was in no mood to be subservient. Anyway, she should have been pleased that I knew who I was – none of the others seemed to know who *they* were. It showed the kind of confidence she'd feared was lacking in me the last time we'd spoken. I decided not to read her letter until I got home – there was only so much criticism I could take on my own in one day.

As soon as I walked through the door and heard my mother welcoming me, I tore open the envelope. I had never received a letter from Miss Grout before. When I saw her Christian name scrawled across the bottom of the paper, I wondered if I'd been mistaken. Perhaps it wasn't about my cardigan after all. Perhaps it was a thank-you note for the book I'd left for her. She needn't have thanked me, I thought with a smile, as I began to read the letter:

Dear Harriet,

Many congratulations on winning the Face of London competition. I would never have expected it of you of all people. [Poor, unassuming Miss Grout.]

Now that you're such a celebrity [Celebrity? *Moi?* Please!] I wondered if perhaps you would like to give a talk to some of the other pupils and their parents at the end of our next PTA meeting on Thursday. The evenings are often quite dreary and long-winded – I'm sure we could all do with some light relief and a laugh at the end of it, so obviously I thought of you and your little book.

Best regards,

Scarlett Grout.

PS You would only need to speak for about ten minutes, with another five to answer any questions.

I was taken aback. I could hardly believe it – Miss Grout a 'Scarlett'! A million Rhett Butlers would have missed that one. As I read her letter a second time I began to see her in an entirely new light. Underneath that dour, overweight exterior, all frowns and misunderstandings, lurked a feisty, exciting, bold, vivacious Scarlett just waiting to come out. Everything suddenly fell into place – her desire to understand me, her fascination, against her better judgement, with my Meditations, her passion for a share in my limelight.

My God, how this woman needed me – and I wouldn't let her down. As soon as I reached the sitting room I took a sheet of paper from the desk and wrote:

Dear Scarlett (if I may call you that now we're pen pals)
[She'd like that.]
I would like nothing better than to help you out with your dull little evening. You can always rely on Harriet Rose, no matter how jaded and dejected you are feeling – remember that, Scarlett. I am here for you.
HR.

First thing in the morning I would push the letter under her study door.

'I've had a letter from Miss Grout,' I said to my mother, over tea and one of her drop scones, homemade with a hint of lemon.

'Oh? What did she want?' she asked.

I passed her Scarlett's letter.

'Unbelievable!' she exclaimed, and passed it to Nana.

'I know. I couldn't believe it either,' I said.

'What a nerve!' my mother went on. She seemed more surprised by the name than I'd expected.

'It certainly shows a different side to her,' I suggested.

'I'd always suspected it, the old bitch!'

'Really?' I said. 'I expected an Edith or a Gertrude.'

I was about to explain that there was no point in holding grudges against a woman in need just because she had an inappropriate Christian name when Nana said, 'A laugh at the end of the evening? She only needs to look in the mirror for that! What is a PTA evening, anyway?'

'Prats Touting for Attention, I think it stands for,' my mother suggested.

Her experience as my publicist should have extended her knowledge of events a little better than that by now. 'Parent Teacher Association,' I corrected her, as tactfully as I could. 'And I've just written to Scarlett to say I'll do it.'

'I thought you had more sense,' were Nana's last words on the matter, with which my mother wholeheartedly agreed.

So it was that the fate of the PTA evening was sealed for the following Thursday.

My mother seemed unusually anxious about the evening as it drew near and insisted that she and Nana should be seated in the front row.

'It's only a talk,' I pointed out. 'I'm not winning a BAFTA.'

'Think carefully about what you're going to say,' she encouraged me, 'and if you don't like a question, remember, you don't have to answer it. Just raise your eyebrows and look towards the ceiling, as if the question was unworthy of an answer, and say nothing.' She showed me the look she had in mind, and Nana added that if anyone said anything to upset me she would be there to tell them to 'drop dead' and show them her hatpin. They both seemed encouraged by all this, but I have to say it left me feeling a little deflated. Until then I had thought of it as an exciting opportunity to publicise my book and perhaps even help others with advice on the publishing industry. But now, suddenly, it was beginning to feel as if I was on my way to be interviewed by Jeremy Paxman.

'I'm only speaking for ten minutes, with another five for questions,' I reminded them, as much to reassure myself as them.

'Ten minutes can be a long time,' Nana replied comfortingly.

'And is "Scarlett" going to introduce you?' my mother asked.

'I don't know. I expect so,' I said.

My mother and Nana exchanged a furtive glance which I couldn't quite work out.

I was too trusting, that was my problem. I needed to open my eyes a little. There was no point in acquiring vast quantities of knowledge about philosophical theories if I knew nothing of more practical, worldly issues, such as men. I couldn't deny it – I was a novice where affairs of the heart were concerned. Not that I lacked a certain natural allure, an instinct for the rules of attraction. My difficulty was knowing who was worthy of them. There had been times, I admit it now, when the line of Miles Brown's jaw had seemed appealing, especially when he was biting into a Snickers bar. But, as I'd written in Meditation 62, while away from school with measles – which, ironically, I'd caught from Miles himself – 'Absence makes the heart grow wiser.' By the time I'd returned to school and he'd greeted me with 'Hello, Harriet, you're looking well fit again – fancy a snog?' I knew unques-tionably that I'd been very much mistaken.

Somehow, though, Jean Claude had seemed different. And not just his looks or the way he said my name. He was a thinker, he wanted to understand me, he listened to what I had to say. Or so I'd thought. But what did I think now? Did he want an answer to who 'I am' and, moreover, who was he?

I removed the black cardigan I had chosen with such confidence that morning and hung it carefully in my wardrobe, feeling the silver 'I am' with my right forefinger. Not 'I was', not 'I shall be', not 'I might have been', just 'I am' – now, here, today, I am. It said it all, but was Jean Claude really listening? Was he searching for the essence of Harriet Rose?

I changed into my white towelling dressing-gown, with 'Tegfold Hall Hotel' embroidered on the pocket, which Fiona had left for me as a parting gift, along with a pair of matching white towelling slippers several sizes too big.

'Why?' That all-encompassing question, that searching, probing 'why', crept slowly back into my mind where all my thoughts and hopes and fears lay buried. Why would a thinking, sensitive philosopher, as Jean Claude professed to be, listen to the ramblings of an airhead like Charlotte Goldman and possibly even invite her to my launch party? And why would a thinking, sensitive philosopher, as I professed to be, give Jean Claude the time of day after that?

I was still working on an answer when I heard the phone ring. I knew before I heard my mother's voice shout, 'Harriet,' that it was him. He had said he would call this evening, and in that respect he was reliable, if in no other. And I, in my infinite wisdom, had said I'd be in.

It wasn't like descending Tegfold Hall staircase. There was no *Sir Peregrine Small* for me to observe, no Frenchman running to help me with my luggage, no black and white marble floor in the hall. But

Jean Claude was there, at the other end of a telephone line, and Harriet Rose was still waiting to be received. And all that separated the two of them as she picked up the phone was that ever-present, all-encompassing 'why'.

'Hello,' I said, 'this is Harriet Rose,' as if he didn't know.

'*Bonsoir*, Harriet Rose,' he replied. 'I am Jean Claude.'

What do you say when there is so much you could say but, like drumsticks that can't find a drum, the words don't seem to come? (Meditation 51) 'How are you?' It was a start.

'My head is still swimming from the helicopter,' he replied, with a laugh.

'Oh dear,' I said, then waited for him to go on.

'I said I would phone you this evening to arrange when we can meet to discuss Descartes.'

Did he really think I'd forgotten the reason for his call? 'Yes,' I replied, 'you did,' and then I reverted to silence. It wasn't intentional: I didn't know what to say.

'I wondered if perhaps Thursday would suit you, maybe at six o'clock – just before the weekend?'

His precision was to be admired, if nothing else. 'This Thursday?' I said, as if he could mean any other. 'I'm sorry, I can't, I've been asked to give a talk.'

'I should have guessed a celebrity like you would be busy,' he said, and I sensed an air of disappointment in his voice. 'Where is your talk? I would have liked to hear it.'

'After the PTA meeting at my school.' I knew I could have made it sound more exciting, but having to do that would have destroyed what I wanted to achieve.

'I expect you will be there with your family?' He was wondering if Nana would be there.

'My mother and Nana will be coming, and there'll be parents and teachers, of course.'

'You'll make it an interesting evening,' he said, which made me wonder whether he remembered our conversation in the bistro – 'What do you want to be when you leave school?' he'd asked. 'Interesting,' I'd replied, and he'd said, 'You already are.'

'I hope so,' I said, and feared I was softening.

'I know so,' he replied, and I almost invited him to come. 'It's a pity because I'm going to be in France after that – I'm staying with my father and stepmother for the weekend.'

'Oh,' I said, 'you'll enjoy that.'

'Perhaps when I get back we could . . .'

That way of leaving his question incomplete.

'Perhaps,' I said, then waited.

'Well, *au revoir*, Harriet.'

'Goodbye,' I said, and he was gone.

It doesn't take long to get from Monday to Thursday. Three days. Seventy-two hours. Four thousand three hundred and twenty minutes. Two hundred and fifty-nine thousand two hundred seconds. And every second I wasted in wondering who would be at my talk – how it would feel to address my teachers and the parents of my classmates, what questions I would be asked – was a second less for me to prepare what I would say. And that, after all, was why I'd been invited: they all wanted to hear what Harriet Rose had to say.

One certainty was that Scarlett Grout would be there, encouraging me and listening to my every word. If ever within those two hundred and fifty-nine thousand two hundred seconds I felt nervous, all I had to do was picture Scarlett and my nerves were gone. That's what being admired and needed does to you: it takes you to heights you could never reach on your own.

First thing the following morning, after assembly (and I made sure for once that my mother got me there on time), I pushed my hand-written letter under Miss Grout's study door. She would open it, I knew, with that misunderstood smile and scan the words through her thick-rimmed glasses for a sign that I'd be there. Perhaps I should have made the letter shorter – a simple 'Yes' between Scarlett and me would have done.

By Thursday morning, with only nine hours to go, her absence of response was beginning to concern me – could I have pushed my letter under the rug? Was she having difficulty reading my writing? Should I have left a voicemail message instead?

I decided to have a word with her after assembly, mention casually that I was fully prepared, ask her how many copies of my book I should bring with me, tell her not to worry if the press turned up again. But, as I had stressed in Meditation 39, plans had a habit of unplanning themselves when you least expected it – perhaps that was part of the Plan, the greater Plan that none of us can see.

In assembly Miss Grout's voice sounded deeper than usual, and she spat out her words as if they were blocking her throat. Not just the notices about detentions either but happy matters, like Miss Mason's leaving party. I was only half listening when I heard her mention 'Harriet Rose', followed by 'PTA meeting this evening' and 'giving a talk'. By the time Miss Grout had my full attention, there was little left for her to say. 'Strictly speaking, the meeting, as always, is for parents and teachers and I really would like to keep it that way. But in the unusual circumstances of Harriet's little talk afterwards, I am prepared to allow a few of you to attend. Purely on a first come, first served basis, of course.' Then Scarlett emitted some of her nervous laughter as she scanned the room to make sure I was there. 'The first ten to give their names to Harriet after assembly may attend this . . . enlightening event.'

I knew what she was trying to do – make me sound important, encourage the others to recognise my status. 'Give your name to Harriet' meant that I would choose them. 'Enlightening event' meant 'give her acclaim'! That must have been why they applauded when she had finished. And why Charlotte Goldman was the first to hand in her name. She was followed by Jason Smart, Miles Brown and a few of the older girls, who were keen to know if the TV cameras would be there.

'Harriet doesn't need television cameras,' explained Celia Moore. 'She's already done all that.' I made a note to ensure that Celia had a good seat.

The day came. I say it as if it were any old day, a date in a diary, a page in a book, but it was not just *a* day: it was *the* day. The day for triumphs, the day for disasters, the day for hope, the day for despair, the day for talent, the day for envy, the day for roses, the day for weeds.

I knew my mother was taking my PTA talk very seriously when she came downstairs in her navy pinstripe suit, which she usually saved for what she called 'power dressing'. And Nana had on a black and white coat that I had only seen her wear for my father's funeral. It wasn't looking promising. As for me, I took the unusual decision to wear my school uniform. It might sound silly, but I felt it would put the book into a more understandable perspective.

'You can't go in school uniform, not when all those people are going to be there,' my mother had urged me.

'Why not?' I had asked.

'Because it's a social event. Because you're a beautiful girl who is a guest speaker and a published writer. Because Charlotte Goldman might be there and she won't be in school uniform.'

I remained adamant about the school uniform right up until her last point. She could see that. It wasn't fair. Why did my face have to be so expressive?

'You think you have all the answers,' I had snapped, somewhat irritated by the fact that she was always right. 'What do you think I should wear?'

'It depends on the sort of statement you want to make,' Publicity explained. 'Which aspect of yourself would you like to emphasise?'

'We should bear in mind,' I said reflectively, 'that I'll probably be on the stage, sitting next to Scarlett, so I don't want to wear anything that clashes with her style.'

When my mother suggested my military jacket and matching khaki trousers, I could see instantly what she had in mind. Two generals side by side, raised above a roomful of corporals and inspiring them with their confidence, encouraging them with the strength of their words.

'I like that idea,' I said, with a smile of satisfaction. 'I think I'll wear my flat black lace-up boots to accessorise the look.'

But my mother thought that a subtle hint of femininity might make me more approachable, especially when it was hidden away quietly under the table. So I wore instead my black leather sandals with the ankle straps, which had made such an impression on Jack in the Smalls' library. And as the trousers covered most of the ankle straps, his toothmarks were barely visible.

'How do I look?' I asked, as I entered the sitting room where Nana and my mother were waiting for me to change.

'Beautiful!' my mother said happily.

'That Scarlett Grout doesn't know how lucky she is,' agreed Nana, which gave me a fair degree of comfort – I'd feared the military look might be lost on Nana. 'You could win wars like that,' she went on. 'You'd wipe out the opposition with just one glance.'

'Fortunately, there won't be any opposition this evening.' I laughed, but my mother and Nana didn't see the funny side.

Then my mother got out her digital camera and took a photograph of me standing by the fireplace with my arm on the mantelpiece, like generals do. 'We'll put this one in the album after the pictures of your launch party,' she said, pressing the review button. 'It will show how versatile you are.'

'Just like her nana.' Nana laughed, adjusting in her lapel the thistle brooch she used to wear as a hatpin. 'I put it down to good cheekbones, don't you, Mia?'

'And an intelligent pair of eyes,' my mother said, with a gleam in her own. Then she linked my arm and added, 'Let battle begin,' as we headed for the front door, which I felt was taking the military analogy just a little too far, but I didn't say so. Generals are like that. They listen and reflect without saying too much.

It was almost time. We had left ourselves ten minutes to get there.

'I hope you've practised your speech,' my mother said, with a frown, as she drove us to school. 'I thought I heard you earlier in your room.'

'I've chosen a couple of Meditations that will give them something to think about,' I explained. 'Then I'll say a few words about my writing style.'

'Good idea,' my mother agreed. 'Keep it brief.'

'And speak up,' Nana urged. 'Don't let anyone put you off.'

'It's only a silly PTA meeting.' I laughed. 'I'm used to more challenging situations than this.'

There were times when my family baffled me. Television, radio, the London Portrait Academy, Tegfold Hall Hotel, they'd seen it all. And yet a small, underwhelming school in Kensington was getting them jumpy. It didn't make sense.

True to form, my mother got us to school five minutes late. I was taken aback by the number of cars in the car park – and they weren't any old cars: they were expensive ones, like VWs and BMWs. There was even a brand new black Mercedes coupé with the top down. We parked our unobtrusive silver Peugeot alongside it and walked swiftly towards the gymnasium.

Miss Quick, the deputy head, was waiting by the door and greeted us with: 'You're late! Miss Grout's waiting for you.'

'I notice we're dispensing with the formalities,' my mother replied, with a hint of sarcasm in her raised eyebrow. Miss Quick laughed nervously and introduced herself. Then she led us to the front of the audience and pointed to a row of empty chairs with 'reserved' on them. My mother sat at the end of the row with Nana next to her. That left four empty seats beside Nana, also with 'reserved' on them. How many guests is a celebrity writer supposed to have? I'd feared that two might be overdoing it.

I hadn't imagined so many people would come. There must have been at least a hundred guests seated in the packed gymnasium. They were talking when we walked in, probably discussing their PTA meeting. I counted eight of the ten students who had given me their names after assembly. They were seated together in the second row. Apart from two or three teachers I recognised, I didn't know the rest of the audience.

I could feel my confidence deserting me as I left my family and followed Miss Quick up the three steps at the side of the stage where she showed me to my seat alongside Miss Grout. There was even a microphone for me to speak into, and a glass of water as if I was a panellist on *Question Time*. We made quite a team, Scarlett and I, side by side above all the others. I smiled at her with the familiarity of a friend, but she must have been caught up in her own thoughts as she didn't smile back. It wasn't until I sat down that I realised how quiet everyone had become. In fact, the only sound I could hear was my heart beating and some muffled laughter coming from the pupils in the second row.

Miss Grout tapped the microphone with her forefinger then turned to me and said, 'Say something into the microphone, Harriet.' It was what they describe in media circles as a sound test. I said the first thing that came into my head:

> '*Odi et amo: quare id faciam, fortasse requiris.*
> *Nescio, sed fieri sentio et excrucior.*'

'What was that?' Miss Grout whispered.

'My favourite Catullus poem,' I replied.

Miss Grout tutted and shook her head. 'Can everyone hear Harriet at the back?' she called out without the assistance of a microphone.

'Yes, but we haven't a clue what she's talking about,' a man shouted back and everybody, except my two guests, laughed.

'Harriet,' Miss Grout whispered again, 'for goodness' sake, think of something sensible to say this time.'

But to me Catullus was sensible — in fact, he was considered by many to be one of the greatest Roman poets. 'What sort of thing did you have in mind?' I whispered back, careful to cup my hand over the microphone so no one else could hear.

'Just say cheese or count to three.'

'And that's supposed to be sensible?' I asked.

'Look, don't bother,' Miss Grout snapped. She must have been feeling nervous too. I'd have to tread more carefully.

'Hello,' I said into the microphone as sensibly as possible. 'I hope your PTA meeting wasn't as dreary and long-winded as Miss Grout expected it to be.'

'That's enough, Harriet. I'll do the introductions,' Miss Grout interrupted. 'Harriet Rose is a pupil at the school so many students and teachers here this evening will already know her. But I'm sure some of you parents are saying to yourselves, "Harriet Rose, who's she?" And I have to admit that until recently even I barely knew who she was.'

There was a ripple of laughter, which seemed to encourage Miss Grout, and her voice became louder. 'Other parents among you know exactly who she is and I know there has been a lot of talk within the school about the publishing of her book *The — The —*' she fumbled through her notes then went on '*— The Infinite Wisdom of Harriet Rose, A Collection of Meditations*, which, surprisingly, won her the title Face of London on *London Live*. Those of you who have time to watch early-evening television may have seen it.'

She laughed as if she thought this was very amusing indeed.

'There has also been attention around the school from local and even national newspaper journalists, which I must say has amazed me. One or two parents have telephoned to ask my position on all the publicity Harriet has been getting, and the impact it might be having on other students. Anyway, all this fuss over a little — over Harriet's Meditations made me think that the best solution all round might be to invite her here so you can fire any questions you have at her, rather than at me. Please don't hold back. But, first, I agreed that Harriet could say a few words to you. I won't spoil your enjoyment of the evening by telling you too much about Harriet's efforts. Instead I shall let them speak for themselves, and you can draw your own conclusions. I'm sure Harriet will be delighted to read a few of her Meditations and tell you a little about the art of publishing – and we are most fortunate to have not only Harriet here this evening, but also her publishing team, her mother and grandmother, whose enthusiasm for Harriet's writing must surely be applauded. So, I give you . . . the celebrated, the unforgettable Harriet Rose.'

It was not the introduction I'd expected. Suddenly I felt trapped, cornered, like a poor sheep led innocently to market. That was when it dawned on me. I had overestimated Miss Grout. She was no soulmate. She wasn't my friend. She didn't even admire me. I felt betrayed, misled, cajoled into this absurd event. She hadn't wanted to promote my book or the reputation of the school. She had no desire to hear about the world of books and publishing. She just wanted to rid herself of the problem my book and I had become. Parents had been telephoning her about me! What sort of parents would do a thing like that, for goodness' sake?

Just then the door at the back of the gymnasium was flung open and Charlotte Goldman walked in with her father. I had seen him at the school before, when Charlotte was playing the leading role in *My Fair Lady* at the end of the second year. She'd got the part because of her strong singing voice; otherwise they would have given it to one of the older girls with a proper figure. Personally I didn't rate her voice. I thought it was as flat as her chest. I preferred mine. At least I could sing in tune. But just because I refused to smile while I was singing and I wouldn't make silly hand movements and tap my foot, I hadn't been given a part at all.

Mr Goldman was a short man. I realised, as I watched them walk purposefully to the front row and sit down next to Nana in the seats reserved for my guests, that he and Charlotte were the same height. In fact, Mr Goldman looked like a bald, overweight, bespectacled version of his daughter. Their features were the same – the pronounced chin, the darting brown eyes and the large, pouting mouth that looked as if it had taken years of saying 'more!' to formulate.

I had no choice. I had to address the audience as I'd practised. There was no way out, unless I used a Charlottian tactic and pretended to faint. But, no, I was Harriet Rose: I would face them and their questions, whatever they happened to be. Besides, I had my mother and Nana with me if it got difficult.

I cleared my throat and took a few moments to compose myself. I needed to make eye-contact with my audience before I began, draw them in with my azure gaze from the start. From my raised position on the stage, I could see them clearly – curious, frowning faces, young and old. Somehow they seemed to lack the warmth I was used to finding in my audiences. And the sophistication was certainly missing too. 'Bland' was the word I would have used to describe them. A 'tea and biscuits' rather than 'champagne' crowd.

Miss Mason was at the back, hiding behind her powder. Beside her, Mr Shaw was sucking his teeth.

Where was the glamour, intelligence, *savoir faire* I was used to? Surely there must have been someone with a hint of style? My eyes fell on a couple in the centre. She was small and round, he tall and slim. And yet there was a certain similarity about them, the poise, the dark hair, the understanding brown eyes. A female who gave real meaning to the words '*à demain*' and a male whose principle seemed to be '*aujourd'hui*'.

'"May today be filled with joy
So that tomorrow it can join
A multitude of happy yesterdays . . ."

'That is Meditation Forty of my collection.'

I hadn't meant to start with that one. In fact, I hadn't planned to recite it at all. But seeing Madame du Bois and Jean Claude sitting there together, it somehow seemed an appropriate way to begin, almost a welcome. He had obviously made a great effort to be there. He deserved that much. That was why I addressed it just to him directly, as if the others weren't there. It didn't take Row Two long to notice: they all turned round to watch and stare. I could sense the other girls' excitement over Jean Claude, without even seeing their faces. And Jason Smart was on the edge of his chair. They'd be talking about it for weeks.

I paused to give them time to finish their noisy whispering and let the relevance of my intimate look sink in.

'Descartes said, "I think therefore I am," but do you?' The use of a question to encourage them to reflect was a technique I had picked up from Socrates. 'Are you in danger of not engaging your brain?' As I'd already addressed a Meditation to Jean Claude, I thought why not direct another at Charlotte Goldman? The art of illustration was another Socratic ploy, after all. 'Remember that for every theory its opposite is never far away. And the opposite of Descartes' theory would be, "I don't think, therefore I'm not."'

It was going well. Some, like Charlotte, were listening open-mouthed, others were whispering again. I pressed on, 'I have started with a Meditation about René Descartes because he is a philosopher I admire, and his views have influenced my own. For those of you who are unfamiliar with the philosophy of Monsieur Descartes, he believed he was able to prove that the soul existed independently of the body. That is, he was a dualist, unlike many of his contemporaries in the seventeenth century and right up to the present day, who believe there is no separate entity, "the soul", but that we are purely physical, material beings, who cease to exist entirely when we die. Which brings me to Meditation Forty-seven: "I like to believe that the mind, the soul, exists independently of the body, something eternal that lives on when our bodies have ceased to exist. Yet, when I look around me, I fear this cannot be so when the souls of so many have ceased to exist while their bodies live on.""

There was a particular reason for me staring as I did at Jean Claude's broad chest when I looked up – and it wasn't because he was now leaning forward as he nodded his agreement enthusiastically at me, although that probably helped me to spot it – the writing I'd missed before. It was in large white letters, highlighted against the black of his T-shirt, like a message of hope and anticipation in an otherwise dreary world. Only I could know why he'd chosen those particular words. Only I could picture him describing what he wanted to the T-shirt printer. Only I could understand how important it must have been to him. It read 'Why not?'

I looked away hastily, fearful that he would see the changing colour of my cheeks – and, worse, that some of the others might. Row Two were staring at me again, and I was certain I'd seen Charlotte turn round. It was Miss Grout's exaggerated glance at her watch that brought me back to where I was supposed to be. I must have been taking too long. Ten minutes she had said. It felt more like fifty. I had given them all something to think about. It was time for me to wind up.

'The greatest influence on my writing style was Marcus Aurelius.

He inspired me to formulate my reflections about my life, the people around me, those I admire and what matters to me. Like Marcus Aurelius, I have numbered my Meditations so that each one can be read individually – separate, yet part of a whole. I want to read one more Meditation to you before I finish and I hope you will reflect upon it before you ask your questions. It is Meditation Forty-five:

> '"I didn't ask to be born.
> I didn't choose my name.
> I had no say in the colour of my eyes,
> Or the texture of my hair.
> Nor will I decide the day I die.
> But I do choose my words,
> And I do create my thoughts,
> And I do take responsibility for my actions.
> All these are my own.
> Judge me on these alone."

'Thank you all for listening.'

I scanned the rows of familiar and unfamiliar faces through eyes tightened to slits with scepticism and irony, defying them to ask a question. I hadn't asked them to come. I hadn't even asked to be there. In fact, all of a sudden I questioned what I was doing there at all. I didn't need this: my book was selling without it. I was an author who had addressed an A-list crowd at the London Por-trait Academy. I didn't need a minor school in west London to further my career. Just who did these people think they were, anyway?

I could hear Miss Grout's voice as she urged them to ask a question – just one, surely someone must have a question, a comment, then – something?

I had never considered the concept of silence until then. Seconds, minutes of wordless spaces filled with fearful anticipation. I became conscious of a large round black and white clock on the wall facing me. There were four numbers on it – 3, 6, 9 and 12. The hands were long black arrows, searching out their targets with bloodthirsty calculation. Suddenly I could hear the second hand ticking its way round the circle like a heart monitor. As each second passed, the clock drew me into itself until I had almost forgotten I was in a packed school gymnasium, waiting to answer mundane questions from uninterested parents and their pubescent offspring.

I counted one hundred and thirty-five seconds before the first question. It was the voice of a woman, somewhere towards the back, hidden behind a block of taller, wider parents with big hair. 'I was wondering, Harriet, how old are you?'

I had spent the previous days trying to guess what the questions might be so that I was ready for them all, but my age had not been one I had anticipated.

'Fourteen,' I replied, then fell back into my comfort zone: 'Why?'

But it was Miss Grout who responded: 'You're supposed to be answering the questions, Harriet, not asking them.'

I said nothing and waited for the next. I did not have to wait so long this time – it was from Jason Smart. He didn't just ask me his question, he shouted it at me, even though he was only two rows from the front. 'Now that you're, like, famous and on telly and everything, do you think there's any chance you'll get free tickets to a Chelsea match?'

They all laughed, as if Jason had made a joke – but I knew his face well enough to realise that he hadn't meant it to be funny, so once the guffaws had subsided I replied, 'If I do, I promise I'll give them to you, Jason.'

I had expected him to be pleased, but even I was taken aback by 'You're a star, Harriet!'

Was that it? My first literary evening built on the back of an ageist mother and a teenage football fan? It wasn't exactly *The South Bank Show*.

'Come along, all you parents out there,' smirked Miss Grout, 'I know some of you have questions to put to Harriet.'

I was certain she looked at Mr Goldman as she spoke, but he didn't see her because he was too busy making notes on a lined pad he had on his knee. I could see only the crown of his head, which was shiny and red as if a lot of deliberating was going on inside it. Not a family trait, I remembered thinking. Then, just when it seemed there would be no more questions, he stood up, his notepad in his left hand, exchanged a glance with Miss Grout and said, in a deep, confident voice, 'I have a question to put to Miss Rose.'

'Yes, Mr Goldman.' Miss Grout sat back contentedly as if she had been drowning and someone had thrown her a lifebelt. Then she smiled encouragingly at him to continue.

'You have referred to both Marcus Aurelius and Descartes this evening in most favourable terms,' he began.

'I have,' I replied. 'I admire them both.'

'And you have quoted from your book a Meditation that refers specifically to Descartes.'

'That's right,' I agreed, with caution, remembering that Charlotte's father was a lawyer. I looked him firmly in the eyes, which, were magnified behind thick round lenses. 'So far we seem to be in agreement.'

'I'm glad to hear it,' he said, with a wry smile. 'You have also said that you modelled your book on the works, the meditations, indeed, of Marcus Aurelius. Is that correct?'

'It is,' I replied.

'And you have presented us with some of your own Meditations, one of which demonstrates that you, like Mr Descartes, are a dualist.'

He had placed an exaggerated emphasis on 'Meditations'.

'I am,' I said.

'Another seems to suggest that you hold with the view that we have freedom of choice, as far as our decisions and actions are concerned, and that we can therefore be held morally responsible for those decisions and actions.'

'Yes,' I said, wondering whether I could truly be responsible for the action of tensing my leg muscles as I spoke.

'Which it would be difficult to hold if our decisions and actions were determined?'

'Difficult but not impossible,' I replied hesitantly. I hadn't expected a cross-examination. Was he trying to trip me up?

'So far, there is nothing remotely original in the views you are presenting. To be precise, they are other people's views.'

'Many philosophers are in agreement with them,' I said.

'Yes, indeed,' he replied, removing his glasses as he spoke, 'but, Miss Rose, you are a fourteen-year-old schoolgirl who has only been studying philosophy for, what, two, three years?'

'Nearly three.' Charlotte answered her father's question as if she had been awaiting it for some time.

'Quite!' her father repeated, with a furtive grin at his daughter. 'Nearly three years!'

'I have learned a lot in that time,' I said, attempting to sound confident but fearing that my quivering lower lip might have given me away.

'I'm sure you have,' he answered, looking knowingly at Charlotte, who appeared, from what I could see, to wink at him, 'but really enough to publish your own philosophical beliefs? And to encourage others to actually buy this book of your – let's be honest – elementary approach to complex theories that have taken great minds many years to arrive at? It is sheer delusion to believe that a puerile book such as this could be a success. Sheer delusion!'

On *Question Time*, David Dimbleby interrupts members of the audience who go on too long, but Miss Grout merely poured herself a glass of water, without pouring one for me, then sipped it slowly. I could feel a blush spreading across my face and into my ears but I couldn't close my eyes and count to ten, not with them all watching me, especially Jean Claude. I could see Mr Goldman's lips articulating their way through sentence after sentence but in my state of anxiety I could make out only the occasional words . . . 'Marcus Aurelius' and 'Roman emperor' and 'Harriet Rose' and 'self-delusion' and 'for your own good'. I had to say something. All I could manage was a lame 'But I won the Face of London competition,' more to reassure myself than to persuade Mr Goldman and the others.

'In all likelihood, you got the sympathy vote,' Mr Goldman replied, then he sat down and Charlotte patted his flabby knee.

I knew I was angry inside, but my only thought was, Why isn't my father with me rather than Charlotte Goldman's?

I was conscious peripherally, through what was left of my focus, of a commotion in the front row. Nana was trying to get to her feet and reach for her hatpin at the same time while my mother struggled to restrain her. But that didn't stop Nana shouting, 'It's obvious what your problem is – you're just jealous of Harriet and her book!'

And my mother added, 'Especially when you only have an airhead for a daughter.'

Uncharacteristically Charlotte just threw back her head and laughed out loud at the suggestion, while her father rearranged his lips into a patronising smile. In an instant my anger turned to fear and humiliation. Perhaps Mr Goldman was right. Maybe I'd got it wrong.

Then I heard another voice speaking from somewhere in the middle of the room: 'I would like to answer that last point.' It was Jean Claude. 'I am a student of philosophy at a sixth-form college in South Kensington. Unlike Harriet, I have been studying the subject in detail for several years.'

Surely, I thought, Jean Claude isn't going to join in the attack.

'Of course Harriet has not given us a philosophical dissertation in her book. I do not believe, and she can correct me if I am wrong, that that was what she set out to do.'

Of course it wasn't. It was obvious. Why hadn't I thought of saying that? But there was more.

'Not only am I a philosopher, I am also a Frenchman, a country-man of René Descartes, as Harriet might say. I feel, therefore, I speak with some authority on the man.'

As he spoke I felt the blush disappearing from my face.

'I, too, believe in the existence of the soul as an entity independent of the body. It is a common belief. Descartes did not have – how you say? – a monopoly on it. Poets and theologians are also fond of the subject, just like Harriet Rose.'

I threw back my hair, which I felt at that moment was hiding too much of my face. Miss Grout dived to avoid it.

'I have read Harriet's Meditations and I found the book refreshingly original. I don't know whether the questioner has read it, but if he has, he will know that it is not just concerned with philosophical theories, it covers many subjects of importance to the writer as a teenager – which I am also – who is experiencing aspects of life for the first time.'

It was exactly what I'd been thinking. I had no idea his English was so good.

'And by the way,' it was Jean Claude again, 'I voted for Harriet to win the Face of London competition and it certainly wasn't a sympathy vote.'

Everyone – even Nana and my mother – was stunned into silence.

Eventually Miss Grout cleared her throat and said, 'Well, I knew Harriet had her publishing team with her this evening but I had no idea her agent was here, too. Most admirable.'

'I would consider it an honour to be Harriet's agent, but from her success so far it does not appear that she needs one, does it?'

This time it was Charlotte Goldman's turn to go red. Not that her father noticed – he was too busy making frantic notes.

I hoped Miss Grout would see this as the perfect moment to draw the event to a conclusion and I think that would have been her intention if a woman in the middle row, not far from Jean Claude and Madame du Bois, had not called, 'Just one more question!' She was quite a young parent, smartly dressed but unassuming, like a woman who has confidence in herself. She was seated next to Celia Moore, which I found particularly reassuring. 'I wanted to ask, Harriet – how many copies have you sold?'

Diana Janney

I moved my lips to answer but nothing came out. I must still have been in shock. Fortunately, Nana came to my rescue: 'So far there have been one thousand eight hundred orders, six hundred from fifty-four branches of Waterstone's,' she announced, reading from her big red invoice book, which she never let my mother or me see, 'including several re-orders, and one thousand one hundred and ninety-five orders from independent bookshops, and libraries, and book signings, and five from my dear friend at Pipers in Piccadilly.' She closed the invoice book proudly and sat down, glaring at Mr Goldman, who was busy putting on his shiny suit jacket and locking his notebook into a crocodile-skin briefcase.

'I'm sure Mrs Moore was not expecting quite such precision – a rough estimate would have done.' Miss Grout's irritation was becoming easier for me to spot now that I had recognised it for what it was.

'I thought headmistresses appreciated precision,' Nana replied sternly.

Miss Grout had had enough. The right side of her face was twitching and her reading-glasses had steamed up. It was time for her to bring the evening to a close.

'Thank you all for coming,' she said politely. 'There is tea and biscuits in the vestibule for any of you who have not already had enough!' And she laughed that laugh again. And that was it. No thanks to the guest speaker, no congratulations on my success, no reference to the book. Just luke warm tea and soggy biscuits in the vestibule. Then she got up – Scarlett – and walked down the steps and out of the gymnasium followed by a scuttling Miss Quick. That left me alone on stage and determined to make an impressive exit in spite of Scarlett's dismissal of me.

264

The audience had not moved from their seats. They were all watching me, transfixed by what had occurred. I sought out the front row for friendly faces – my mother, Nana . . . but where was Nana? There was an empty space next to my mother where she had been. Mr Goldman and Charlotte had gone too. I pushed back my chair in an effort to get up. But my legs, which had remained firmly crossed throughout my interrogation, seemed to have lost all life and had locked in the seated position. I was marooned on stage in a gymnasium packed with teachers, parents and students all gawping at me. Had they noticed? What should I do? They were waiting for me.

I picked up a pen and pretended to write something, anything, until they went away, leaving me and my limp legs alone.

'Help,' I scribbled on a scrap of paper Miss Grout had left, with the title of my book on it in capital letters. I picked up the paper, careful to turn it sideways, and held it out so that no one but my mother could see it. In an instant she was beside me on the stage, chatting as if nothing had happened, as if I hadn't been humiliated by Mr Goldman in front of an entire audience, as if Nana hadn't disappeared – probably in search of Mr Goldman and Charlotte, hatpin at the ready – as if my legs hadn't just given way under the stress of it all.

'It's my legs!' I whispered. 'I can't get them to work!'

'Rub them hard under the desk while I keep talking,' my mother directed me, moving to the front of the desk so that only the guests at the side of the gymnasium could see me. 'You were marvellous,' she went on, 'really good. And you read your Meditations beautifully.'

'You shouldn't have let me do it!' I snapped. 'You should have warned me against old Grout and the Goldmans. I thought mothers were supposed to have a protective instinct – what happened to yours?'

I could feel pins and needles now, all the way up my legs, and the rest of me was just as prickly. 'I wish you hadn't bothered publishing my Meditations in the first place. You've made a laughing stock of me. I've been seen by the entire capital on *London Live* as the recipient of the sympathy vote and I didn't even know it. Why else would anyone have voted for me? Who would really want to read my – what did that old baldy say? – my elementary approach to complex issues? Only you and Nana, that's who!'

'Harriet, you're not seriously going to listen to what some jealous little man like Mr Goldman has to say, are you? I thought you had more sense. A beautiful intelligent girl like you – it would be like Snow White taking advice from Dopey!'

My mother always knew how to bring me to my senses, even in the most tragic circumstances. Of course, she was right, and the packed gymnasium thought so too. It was their loud applause which alerted us to the fact that they had heard our every whisper through my microphone. I should have covered it with a hand in case it was still switched on – I was a professional now, after all.

'Bravo!' someone shouted from the back of the hall. 'Bravo, Mrs Rose!'

My mother turned to face them with a bow and a smile. Then she helped me down the three steps where Jean Claude held out a hand for me.

It wasn't fair. When I needed one of Nana's big white handkerchiefs up my sleeve it wasn't there. They mustn't see me crying in Row Two, I thought. They might think I'm a Charlottian attention-seeker. But there was no escape.

'I'll take her home,' my mother said to Jean Claude.

'What can I do?' he asked.

'Try to find Nana,' she answered. Then she took my arm and ushered me out of the school and into our car. *An Audience with Harriet Rose* had come to an end.

34

'I want to be left alone,' I told my mother when we got home. 'I need time to think.'

'I'll be in the kitchen making *coq au vin* – your favourite,' she said, as she adjusted my pillow on the sofa and pulled my duvet round my shoulders. 'Watch some television – it'll take your mind off everything.'

But how was I supposed to do that when my mind was filled with Mr Goldman's words? And not only his actual words: there were also the ones I feared he might have used and I'd forgotten, and the ones I could imagine the rest of the audience using after I'd left. And then there were my words, the ones I should have used but hadn't. And the ones I'd used in my book, which should never have been seen.

What was the point of them, anyway? Adolescent ramblings without substance, puerile reflections on the world around me, no matter what Jean Claude had said. Who was Jean Claude, anyway? Could I *really* trust what he had to say? And I was no philosopher – three years' study and a school prize hardly made me Bertrand Russell. What were my theories? Where was my critique? Who would ever refer to the Rosean school of thought? If only my father had given me a watering-can instead of a pen I might have had a flower named after me by now. Instead I was pining for my own argument. It was his fault – my mother's and Nana's too: they shouldn't have encouraged me to write, the three of them. They had made a fool of me. Why couldn't they have bought me an iPod for my birthday like normal families? If they hadn't gone and published my daft thoughts none of this would have happened. The press would have left me alone, the whole school wouldn't be talking about me, and Scarlett would have continued to ignore me completely. Didn't anyone realise I wasn't the type for celebrity status? I should have had to struggle with exams and mortgage payments, I should have received numerous rejection slips from publishers and agents who didn't understand the message I was trying to get across before I'd reached this stage. I was fourteen, for goodness' sake. What do fourteen year olds know about television appearances and media attention? My family should have protected me, not hurled me headlong into the jaws of fame, as if I was some product of a North London stage school.

I would have to sit my mother and Nana down and have strong words with them when Nana got back with Jean Claude. I took my pen from my notebook, which my mother had left by my side, and jotted down exactly what I wanted to get across to them, not bullet points like Mr Goldman's, but expressions of the way I was feeling. Rosean arguments of insecurity. It was important to me that they understood. I numbered them, as I had my Meditations, but these points led to a conclusion, which no one, not even Charlotte Goldman, could fail to understand.

1. I am grateful to my family for their love and support and encouragement.
2. Without that love and support and encouragement I would not have written my Meditations.
3. If I had not written my Meditations, my family would have been unable to publish them.
4. If my family had not published my Meditations, I would not have suffered this evening's humiliation.
5. Humiliation made me feel unhappy.
6. Most great philosophers recognise the importance of happiness as a goal.
7. I am not a great philosopher.
8. Even people who are not great philosophers can appreciate the goals of those who are.
9. I want to be happy.
10. Conclusion: keep that bloody Mr Goldman away from me in future.

I read it through to make sure there were no logical inconsistencies. There were not. I was quite happy with the argument, especially its conclusion. They would understand when I read it to them, I was certain. All I needed now was for Jean Claude to bring Nana home.

But where were they? I looked at the clock on the mantelpiece. It was eight thirty. My mother and I had been back for more than an hour.

'We shouldn't have left them at the school,' I said to my mother, who was watching for them through the window.

'I wanted to get you home,' she said. 'I thought they'd follow in a taxi. Not even Nana should take this long to find.'

'You know how nippy she can be when her mind's set on something,' I said. 'Look how she was on the first day of the Harrods sale – gone for hours.'

Gone? Had I said *gone*? Could Nana have *gone*? I had feared as much that day over breakfast at Tegfold Hall. She was the oldest – it was obvious she would go first. But not so soon, and not like this. I should have thought of it before.

'Nana has *gone*!'

'I think we both know that!' my mother said, with a hint of irritation.

'Not just gone,' I exclaimed. '*Gone*. Finished. Departed. On her way out.'

'Don't be so dramatic, Harriet,' my mother snapped.

'Why else would she not have come back by now?'

'Because she's dramatic, like you.'

But I wasn't dramatic – I was a realist, with perhaps a touch of idealism from time to time. That is, I saw the world as it was, with a suggestion of how it ought to be. And in an ideal world, Nana would have been with us, sizing up Jean Claude and telling me I could do a lot better.

'He read your Meditations to Charlotte Goldman,' she would have said. 'How can you trust someone who reads Meditations to a girl who thinks that Meditations are what you do to relax before bedtime?'

My mother decided that the *coq au vin* couldn't wait any longer. She carried it in on a tray and we started to eat.

We were silent for a while, pretending not to worry. Eventually my mother said, 'I'll go back to the school and look for them.'

'And leave me here to worry on my own? I'm coming too.'

When we got there the doors were locked. Even the notice announcing my talk had been taken down and replaced with one that read: 'All deliveries to the tradesmen's entrance at the rear.'

'Where does Jean Claude live?' my mother asked, as we climbed back into the car in an empty car park.

'South Kensington somewhere,' I replied. 'I don't know the exact address.'

'You should never go out on a date without knowing someone's address and telephone number,' my mother said.

But this was no time for lectures: Nana was a missing person.

'What about bookshops?' I suggested. 'She might have gone to see if the one round the corner wanted to order any more copies. They're open until late.'

My mother thought this a good idea so that was where we headed. There were only a few people in the shop, and none was Nana. I spotted several copies of my book stacked on a table of new titles.

My mother picked up a couple and placed them on another table marked 'Master Works'. 'That's where they belong,' she said, and we walked out.

When we got back I half expected to find Nana at home, making herself a cup of tea, but the house was as empty as we'd left it. And there were no messages on the answerphone.

'I'll be so angry with her if she's all right,' I said.

It didn't come out exactly how I'd meant it, but my mother understood. 'Maybe they went for something to eat,' she wondered lamely.

'At midnight?' I replied. 'She's a seventy-four-year-old grand-mother out with a sixteen-year-old Frenchman.'

'Why not?' asked my mother. 'It's not Cinderella we're talking about.'

Eventually I agreed to go to bed. My mother said she'd wake me if there was any news.

News. I'd waited for news before. Last time it had been preceded by 'bad' and was followed by the final six months of my father's life. We couldn't go through another loss. Nana had to be safe. I tried to sleep but it was impossible. My heart was pounding so loudly I kept thinking it was the front door.

By early morning my mother had worked out a plan. I should have known I could depend on her in a crisis. There was only one problem: it involved Bill. He, it seemed, was the answer – the solution to a problem that was out of our control.

'Bill? This is Mia Rose – Harriet's mother. I'm sorry to ring you so early.' It was a promising beginning but I still couldn't see where it was leading. 'I wondered whether you could help us. I wouldn't ask if it wasn't an emergency.'

She closed the sitting-room door so I didn't hear any more.

It was not until later in the morning that I understood. My mother was sitting watching breakfast television when I finally returned to the sitting room. 'Do you really think it's appropriate to watch television as if nothing's happened?' I asked angrily, partly because she had shut the sitting-room door when she was on the telephone to Bill.

'Listen!' she exclaimed, as if I would be interested in morning television. I walked towards the set to switch it off. I already had my finger on the switch when I saw her face – serious and demure in her black and white turban hat, with a telephone number across her chest. 'If you have seen this woman please telephone us on the number at the bottom of your screens. We understand that a five-thousand-pound reward has been offered for any information leading to her safe return.' Bill's voice sounded serious, as if he had his head tilted to one side again.

'So that was your plan,' I said, taking my mother's hand. 'I knew you'd think of something.' We held on to each other and I sobbed into a white handkerchief that my mother passed me.

'I e-mailed a photograph of her to Bill. He said it should be the most recent one. I hope people recognise her if she's taken her turban hat off.' My mother started to cry too.

The phone rang and we jumped up to answer it.

My mother got there first. 'Hello, Bill. Any news yet?' I could tell by her face that there was nothing positive. There had been only one possible sighting of Nana – at a pub called the Cornish Yarg. Although the Cornish Yarg sounded highly unlikely (Nana didn't like pubs – she said they encouraged men to act 'funnily', widening her eyes, looking heavenwards and crossing her arms tightly over her chest), we thought we'd better check it out.

'The Cornish Yarg?' I repeated, once my mother had finally come off the phone to Bill. 'What sort of stupid name is that for a pub in the centre of London?'

'Apparently it's a cheese,' my mother explained. '"Yarg" is "gray" backwards.'

'Why would anyone want to call a cheese after "gray" backwards? Was that why you were laughing on the phone?'

'Laughing?' my mother repeated. 'I don't remember laughing.'

'I distinctly heard you laughing,' I said. 'I remember thinking that Nana's disappearance was hardly a time for amusement.'

'I remember now,' my mother recalled. 'Bill said the person who invented the cheese must have been dyslexic.' And she gave a little laugh to persuade me.

'And you thought that was funny?' I asked sternly.

'Not really, now I think about it. It was probably nerves.'

'Well, we'd better go and check out this pub straight away. If it was Nana, she won't be in it for long. She probably just went in to use the loo.'

'We'll get a taxi. The driver will know where it is.'

'Did Bill give you directions? It sounds like the sort of place he'd go to.'

'Just that it wasn't far from his studios,' she said.

'I knew it!' I replied, and we went out in search of a taxi.

Reassuringly, the driver recognised the name immediately. We glimpsed the sign before we spotted the building, a rectangular board swaying to and fro with a depiction of a large round cheese in the middle covered with what appeared to be nettles.

'That's the Yarg!' the driver said, pointing towards a dark, gloomy building on the street corner with tinted windows and black shutters.

'Take me back!' I shouted. 'I'm not going in there!'

Fortunately the driver thought I was joking and laughed, while my mother took my arm and pulled me out of the taxi.

We should have known not to go inside when we saw the hand-written 'No Vests' sign pinned to the swing door entrance. It was at an angle, held up with a piece of Blu-tack – or chewing-gum, I couldn't be sure which. My mother looked uneasily at me and tightened her grip on my arm.

'I'll wait outside,' I said, turning to go back through the swing door.

'I think you'd be safer in here,' my mother replied. And I could see she had a point.

Together we checked the ladies' room, which had a pink loo and matching wash-basin with a single tap that didn't stop running. There was no sign of Nana.

'She wouldn't have come in here even if she was bursting,' I said, holding my nose and walking out.

Then, just as we were heading for the door, in walked Bill, all rushed and sweaty and full of himself. 'I thought I might find you two here before me,' he said, with the familiarity of an old family friend. 'Any sign of Nana?'

Nana? Who did he think he was, calling her 'Nana'? How could anyone be so presumptuous? 'No,' I said sharply. 'As I thought, my grandmother isn't here.'

'Well, why don't we have a drink as we're here?' he said, and to my amazement, my mother agreed.

We found a semi-circular sofa in the corner of the snug, large enough to take my mother and me but too small to admit Bill. But that didn't bother him. He pulled up a stool and sat across the table from us, rocking to and fro, with a Nike-clad foot on the crossbar, in a way that made me feel like asking to be taken back to dry land. 'Isn't it great?' he was saying, and I prayed he wouldn't mention cheese. 'The Yarg's been here for years. Chris, the land-lord, is an old mate of mine. We were at college together.' Bill waved with familiarity towards a man behind the bar, who waved back at him with a cigarette between his fingers. Then Bill walked over to Chris to order his pint, wine for my mother and bitter lemon for me.

'We should be looking for Nana,' I used the opportunity of his absence to point out.

'I know,' my mother agreed, 'but we have to be polite to Bill. He put himself out to get that photo of Nana on television.'

That made me feel small. I should have realised she was only being polite. Bill was on his way back. I gave him a half-smile. That should be enough.

'How's your book doing, Harriet?' he asked, as he gulped his pint.

I could tell by the way he asked the question that he wasn't interested in my reply so I didn't give him one, and he didn't notice. My mother did, though.

My mother noticed everything, especially when it concerned me.

'So, when did you last see Nana, Mia?'

If he insisted on calling her 'Nana', he should have been asking me.

'Last night,' my mother replied. 'We were at a PTA meeting at Harriet's school.'

'Well, that would be enough to bore the socks off anyone,' Bill said, swilling his beer. 'She'd probably just had enough.'

'I was speaking at it,' I said, looking him straight in the eye, as Nana and I had seen John Wayne do in similar situations.

'Oh,' Bill said. Just like that. 'Oh,' followed by a long embarrassed pause while he took out and lit a cigarette.

'We were having a wonderful evening,' my mother felt the need to explain, 'until towards the end.'

She shouldn't have reminded me when I was trying so hard to forget.

'Why? What happened at the end, Harriet?' he asked, with a bemused smile. 'Did you forget your lines or something?'

'Harriet never forgets her lines,' my mother answered frostily, and I felt more at ease with the way the conversation was going.

'Oops! Sorry, Harriet! I've been ticked off!' He placed a wide hand playfully over his mouth.

I could tell from the way my mother was looking at me that it was my turn to speak up. 'There was an extremely rude man at the event, who didn't seem to understand my work at all.'

'You get those when you're in the media, love.' He was trying to impress my mother with feigned sincerity, but I saw through it.

'Everyone was caught up in my philosophical debate with him, so we didn't notice when Nana left the room.'

'What happened to the bloke?' It wasn't exactly *Inspector Morse*, but at least he was keeping up.

'He left too,' my mother said, 'although we're not sure who went first. Suddenly they were both gone. I asked Jean Claude to go and look for her and—'

'Who's Jean Claude, then?' he interrupted with curiosity.

What business was it of his? 'He's a friend,' I said, 'a fellow philosopher.'

'You mean he's your boyfriend,' he said, simplifying a complex situation in the way I was beginning to associate with him.

'The point is,' my mother intervened, and I could see from her face that he was annoying her too, 'she didn't come home last night, and that's just not like her. I've telephoned everyone I can think of, even the local hospitals.'

She whispered the last part because she thought I didn't know. But I did. I'd telephoned them too.

'And the response to the photograph you put on television this morning isn't what I'd call encouraging. But thanks anyway.' My mother had reached the point when she was about to tell him we were leaving. I could tell. 'It was very kind of you, but if you don't mind, Bill,' she said in her best publicist's manner, which neither Nana nor I could ever have achieved no matter how much we practised, 'Harriet and I should be leaving. Harriet has already missed half a day's school.'

'You little skiver!' Bill said, as we got to our feet.

'Actually, no,' I said. 'My teacher told my mother I could have the morning off under the extremely unusual circumstances.'

'Oh, I see,' Bill said, but I don't think he did.

'And thank you for the drinks,' my mother added. 'They were just what we needed, weren't they, Harriet?'

'Yes,' I replied.

'I'll stay on and have a quick one with Chris. I'll let you know if we hear any more about Nana.'

'You didn't thank him for the gladioli,' I whispered, as my mother and I made our way across the crowded smoky pub to the exit.

'Best not to,' my mother replied.

'I thanked Jean Claude for my roses,' I confessed.

'That was different.'

Sometimes my mother could be difficult to follow.

'Why?' I asked.

She hesitated then replied: 'Because you won't mind if he sends you some more.'

It sort of made sense.

There was only one message on our answerphone when we got home from the Cornish Yarg. It was not from Nana or Bill.

'I am Jean Claude. I must speak with Harriet.' Like a fool, he had not left a telephone number.

'What an idiot!' I exclaimed.

'Don't you think you're being a little hard on him?' my mother asked.

But I was in no mood for Anglo-French relations.

'You'd better go to school this afternoon and see if you can find Madame du Bois,' my mother decided. 'There's always a chance that Jean Claude found Nana last night.'

'Surely he would have said so in his message?'

'You can't always tell with foreigners,' my mother replied knowingly.

'You won't go anywhere without telling me, will you?' I asked, as I left the house. I wasn't taking any chances with the last member of my family.

'No, I promise,' she said. 'And don't worry. I'm sure Nana will be all right.'

She wasn't really sure – I could tell by the way she couldn't look me in the eye when she said it. She just wanted me to go to school so I wouldn't see her cry.

I walked slowly to school, looking through shop windows and in doorways as I went. I didn't really expect to see Nana, but the looking gave me hope. She wasn't gone, just somewhere else, and if I kept looking, some day soon I would find her, standing in her black and white overcoat and turban hat with her black leather shopping-bag under her arm, saying: 'Don't be so daft, Harriet. Did you think I wouldn't come back?'

It wasn't until I entered the classroom and found that maths had begun that I remembered. It was Friday. Which meant it was Madame du Bois's day off. The rest of them stared at me, open-mouthed, as I walked in. I sensed they'd been talking about me all morning. They probably hadn't expected me to come in.

I sat down at my desk, aware of their eyes still upon me. The superstar Harriet Rose had arrived. Did you hear of her humiliation last night by Charlotte's father? And the glance she exchanged with that French friend of hers, Jean Claude! He was the good-looking one from the helicopter, sitting with Madame du Bois in the middle row. Were you there when he spoke up about poor Harriet? Did you see her face when she couldn't move from her chair?

'I saw your grandmother on television this morning.' The unmistakable whine of Charlotte Goldman indicated that maths was over.

'Harriet's grandmother?' came Jason's predictable response. 'Don't tell me she's written a book as well! What's it called – *The Meditations of a Wilting Rose?*'

The others seemed to find this particularly amusing, except Charlotte who said, 'Don't be so rude to poor Harriet. Her grandmother looked like a lovely old lady, even if she was wearing a funny turban hat and sunglasses.'

'It takes style to wear a turban hat and sunglasses,' I replied sternly. 'Something your type would never understand.'

'And what type is that exactly, Harriet?' quivered Charlotte.

'The type who gatecrashes other people's launch parties in frothy pink frills with matching lip gloss.'

The rest were amused by me now. I liked that. So I continued, 'The type who never forgets their waterproof mascara in case they have to cry for attention.'

That remark didn't cause quite so much raucous laughter as the first – they must all have been wearing waterproof mascara.

'Have you found her yet?' asked Miles, in an uncharacteristically compassionate tone.

'Have you lost your nana?' Jason laughed.

'There's a five-thousand-pound reward for anyone who finds her,' sniggered Charlotte.

'Five grand!' exclaimed Jason. 'So what are we doing sitting here?'

The whole of Class 3B surged towards the door and ran noisily down the stairs as the school bell chimed the end of the day. I hung back as they raced through the school gates down the drive towards freedom. I could hear Jason's voice bellowing the likeliest places to find an elderly woman who had not come home all night. Some were laughing while others chastised Jason for his stupid sense of humour. But it didn't bother me, even if the jokes were at my expense. I knew what Nana would say: 'Don't worry, Harriet, they might be laughing now, but you'll have the last laugh.'

The trouble was, it seemed that everyone had had the last laugh but me: Charlotte Goldman seemed to have managed to seduce Jean Claude when all I could manage was a date in my helicopter while he had his ears stuffed with cotton wool; Charlotte's father had reduced me almost to tears in front of a packed gymnasium at the end of my PTA talk; our five-thousand-pound reward for Nana's return had led only to a drink in a seedy pub with an ageing Lothario; instead of being top of the class in French I had sunk into oblivion with only a short intermission when I had confessed my French adventures with Jean Claude to the whole class and the teacher who had turned out to be his mother; even the *Guardian* had mistaken what was no more than a subtle sense of humour for the responses of a precocious fourteen year old; and my own dear nana, who had never before let me down, had disappeared without a word into the chaos of London. I had even been duped into believing that these very school gates had heralded a celestial message when all they had announced in reality was a bunch of crummy reporters from the local newspapers. My life seemed destined to be one long sack race. What had become of the feisty, exuberant Harriet Rose in the red bikini? Where was the girl in the black cardigan that read 'I am'?

Fourteen was too young to be disillusioned. You needed a string of broken relationships and a weight crisis for that. No, my family was not the type for disillusionment. There was more to us than the sum of three pairs of steely blue eyes. We were a trilogy of hope against despair, joy in the face of tragedy, humour in the depths of sorrow.

I took a deep breath, pulled back my shoulders and strode through the wrought iron school gates with a look of determination, as if a new life lay on the other side. Somehow I sensed it did, even before

I became conscious of the laughter subsiding, replaced by excited whispers and nudging elbows.

'Isn't that the bloke from the helicopter who was with Harriet at her talk last night?' asked Jason.

'I know him too,' Charlotte announced proudly. 'That's Jean Claude.' She adjusted her hair and walked confidently down the drive towards him.

'So who is he?' Jason called after her.

'I met him at Harriet's mother's health club ages ago,' she shouted back, as if Jean Claude had nothing whatsoever to do with me.

'How's his French kissing?' asked Jason, with the maturity of a tadpole.

'None of your business.' Charlotte laughed, looking down at the ground to hide the embarrassment she did not possess.

'Well, he's coming now, Charlotte, so you'd better be ready for him,' Jason went on, simulating a snog on the back of his hand.

What could I say? She probably did know more about his French kissing than I did.

I forget who it was who shouted, 'Here he is!' but I remember very clearly what happened next. Jean Claude made his way towards Jason, Charlotte and the rest while I hid behind a large oak tree, like the wise old owl, and waited to find out what he was doing there, in case he had arranged to meet Charlotte.

'*Bonjour,*' he said quietly. '*Je m'appelle Jean Claude — Jean Claude du Bois.*'

There was a high-pitched gasp of surprise from everyone except Jason, who clearly had not put two and two together or, if he had, was not particularly impressed. 'So?' he said, in his finest English accent. 'What about it?'

'You know my mother. I was with her last night at the PTA meeting.'

'And who exactly is your mother?' Jason enquired.

'Madame du Bois – your French teacher,' Jean Claude replied, somewhat indignantly. I liked indignant. It suited him. It made him seem more mature, unless it was just the contrast he made with Jason Smart.

'Hello again, Jean Claude!' Charlotte did not only speak, she actually walked right up to him. But I was the one he'd stood up for last evening. I was the one to whom he had sent red roses. I was the one he'd come seventy miles to Tegfold Hall Hotel to find.

'I am looking for Harriet,' he said. 'Harriet Rose. Is she here?'

I peeped out from my hiding-place behind the tree, like Eve in the Garden of Eden.

'I'm here, Jean Claude,' I said. And he smiled.

Nobody missed that smile – not even Jason. It transfixed them, like the end of a long-running drama serial. Each one turned their gaze from Jean Claude to me and back to Jean Claude.

And all the while Charlotte stood beside him, not knowing what to do next. How could she? No women's magazine would have thought to cover this one.

Jean Claude knew what to do, though. He walked right past Charlotte towards me, oblivious of the exclamations and sharp intakes of breath. In seconds he was beside me, as if my front tooth had just gone through my lower lip again – which it might well have done, but I wouldn't have noticed.

I don't know what I expected him to say, but I have to admit I was as surprised as everyone else when he said, 'You owe me five thousand pounds.'

Charlotte Goldman's relief was short-lived, however, when he went on, 'It is my reward. I have found your nana.'

I cannot honestly say it was only the joy this news brought me that caused me to throw my arms round him, but it certainly had a lot to do with it. I did find Jason's cheer rather embarrassing, though – he didn't even know my grandmother, for goodness' sake! And if the rest of the class chose to join in with him – well, what did it matter? This was my day and nothing was going to spoil it, not even Charlotte Goldman saying, as I removed my arms from round Jean Claude's neck, 'I hope you enjoyed that, Harriet – it cost you five thousand pounds.'

I did not need to respond. Once again Jean Claude did it for me: 'I want no reward from Harriet,' he said. 'Her happiness is reward enough for me.'

That shut her up. In fact, it shut up everyone, even me. I had a thousand questions to ask him, yet I could not voice a single one. I tried, but my lips seemed as paralysed as my legs had been. All I was able to manage was a solitary 'Where?' followed by stony silence.

Fortunately, Jean Claude seemed able to see the funny side. 'First I find your nana and now I find Cratylus again, too!'

His deep Gallic laugh contrasted with Charlotte's high-pitched tones when she said, 'Not that silly old Greek philosopher Harriet's so keen on!'

In seconds the blood had surged back to my paralysed lips: 'And I thought the only philosopher you'd heard of was Snoopy,' I said, which caused Jean Claude to laugh his Gallic laugh again.

'You sound like Anne Robinson,' was all Charlotte could manage.

'And you are the weakest link!' I replied, as Jean Claude took my arm and led me towards the car park. 'Goodbye!'

I knew they would follow us. Part of me hoped they would – I didn't want them to miss anything. When we reached the car park, he stopped – to look for his moped, I supposed. I took the opportunity to ask him the question to which I had been longing for an answer: what had happened to Nana?

'When your mother asked me to find your nana last night I thought it would be *très facile*. I looked in the likely places – in the car park, by the tea and coffee table in the vestibule. I even waited outside the lavatory. But, alas, I could not find her. I was about to give up and go home when I noticed through the open door to the gymnasium some movement on the stage where you had given your talk. I entered the gymnasium and walked to the stage and *voilà*! There she was, your grandmother!'

I wished he could tell it another way. He was beginning to sound like Monsieur Poirot.

'She was reading a copy of your Meditations.'

'Miss Grout must have left hers behind,' I suggested.

'*Ah, oui, possible*.' He pronounced 'possible' the French way and I could hear Jason imitating him in the background.

'She was wiping her eyes with a handkerchief so I knew at once she was very upset and I was cautious to disturb her. I waited until, eventually, she looked up, and saw me and smiled.'

Jason was pretending to play the violin and Charlotte was pretending not to laugh.

'I helped her down the steps from the platform and I was about to bring her home when we heard a noise – a knocking. It was coming from the gymnasium door. Just a light knock. Like this.' Jean Claude tapped on the back window of a parked taxi I hadn't noticed to illustrate his point. 'I wasn't the only person looking for your nana. One of the parents was searching for her too.'

The taxi door was thrown open forcefully by a hand I couldn't fail to recognise. Then a voice I'd feared I might never hear again said, 'Was that my cue to get out, Sacha? I thought we were just picking up Mia, then taking Harriet home. What a time you've been!'

Out jumped Nana, with the sprightliness of a teenager, adjusting her turban hat, which had caught on the roof of the taxi in her haste to get to her feet. My mother, who was inside, like a messenger of the gods, had joy mixed with relief in her eyes. 'Nana wanted to come straight here,' she said. 'Didn't I say she'd be all right?'

No Meditation could ever describe the happiness I experienced at that moment. It would take a true genius of the pen to get close to it. All I can say is that Nana had gone and now she was back and anyone who truly knows what it is to lose someone will understand how I felt.

'I looked everywhere for that Mr Goldman!' she exploded, like a volcano that had waited too long to erupt. 'He's lucky I couldn't find him.'

Audacity being a Goldman family trait, Charlotte intervened: 'He can't have been easy to miss – he was driving the brand new open-top black Mercedes coupé.'

Nana turned round to face her head on: 'Is that how all his hair blew off?' she snarled, then resumed her narrative. 'But every big . . . ugly . . . grey . . . boring cloud,' she paused before every adjective to cast her steely eyes on Charlotte, 'has a silver lining.'

'Your nana wanted to tell you the news herself,' said Jean Claude.

'News?' I said, with trepidation, shaking all over my body. 'What news?'

'Not all the parents last night were like Mr Goldman,' said Nana. 'Some of them had good sense and judgement.' I was starting to feel sorry for Charlotte. 'One in particular.' Nana had a way of speaking as if she was addressing a whole nation. 'Her name is Mrs Moore.'

'Celia Moore's mother?' It was more of an exclamation than a question.

'That's the one!'

'A very nice lady,' Jean Claude added. 'She invited your nana and me to her home for dinner.'

'Was Celia there?' I hoped I sounded nonchalant – I didn't want him thinking I was worried he'd noticed Celia's breasts.

'No. She went to revise for her exams.'

Good old Celia. She deserved her success.

'Mrs Moore wanted to know all about your book,' Nana said proudly, 'and I was the woman to tell her. Every detail. Every sale. I had all the information with me in my invoice book. It couldn't have been easier.' I feared that Nana might have tested the limits of Mrs Moore's hospitality.

'I'm sure she didn't want to hear all that,' I suggested in a whisper.

'Right through the night we talked. And she read your whole book while we were there.'

It was sounding more and more unlikely. If Jean Claude hadn't been there too, I would have feared that Nana was going funny.

'Then, first thing this morning, she drove us to her office.'

'Her office?' I repeated, conscious of the others' sniggers, which, frankly, I found perfectly understandable.

'To prepare this.'

She handed me an official-looking document. It had my name on it. And the title of my book. And a figure. A very large figure. In numbers and words. The rest of them gathered around me in an attempt to glimpse the document.

'It's a contract,' Charlotte announced. 'I've seen my father prepare them like that. Is Mrs Moore a lawyer too?'

'No!' exclaimed Nana. 'Mrs Moore is a director at one of the leading publishing houses in the world. And this,' she took the contract out of my hand and waved it at Charlotte, 'is a contract for the purchase of the rights to Harriet's book – you know the one,

Charlotte, the puerile book that Harriet was deluded enough to believe might be a success.'

I couldn't make out Charlotte's muttered response. It really didn't matter. Nana was back and she had achieved something of which she was as proud as I was. That was why she had stayed away for so long.

'When I knew Mrs Moore was interested in your book, I promised myself I wouldn't come back until I had a contract in my hand. I persuaded the publishers to have it drawn up extra quickly because of all the media interest. It's what you deserve, Harriet! And you don't have to worry any more about all those extra orders your silly old nana went and took.'

'There's nothing silly about you!' I cried, hugging her to me as if I meant never to lose her again. 'You're the cleverest, dearest nana in the world.' And none but a fool would have disagreed with me. Jean Claude certainly didn't. In fact, when I looked at the two of them, it appeared that over the past day they had made up their differences.

Nana rummaged up her coat sleeve for a handkerchief, then continued, 'I couldn't have done it without the help of this Frenchman here!'

My mother remained tucked away in the taxi, struggling to put on a pair of big black sunglasses before a tear showed that she could be dramatic, too.

'I tried to telephone you this morning,' said Jean Claude, 'just to tell you not to worry, without giving away your nana's secret, but you were not in.'

'That must have been when we were having a drink with Bill at the Cornish Yarg,' I said, looking into the taxi at my mother, who nodded.

'What?' shouted Nana. 'You went out for a drink with that roving-eyed reporter when your poor old nana had been missing all night?'

I was about to explain that Bill had only been helping my mother and me to look for her when I noticed that Jean Claude seemed uncharacteristically irritated by the reference to Bill. So instead I said, 'Bill's really quite nice when you get to know him.' My mother gave me a wink of approval, and I winked back at her, as if we'd said simultaneously, 'That'll teach him!'

An inquisitive Jean Claude went on, 'You didn't return my call.'

I knew what he was asking: 'How long were you out drinking with this roving-eyed reporter?' So I said nothing.

'I took your nana home to my mother for the rest of the morning, and she looked after her while you and your mother were out. I think they have become the greatest of friends.'

'That would be Madame du Bois, our French teacher?' Jason Smart confirmed, as if it was an entirely acceptable practice to listen to other people's conversations.

'What would I have done without my lovely little French friend and her son here?' Nana said reflectively, patting Jean Claude's cheek.

Encouraged by this sudden show of affection, I risked saying to Nana, 'It was good of Jean Claude to help you like that, wasn't it, Nana?' Perhaps, deep down, I had the makings of a good publicist after all.

'Your grandpa would have said Jean Claude was the lucky one!' Her pale blue eyes twinkled with witty rebellion, but I could see that she had warmed to him.

'And he would have been right,' Jean Claude agreed.

That made Nana laugh. Everything was getting back to normal.

'I can't thank you enough,' I said.

'Perhaps you can,' Jean Claude replied. Half of my schoolmates jeered and the rest remained silent. 'You could agree to come on holiday with me to France this weekend. My father and stepmother have a large villa on the Côte d'Azur that they keep for holidays, with a very big swimming-pool the size of this school, and beautiful views of Provence. Say you will come, Harriet!'

'Say you will come!' Jason taunted.

'On one condition,' I answered. 'That Nana and my mother can come too.'

'It would give me great pleasure,' he said, and I sensed Charlotte Goldman turning the colour of her party dress.

To anyone who finds the ending too like an American movie and would have preferred more of a Jane Austen, it should be pointed out that Harriet Rose thought so too. Which was why, the following morning, she explained in her most demure Elizabeth Bennet accent that she had had second thoughts about the holiday in France at Jean Claude's father's villa with a swimming-pool the size of her school. It was not that she didn't want to go, or that she didn't like him, because in fact she found him very charming and *sympathique*. Rather, she was unable to entertain the prospect of a romantic liaison with a man who had chosen to read her Meditations to someone like Charlotte Goldman – a manipulator, a tactician, an airhead. And although she realised that 'airhead' was not a word that Jane Austen would have used, she felt that on this particular occasion no other word would do. Jean Claude, in a manner not dissimilar to a Jane

Austen hero, smiled just a little, as if he was the owner of a very amusing secret, the effect of which was almost to encourage the heroine to walk away and never speak to him again. But she did not.

Instead she listened intently as he recounted to her a conversation he had had with Charlotte Goldman on the evening of the book launch. Charlotte, having bounded over to him like a pink blanc-mange ('blancmange' in fact was Harriet's contribution to the narrative, it being a French word that Jean Claude would easily understand), had asked him whether she might borrow his copy of Harriet's *Infinite Wisdom* as she had arrived late and they had sold out. Naturally she had promised to return it to him once she had read it – it was her *Cosmopolitan* seduction rule number one. Jean Claude, however, had told her he needed his copy – as part of his induction course at his sixth-form college, the philosophy students had been invited to take part in a talk entitled 'Reflective Recitations'. It was to be held one evening, open to the public, and he had decided to read from Harriet's Meditations, then say a few words about them. He was certain he had not told Charlotte which day the event would take place – he had already been bitten by the odd mosquito *française* in his native country – so he was extremely surprised when Charlotte came up to him after the talk 'to say hello' and tell him that she thought his recitation was 'brilliant'. It will come as no surprise that Jean Claude's noble response was that it was not his talk that was brilliant but Harriet's Meditations, with which, naturally, Charlotte agreed. He had added that he would be grateful if Charlotte would convey to Harriet the message that he hoped she would not mind that he had read from her *Infinite Wisdom* without her consent but that he had tried to telephone her several times unsuccessfully after she had left the book launch so abruptly.

Of course, Harriet did not want to point out that Charlotte

The Infinite Wisdom of Harriet Rose

Goldman had conveyed no such message to her but in the circumstances of her treatment of her misjudged hero, there was very little else she could have done. And it is on this ebbing tale of enlightenment that the curtain must fall, lest the reader should intrude upon Harriet's modesty as she and Jean Claude grappled, like true philosophers, with the mind-body problem.